LYKANTHROPOS

LEE PLETZERS

ISBN: 095828931X
EAN-13: 9780958289313

The version printed via CreateSpace

Writers Press / Triskaideka Books
PO Box 38646
Wellington mail centre
Lower Hutt 5045
New Zealand
http://triskaidekabooks.co.nz

For Ami, Lewis, Connor
Love forever

Prologue

New Zealand. 1980.

The 'Hammer Horror' movie played on the old black and white television, which sat on top of a scarred dresser. Nine-year-old James Dennett watched the movie lying in bed under a thick, heavy quilt. The cold winter air in his small room threatened to break though the comfort of the quilt as his sleepy eyes stared at the TV.

The movie was yet another portrayal of the werewolf story, one of the many versions he had seen. James was hooked on the Lycanthrope myth, and this one, like the others, had him hook, line, and sinker. As the story progressed, the small boy found himself clutching the blankets tighter and tighter, drawing them up until they finally covered his eyes.

A noise from outside caught his attention.

At first, he thought it was his father returning home late from work, but that couldn't be. It would never be. Dad died violently at the jaws of a dog and was never coming home again. Died saving his life. The only thing he had of his father was a handmade wooden chest, half filled with toys — all of which he'd given up playing with. They remained there as a memory only.

Outside, the sound repeated. Again his attention was drawn to it. It sounded very close. James threw the covers off and knelt on the bed, facing the green and white pin-striped curtains.

The old house creaked, a sound that made the boy's heart skip a beat.

Again that sound -- closer now.

It sounded like someone slowly rubbing two pieces of sandpaper together. Someone walked on the loose gravel of their driveway. The soft click of the gate lock was thunder in his ears. It was past midnight, who'd be visiting at this hour? He carefully pulled the curtain open.

A harvest moon hung high in the night sky.

On the left-hand side, halfway down the driveway, was a block of brick and tile apartments. Trees ran down the right-hand side. The moon threw eerie shadows across the driveway and against the side of the apartment's three-story wall. To his right was his mum's garden. Behind the garden was a hedge that grew around three-quarters of the back of the house, and behind that was Saint Mary's Primary School and tennis courts.

James couldn't find a trace of anyone out there; although he was sure he'd heard the gate close. The brightness of the light from the television set flashed against the left side of his face. He could see the television's image reflected against the window. Then the scurrying of rats in the roof caused him to look up. Thus distracted, he released the curtain and decided to continue watching the horror movie. On the television, four pretty girls walked along a dirt road huddled together as they crossed the Moors. They looked scared, tired, and cold.

Something hit the side of the house and landed with a wet thump on the balcony. The blood in his veins froze; the air in James' lungs became ice. He shakily opened the curtain and peered out.

Nothing seemed out of the ordinary.

A sudden movement caught his eye. He turned to face the brick and tile apartments. A dark shadow grew tall against the bricks, towering over the shadow of the trees. James swallowed hard when he saw the figure creating the shadow.

It stood tall as a bear and just as hairy. Its mouth was open, and from a jaw longer than his hand, long, sharp teeth glistened against the moonlight. It threw its head back and howled at the fat, yellow orb of night.

Petrified, energy fled his body and he fell to the bed. His breath was fast and heavy. He told himself there was nothing out there, but he didn't believe his own lies.

A slow creaking sound filled the room. James knew that sound, had heard it millions of times. He slowly turned and looked at his toy chest. The lid opened slowly, rising inch by inch against its hinges.

A rag doll, dressed like a jester with bells on its hands and feet, jumped from the box, making tinkling sounds. Next a laughing box followed its crackle maddening in the dark. Then plastic trucks and cars, Lego pieces, cards, a box of magic tricks for kids, and a dribble glass tagged after. Tennis balls bounced around the room, and a monkey with metal cones attached to its hands walked around clapping.

The noises of battery operated toys blended with the metal bells and clinking of cones to make an unharmonious sound that threw an eerie blanket of threat over the room. James pushed himself against the wall and held the blankets so tight with both hands that his knuckles grew white. Fear drained all the color from his face.

Suddenly, the television hit full volume and a male voice boomed: "He is the spawn of Satan!"

Licking his dry lips, he glanced at the television, then back at the toy chest. It wobbled side to side, as if trying to tip itself over. The toy chest erupted in flames; thick white and black smoke filled the room, billowed to the ceiling, and engulfed the light from the television, leaving the room in an ash grey haze.

A blurry figure with deep yellow eyes, slowly took form.

The beast howled and leapt, front legs extended, and eyes swelled with hunger.

The nine-year-old boy screamed . . .

* * *

1573 Scotland

Through the dense bush on the outside border of a small Scottish village, it moved. Four heavy paws crushed frozen grass. Thick and heavy breath clouded white as it hit the freezing winter night air. It stopped, spying a hut.

Cold, yellow eyes watched the shadowed movements inside the badly structured stick and straw shelter. It found an advantage spot and waited.

Eventually the crooked wooden door jerked open. A large, stocky man in his late thirties limped to the door and thanked his hosts. He took hold of a long, thick branch axed from a willow to use as a walking stick for his injured leg, pushed the door closed, and headed down the overgrown path.

Sounds.

Pittapat... pittapat...

The sounds echoed through the still night. Phantom moon shadows, flashing, flying, through the darkness amid the surrounding trees and the shrubs. The man glanced nervously at the shadows around him, his heart pounding against his chest. The sounds grew louder and closer, until he could no longer control the fear and slowly turned. His breath caught and his eyes widened. He prayed, knowing it would do no good, but prayed nonetheless.

It leapt.

The weight bowled the man to the ground as Man and beast tumbled head over shoulders. It was quick getting back to its feet. The man saw the fullness of it for the first time. It stood four, no, five, feet tall with shoulders hunched and head low. Yellow eyes leered through the blackness at him.

The man backed up, his legs rubbery with fear. He stared at the beast as it slowly advanced on him. His nerves twitched as horror ate its way through his system.

Feral lips curled back exposing long teeth. It had one purpose in mind. The beast needed to feed.

The man stumbled and fell. The beast leapt. Instinctively the man raised his arm -- bent at the elbow his forearm crossed his face. Long teeth slid through his flesh. The jaw clamped down, severing the forearm muscle.

His scream shook the grass.

Voices.

He heard voices. Large numbers of them growing closer, yelling unintelligible words and age-old chants.

The beast backed away, attention drawn to the adjoining field. It looked at the man's blood seeping from ripped flesh. The voices grew louder. Something sparkled from the moonlight.

Weapons. The voices came with weapons.

It ran.

Seeming to take forever, the group reached and gathered around him in a tight circle; a few others chased after the wolf. The man saw faces he knew surrounding him. The kind, and friendly faces from neighbors and shop owners throughout his town.

"Help me," he begged. "The pain. Me arm throbs with it."

"Aye," an elderly man said. "We'll help ye."

Five people gently lifted him off the frozen grass. The three men carrying weapons returned. The man heard one of them say: "It's done. We got lucky."

"Who was it?" another asked.

"Lyle McLeod. Who be this?"

"Don't you recognize Duncan?" The voice spoke with authority, clearly the leader of the group. He thought he knew this voice but the pain squeezed his mouth shut and killed his concentration.

"We should cut off 'is 'ed," an old voice growled.

"Nay. We wait, see if it takes hold."

"Wait, ye say!"

"Aye, if thou disagree, take it to the council in the morn. There'll be no more death tonight."

Those were the last words the man heard as darkness wrapped around him and stole his conscious thoughts.

* * *

He awoke in a barn stall. Thick iron bars surrounded it. His arm was itchy and as he absently scratched it, he suddenly remembered the attack and checked his arm.

His arm looked completely healed as if nothing had happened.

Through the barn windows, stars glittered in the night sky. The barn doors opened, drawing his attention. A young lad entered carrying a sword that looked too large and heavy for him. He knew this boy but couldn't place his name.

"Lad, let me out of 'ere."

"Nay, I canny do that."

"Pray tell why this be so?"

"Ye be dangerous," he replied.

"Do you know who I be?" The man wrapped his hands around the bars. The lad jumped back a few feet, his eyes grew wide. The man was surprised by the lad's actions, "What's goin' on here?"

"I'll fetch me father, tell him you be awake." The boy ran from the barn, knocking over a pitchfork and scythe in his haste.

The man sat in the hay, legs drawn to his chest and waited. He didn't sit for long. Hearing his name called, he jumped up and returned to grip the bars. The cold iron felt soothing against his suddenly hot palms.

"Ah, there ye be, McDennett. I been thinking 'bout ye."

The man recognized his friend, lean features, and long face to match long, hard hands.

"William," he said quietly, his eyes boring into his friend. "Why I be 'ere? What have I done to deserve this?"

William leaned against the far wall, sighed loudly, and said, "Do ye remember the attack...by the wolf?"

"Aye, I do."

"It weren't no wolf." He took a deep breath. "It were a lycanthrope that got to ye."

Duncan McDennett fell to the floor. Fear and the loss of hope, emotions he had never felt before, surged through his being, throbbing and knocking the reality home.

"No, ye be lying," he whispered harshly. A million thoughts ran through his mind. Running his hands through his thick hair, he said, "I be married. What story did ye yarn?"

"Lassie thinks ye be dead."

Duncan hugged himself repeating the word "No" over and over like a mantra. The chant whispered in a rhythmic tone as his body swayed to and fro.

"Ye broke out three night ago," William continued, unsure if his friend heard him or not. "Ye went home, half changed."

The chanting stopped.

"Lassie?" Duncan enquired.

"Ye raped her but did no serious 'arm. Her memory be reserved of the attack, but she believes it to be ye, returned in animal form." He took a deep breath and continued, "This is why there are now iron bars and you will be watched every night."

"I will become a lycanthrope. How can I be stopped? No one can stop a lycanthrope when it is hungry."

"Aye, that be fact. We will feed you with every cycle."

Duncan's voice grew cold. "Ye shall perish in time. I will not."

"We'll see what is what at that time. I will return shortly." With that William turned and strode out.

Duncan paced the stall. His old life was gone. This he would eventually come to accept, but he would not live like an animal caged behind bars. He felt a strange rage building inside him, a fire he had never felt before and he liked it. It felt like power and fear rolled into one.

He charged at the bars, slamming into them with his right shoulder. The bars rattled against the bolts. Duncan felt no pain. He backed up as far as he could and charged the bars a second time, jumping at the last moment.

His body connected with a thud and the bolts snapped. The bars flew to the opposite wall as he tumbled through. He picked himself up. Three men carrying swords hurried to block the only escape route.

"William, Angus, Michael. Be out of me way."

Angus and Michael backed away and dropped their swords,

but William stood firm.

"No," William said. "Ye will have to go through me, first."

Duncan nodded in understanding. He was a lycanthrope now and as such he had no friends.

He said: "Aye. I will."

And charged...

* * *

New Zealand 1980

In the living room, his mother heard the cries and instantly dropped her Stephen King novel, 'Carrie' and ran with God's speed to her son's room, almost crashing through the door.

She first heard the television and then saw the quivering pile of blankets on her son's bed. His room was a mess, toys everywhere. She stood motionless a moment to take it all in. She watched the TV for a second and the scream started to make sense.

"You shouldn't be watching these kinds of movies," she said in a kind voice, even though she was upset with him for watching television this late with school the next morning. "They'll give you bad dreams."

"Over there." A hand with a pointing finger slid out from under the blankets and pointed to the open chest.

"And what's that, honey?"

"The beast that took daddy."

She remembered the horror movie and her heart went out to him and bled for his innocence. He never understood what happened when it came to his father's death. She felt remorse, not only for her son but for herself as well. James had seen the dog attack and kill his stepfather.

"No love," she said, pulling the blankets down. She wanted to cry at seeing his tear stricken face and red puffy eyes. "That was only a film."

Duncan McDennett moved into the shadows thrown by the apartment buildings. The boy was a full blood, the last of the line. He would have to make this child into what he was. The child possessed the tool that all true bloods have, the power to move objects with his mind.

He morphed to human form, pleased the child had seen him.

Duncan reached down and patted his two companions. They preferred to stay in lycanthrope form. The three of them had been together for two-hundred and seventy-three years. They were good companions and good hunters, and most importantly, they followed his commands.

"Oi, what the fuck ya think you're doing?"

Duncan turned to face a skinny man in his mid-twenties with a three-day stubble and a hand rolled cigarette dangled between chapped lips. The man's arms were covered with tattoos, his T- shirt was torn, and he wore dirty black jeans.

He had sensed this man watching him a long time ago but then the man had left and he had thought nothing more of it.

"Hey, I'm fucking talking to you."

The lycanthrope's growled and twitched. Duncan patted their heads. "Easy now," he cooed.

"Yeah, that's right." The man advanced a couple of steps. "Keep them mutts controlled."

Duncan took a step closer. The man stopped.

"Whatcha think you're doing on my property, man?"

Duncan looked around. He was standing on the grass edge of a concrete driveway leading to another block of flats. He met the man's eyes and said slowly, "Are you looking for trouble?"

"No mate, you're fucking asking for it."

"I see. Would you like us to leave?" He spread his hands out at his sides, indicating the two animals.

"Yeah," the man said, his confidence rising. "Why don't you

and your ugly girlfriends fuck off?"

Duncan smiled. "Very well," he said and turned his back. He took a few steps forward and quietly said to the lycanthrope's: "Dinner."

The beasts rose on their hind legs, lips curled back. They felt the hunger, as Duncan did, but he didn't feed that night.

PART ONE

TO KNOW FEAR, ONE MUST FEEL IT CREEPING ALONG THE SHADOWS...

Chapter One

Since he took up freelance photography three years ago, failure seemed to plague James Dennett. Every week, he would send in a series of photos to magazines across the country. And a month later they would return with the same thank you but no thanks letter. Amazement had ossified inside him when his pictures of an out of control plane, nose-diving into Redwood forest, were rejected. It wasn't a 747 or a Jumbo, only a small twin engines aircraft -- yet it made the news and still his photos were unwanted.

Everything he sent would come back, back to this horrid place, this horrid caravan park set against a dark sheet of ocean, which swirled and flowed onto a golden beach called, 'Opera Sands'. The name was adopted after a weeklong opera took place on a small white painted stage in the 1930's. The stage still stood, old, wrecked, and salt ruined.

The bright morning light momentarily blinded James as he stepped out of the old rusty, small 1960's caravan and slammed the tin door shut. The latch caught and held for once, he thought this to be a good sign to start the day with and perhaps if luck and skill combined, maybe sell a photo or two.

The unemployment benefit wasn't much help, but the caravan was cheap and he got to meet a lot of interesting people. Some were tourists, but most of the others were people like him trying to get by the best they could. He found the tourists liked to be professionally photographed with the opera stage behind them and it was this work, that which paid for his film and developing chemicals.

Crossing the moist dark green, uncut, ankle high grass on Friday morning, he made a 'bee-line' straight to the Caravan Park office, a small side room between the cafe Royal and Mrs. Clemm's apartment, joining the two. He checked his wallet and removed enough cash to pay the rent and sighed at the amount left for the weekly expenses. He didn't have the cheapest profession around, but he loved it all the same.

He didn't like the owner though. Mrs. Clemm was a large woman getting on in life whom always sat on a large round wooden stool behind the shatter proof window with a small cutout at the bottom, for transactions. Her flower pattern dress hung slightly open, as usual, to the third button, allowing more than enough cleavage to show.

Her eyes were fixed on a large romantic novel, one of the hundreds she'd read after taking over the day-to-day running of the park nine years ago. The books were stacked neatly in several piles next to an unused bookcase.

She glanced up from her book and saw James crossing the lawn, almost at the concrete path now, headed her way.

Ethel Clemm hadn't liked the man since he arrived at the park two and a half years ago, unshaven with a camera hung around his neck, a big smile and asking about long term board.

Ethel found she actually hated the man. She remembered telling him; 'Dreams are for fools.'

"Mrs. Clemm?" James knocked on the window. "Rent day?"

Slowly raising her eyes from the novel to him, giving a disapproving frown, she said: "Mr. Dennett, I have some mail for you." She picked up five A4 size envelopes off the table beside her and pushed them through the slot. "Not more rejections, I hope."

"We'll see, Mrs. Clemm," he replied taking the envelopes and handing over the rent trying not to look down her open blouse.

"You'll never make it, you know. I know these things. It's like winning Lotto, four chances in a million."

For an instant, James saw himself reach through the slot, grab her by the throat and throttle the life from her oversized body until she fell limp, and then scream at her: "Do that bloody blouse up, old woman!" He felt it the perfect end for all the insults she'd thrown at him these past years.

On more than one occasion, she started malicious rumors about him and his family. Where she picked up these ideas he had no idea. He decided not to cause any trouble and never mentioned hearing the lies she spread. He wanted to keep a roof over his head. No matter how terrible the caravan was it was still his home and work place.

"I'd like a receipt, Mrs. Clemm."

Quietly she filled out the receipt and handed it to him through the slot with a forced smile. "Here you are, Mr. Dennett."

He folded it and placed it in his back pocket. Today was strange; she hadn't thrown any remarks about his photography. Maybe she was changing her view of things? He doubted it. She hated him for doing what she never had the chance or guts to do - and that was to follow one's dream.

Strolling across the lawn letting his torn sneakers collect moisture on the way back, he tore open the first envelope and found what he'd gradually come to expect; his photos and a 'Thanks but no thanks' reply. He reached his home and stepped onto the first of two concrete blocks acting as steps, and had to force the caravan door open as usual.

He dropped the envelopes onto a small table he had to pull down from the wall and unfold the two legs. A seven-foot curtain hung at the other end of the caravan, from the ceiling to the floor, acting as a door to his bedroom. It was an easy to replace and easy to repair door and very effective.

James stretched out on the tacky orange couch attached to the back wall, unlike the table; this was fixed to the floor by a series of bolts. He reached over the table and read the other letters because there was nothing else to do except dream of grandeur.

The second, third and fourth envelopes read the same as the first and all the others he'd amassed over the past two and a half years, or was it three years now? The fifth rested on his chest as he popped a cushion against the arm of the couch and the wall. Opening the envelope, he pulled out the photos and tossed them onto the table. Two skidded off the edge.

He held the letter folded in one hand and tossed the envelope to the floor, not noticing something slide from it. After a moment's thought he decided to read the 'Thanks but no thanks' letter. It started the same as the rest had:

Dear Mr. Dennett,

Sorry to return your photos, at the moment they are not exactly what we are looking for.

However...

And that's where it became interesting. James swung his legs off the couch and sat upright. He smelt a faint hint of hope. Excitedly he read on...

Judging by the position and texture of your photos, lighting etc. our editor spotted a lot of raw potential and with that in mind we are willing to give you the opportunity for a commissioned two part series of evening shots of Redwood forest and of Opera Sands. We have a writer at work on the history of the forest and the beach.

Please refrain from looming tree shots and animals on dirt tracks, as these would not go well with the article being written.

Naturally, if your work matches with what we are looking for, we would be happy to offer a commissioned contract.

Please note that this has also been offered to twenty other new photographers as part of our yearly drive to find new talent.

Yours sincerely

Joe Phillips

Executive Editor

James noticed that it wasn't signed, but whooping with joy, he didn't really care thinking it was an oversight by an overworked secretary. He read the letter a second time. *I don't believe it,* he thought, reading the letter another two times, excitement rushed through his veins and he pinched himself thinking it was just a great dream. The pinch hurt. This was no fairy tale dream. This was real. Now he was faced with a few problems.

A vision came into his head of what kind of photos to take and he realized he'd need high exposure film. 1600 and 3200 speed was fine and all but not really powerful enough for what he had in mind. He'd need infrared or infra- green film, and the $62,000 question was, where in the hell could he get that and how much would it cost? He was given a deadline and he wanted to get his photos in first and beat the other twenty numb-nuts vying for the same thing.

Pushing the idea aside for the moment, he reviewed the images he had for the kind of shots he could do that would secure a commissioned offer for further work. If the moon were bright, he would use the light reflector, usually used for people shots, to capture an ominous setting. This shot he could use with 3200 speed, 4600 would make it too bright and they did say no animal shots, but to get the shots of dancing shadows on a windy night. That would be perfect, but he had to act fast as others were in the running also. If only he could get his hands on some infra-film.

Using an Internet Cafe computer he could remove a lot of the red or green coloring. Nothing was mentioned in the letter about digitally enhanced photos. He reached down for the envelope hoping the answer was in there, but alas that was as empty as a dry well. In frustration, he screwed it into a ball and tossed it across the room. It came to a stop after bouncing off the white gas powered stove with only one element. Trying to think, he lay on his back and sighed deeply. Opportunity finally knocked on his door and at the moment it couldn't find the key to let itself in.

All his emotions of hope shot through him and came to a sudden halt crashing against an invisible barrier and James cursed for not being able to find that blasted key. If it wasn't one thing it was another. He wanted to scream out as the frustration burned into him.

Getting off the couch and going into his room, James pulled a shoebox from under the bed and put the letter inside. He replaced the lid and slid it back.

He decided to take a shower to wash away the warped emotions he was experiencing and be able to think rationally about where to find the items he required. He went to the cupboard and pulled out the only towel he had. Traveling back to his room, he grabbed a pair of blue jeans; a T shirt and such, then left the caravan and headed toward the shower rooms. Again the tin door's lock held. It was a sign of good luck but then again James always looked for those types of signs in daily life.

CHAPTER TWO

Standing in the shower's concrete cubicle with hot water pounding against his chest and shampoo sliding down his back, James slowly stretched out his hand with his palm up in the direction of the soap holder under the shower head. He closed his eyes and pictured the soap rising out of it, floating through the air and dropping into his hand. With his mind focused on every detail of the bar of soap, he tried with all his might to force that solid object off the soap holder and onto his palm. The task seemed impossible and he believed this negative thought was holding him back, even though, many years ago as a kid he had been able to do it. The memory of making all his toys fly out of the toy box and land on the floor flashed back to him and he involuntary allowed his arm to fall to his side.

When it happened, it scared the living daylight from him. Now he understood it perfectly - telekinesis, the ability to move objects with the power of the mind. It had nothing to do with demons or monsters, as he had thought way back then. Age increased wisdom and he wished the scare had not stopped him from using or perfecting the gift, because now, he couldn't do it. He turned the shower off, not bothering to soap today and entered the changing area unaware the soap had fallen to the floor.

James gave up on telekinesis for the day; after all, there was always tomorrow.

He stood in front of a large mirror and brushed long, brown hair from his bedroom brown eyes. His cheeks and chin were rough with stubble. He decided then and there to let it grow out a bit and see if a beard suited his angular face. He was well built and solid, had even lifted weights at one time wanting to look like Rocky. He frowned when he tucked in his shirt and noticed a junk food stomach expanding. He tapped it a few times, and then pulled out his shirt hoping the hanging fabric would hide it.

Photography was not an easy profession to be in. It had more downs than ups. He had made a decent wage when he worked at the law firm, and took photos as a hobby. It brought in a few bucks here and there and James thought he could make a living doing what he loved. It wasn't working; until the letter arrived with an offer of a full time contract.

Finally, nearly flat broke, opportunity showed itself. His chance had arrived. He couldn't fuck this up, no matter what.

James left the shower cubical and strolled across the moist but drying grass, his mind focused on the film to buy and its cost and he knew it wasn't going to be cheap; this would break him if he didn't get the contract.

Pride kept him from returning to the law office with his tail between his legs begging for his old job. They parted on good terms, and he didn't sense any bad vibes at the leaving party. He smiled at the memory.

He stopped in mid-stride. *What are you doing*, he thought, *you have a job to do with a deadline*. He knew he was right and amended the direction of his thoughts. The three places he had come up with were the Video and Camera Image Enhancement shop (a long shot he knew), Auckland University, and Canterbury University. Canterbury was the best but it was a two or three-day trip. Then he would have to borrow the money to get there and no one he knew, except Carl, would be in a position to lend it to him.

'Risk all or gain nothing,' that was his favorite expression and dammed if he wasn't risking it all now.

Not far from his caravan, with the wet towel draped around his shoulders and dirty clothes in a plastic supermarket bag, he spied the tin door of his home swaying gently in the breeze. He shook his head in disbelief. The worst caravan in the park was his, and it was the only caravan whose door had a mind of its own and rarely stayed closed.

He froze in his tracks. Had he just seen movement inside? There it was again. A shadow moved against the drawn curtain. Someone was in his castle, invading his private space. This situation was a first for him and he wasn't sure what to do. But damn it! That was his home no matter how shitty it was.

'Action. One must take action to protect what is his.'

His legs would not move, frozen into the moist ground. This seemed unreal; it was broad daylight for goodness sake. Then he remembered his photography equipment. He had thousands of dollars of equipment. That got his legs moving.

He crept to the door. Heart pounding against his chest like a sledgehammer, he stepped to the side of the door and waited for the breeze to blow it open so he could charge in.

He inhaled a few quick breaths in an attempt to slow his heart.

Instead, his heartbeat quickened as he quietly stepped onto the first of two concrete blocks as the breeze opened the door. He had too much expensive equipment in there to back away or hide.

James's sneakers squeaked and the sound surprised him causing him to hesitate. Nerves turned and twitched in the pit of his stomach.

No thoughts ran through his mind. His answers to life, the universe, and everything were summed up in the blink of an eye: *Survival.*

All sounds except his heart beat ceased to exist. The survival instinct switched on, his nerves stopped their game and he was fully alert as he stepped onto the second and higher block. He glanced through the gap between the tin door and the frame, scanning whatever was in sight. James tilted slightly forward and looked in the direction of the bedroom, hoping to spot the intruder and get a glimpse at the size of whomever he was up against.

He couldn't see a thing.

James turned toward the direction of where the couch and table sat. They had most likely seen him coming and were waiting.

That's when he spotted a pair of heavy work boots propped up on the corner of the table. Thick clumps of dirt with blades of grass stuck into it dangled from the heavy rubber soles. The boots were tapping together, as if the person was listening to music. The intruder sighed loudly and with the aggression of a bored male.

Unsure of what action he was about to take, James moved forward. Hearing that person's voice instantly put an unfavorable image in his head, and his nerves back worse than before. Perspiring fear covered his forehead and slicked his back. Adrenaline coursed through his veins. The shakes would come soon. James wanted to go back in time, back to the shower with the hot water rolling down his body and the shampoo sliding down his back. What bliss!

His palms were sticky with sweat. The time to act had come.

It was now or never.

Do or die.

James swung the door wide open and threw himself inside, landing in a karate-like striking stance. His right arm was straight and rigid, the fist clenched tight. His left arm was pulled back taunt and ready to strike. And his feet - one back, the other slightly forward, both bent, he was ready for anything. Prepared for the worst.

Unimpressed, the intruder did not move. He lay on his left side with elbow pushed in the old cushions of the couch and his feet softly tapped each other on the table's corner. He said, "Hi, James. Alert as always, I see."

It took a second or two for the image of the intruder to register.

The brown hair patched with long gray streaks. The lean muscular figure, old dirt covered work boots with long thick laces, and the rough tanned face of a man who has led a hard life and worked for everything he had.

The kind, although visually intimidating and often a little slow, Carl Rothsins. He wore a large cross with rosary beads around his solid neck and attended church twice a day, before and after work. He loved God, his wife, and two adopted children, in that order, and he worked long hours to provide what they desired. Luckily, his wife was a woman of few needs and his children grew up understanding they couldn't always get what the other children had. But they never owned a stitch of clothing which was torn or patched. And they were well fed.

It was weird how some people just click together like a perfectly completed jigsaw puzzle, exactly the way he and Carl had the first time they had met, five-and-a-half-years ago, when James worked at the Law firm (he was only a clerk, but that isn't what he told people). He met Carl at Diggs and Briggs Construction Company. When he was still developing his photography skills and had asked permission to roam the site and take photos. It was a Sunday and the place was almost deserted. *Permission granted, but you wear a hardhat at all times and don't touch any of the machines.* He agreed. Damn, working at a law firm had its perks.

He was standing on top of a mound of dirt (without his hardhat) taking shots of the only worker there operating a digger. The man noticed him and waved. Twenty minutes later, they were both sitting on the digger drinking Pepsi. They instantly felt at ease with each other and discussed many things. Carl was the only person to wish him success at his photography dream.

Now his friend had popped around for another surprise visit.

"Carl," James said, startled and relieved. "What's up, mate?"

Carl sighed loudly and somberly replied: "It's me kids." His feet stopped tapping. Slowly and with pain, he said, "Last Wednesday...I finished work early and the wife, well she was out with her friends playing bingo, as she does every Wednesday..."

"Yes," James said, trying to keep Carl on track as he had a habit of wandering away from the subject.

"Sorry," Carl mumbled, swinging his massive legs off the table. He sat up and continued, "Like I said, I came home early, all the lights were on and the TV, but nobody around and you know how I hate wasting power."

"This can't be about wasted power, Carl. Did they crash the car or something?"

"I found Craig and Julie..." He took a long, slow breath. "I found them in bed together."

James had his suspicions so it didn't actually take him by surprise. But it seemed Carl hadn't noticed, or if he had, he had turned a blind eye to it. James acted surprised for his friend's benefit.

"What?" he said, surprising himself with the correct choice of tone and amazement. It came out sounding sudden and strained -- a perfect reply.

"That's right," Carl's voice grew in volume, anger adding a slice to his words. "They were fucking each other!"

Taken aback by the language of the usually soft-spoken Carl, James was caught off guard and at a loss for words. His response was to close his eyes and shake his head in astonishment. In all the years he had known Carl, he had never seen the man this upset, although who could blame him. The children knew they were adopted, had known from a young age. Most parents complained about their kids always fighting and Carl would glow like a child with his first bike and say: "My kids never fought. They were quiet and kind and always played together." Others would comment on how lucky he was. But he wasn't feeling so proud now.

"They spat on God and moral law!" Carl threw the words at James as if he were the devil's advocate. "When I get home tonight and see them together...I don't know what I'll do." Suddenly his voice dropped and he mumbled: "It's been over a week, and..." His sentence trailed off. "I don't even know why I am here. I guess I just thought you might have some advice, what with being an ex-lawyer and all."

James chose his words carefully. "I'm sorry Carl, I'd like to help you, I really would. But I feel this is a situation where I should not interfere. Speaking as a lawyer, it is illegal but there needs to be proof of penetration, like the birth of a child. But they are adopted, which puts us into a gray area."

After a moment's thought, he said: "I guess you're right. This is embarrassing. Imagine a guy in his fifties asking an unmarried guy your age for advice."

James remained silent. In Carl's eyes, he guessed thirty was young.

"I'm not a religious man," James searched for the right words, "but, perhaps … um, perhaps the advice you need can be found at church."

"Sorry, but I cannot tell Father Brian, about this."

"That's not what I meant." James sat on the table's corner.

After a moments silence, Carl whispered: "Yes, yes. I see." His face lit up and the light in his eyes danced again, "God helps those who ask. Ask and thou shall receive." Carl was excited and appeared to be coming around to his old self.

"I guess," James mumbled.

"What?"

"Nothing, never mind."

Carl smiled, "Okay. I should be going," He noticed one of his laces had come undone and he bent down to tie it up and spied something on the floor. The corner of a card stuck out from under the couch, only the tip of it visible. "Hello, what's this?"

James watched his friend closely. Carl had brightened up a little too quickly for his liking. He watched his friend lift a sheet of thick paper off the floor next to his right boot. It was small, roughly the size of an envelope. It was white with a blue frame and some fancy typeset. "It looks official."

James shook his head. "I don't know." But for some reason a thin beam of hope shot through him. Gingerly, he took the paper from Carl's stubby fingers and carefully read it… twice. His lips parted into a large smile.

"Good news?"

"I don't believe it. Lady Luck is back."

Carl looked confused.

James said: "This is a form I need for some film and stuff." He never bored Carl with detail. "I was wondering how to get it and it says here that they are partners with Auckland University's Film Development Lab. It seems that they supply the film for the photographers." He flipped the card over to find several question relating to what he would need and why, plus some general questions for him to put a check mark into a yes or no box. He ran to his room and collected the shoebox, his 'official box'.

He removed the lid and handed the top letter to Carl, who after reading it raised his eyebrows and said: "You're on your way."

James couldn't stop smiling.

"Well," Carl said. "Here's wishing you luck." He handed back the letter, "Thanks for your advice."

With that, Carl rose off the couch and left, headed for the house of God. James watched him walk across the grass, wave to Mrs. Clemm, and then remove a small book from his back pocket. James knew it was a junior edition bible, for it was all Carl ever read. He raised his children based on his interpretation from passages of that book, now it appears the children have strayed from the flock - in a big way. He hoped Carl found the answers he searched for, although he doubted it.

* * *

The cathedral rose high into the sky. It held a bell tower in the steeple, but the bells were old, salt ruined and cracked, and in dire need of repair. But Opera Sands was still a small community and couldn't raise the money required to have them repaired or replaced, so, for the past fifty years they had remained silent.

Carl stopped at the concrete steps. Fifteen of them led up to the heavy large oak doors. Next to the church was a park and he could hear the children laughing and playing, some with their parents, and others with friends.

He remembered a time when he and Martha use to play with their kids at this very park after Saturday and Sunday service and sometimes they would have a picnic if the weather was good.

The memories brought a smile to his face and an ache to his heart. He silently longed for those days to return, but alas, they were gone forever.

Lost in his past memories, Carl didn't notice a young man dressed in black, run up and around him from the corner of the church.

"Excuse me, sir," the young man said from behind, but before Carl had a chance to turn around, he felt a sharp pain in the back of his neck. "My name's Allen. Remember that old man," he whispered into his right ear, and then ran off, tossing a syringe in a nearby rubbish bin.

Confused, and panicked at seeing the syringe, he started to chase the man. Reaching the side of the church, he saw the young man near the end of the park. Colors washed his vision and he stopped. He rubbed the back and side of his neck, there wasn't any pain now and he remembered he was at the church for a reason.

The colors quickly returned to normal. He relaxed and climbed the steps to the door. As he reached the top step, he had completely forgotten about the young man in black. A mild dizziness set into him and he felt his energy drain away. Just standing was bringing on a slight sweat and his legs shook.

Quickly, he opened the door. The church was empty. He walked to the altar and knelt down, clutching the cross around his neck. His eyes were wide as he stared at the effigy of Christ, asking, begging for answers. The cold, hard wood began to take effect on Carl's old knees, but he ignored the steadily increasing pain, and waited for an answer.

For twenty minutes, he knelt with his hands clasped tightly together, before strange sounds surrounded him, sounds of a thousand men, screaming. The effigy of Jesus shook, jerked and pulled away from the cross. Blood shot from the hands as it tore past the nail. The head of Christ turned upward and screamed: "Why? Why me? I did not ask for this, Father. Why?"

It floated in the air, screaming the sentence over and over again. Carl fell back in shock unable to remove his eyes from the image of Christ. Hot, white flashes of light shot from the wall the cross hung on.

The wall crumbled, revealing a desert land behind it. Hot sand stretched for miles meeting red mountains in the horizon. A blazing sun burned above in the clear sky. Suddenly, seemingly to come from nowhere, tanks and soldiers appeared. Bombs exploded, shooting hot sand against the armies. Men fell in tens and a hundred screams of terror filled the air. A bright flash came billowing from the sky and then...all was silent. The tanks stopped moving. The soldiers were gone. The Earth was dead. Howling sounds came from unseen areas. Howls of an animal - an animal in pain. The ground trembled and shook. A large crack appeared down the center and fire shot upwards licking the sky black.

Total destruction.

Then, as quickly as it had started, it stopped. The vision vanished. The church wall was back.

The effigy of Christ, still floating, looked down upon Carl who was crying. The effigy spoke, "When the Jews return to Zion, then all that was won will be lost."

Carl watched in silent awe as the effigy pinned itself back on the cross.

"And the devil must be loosed a season lasting thirty-two months."

He rose off the pew; his sore knees stiffened. Pain shot through them, as he stood erect and stretched. He knew what had to be done and that God had chosen him. He was sad and happy at the same time, if that were possible. He was sad at what had to be done and was happy God had answered him.

Leaving the church, Carl knew the vision was a look into the future. It wasn't nice. He could still hear the sound of thousands of people screaming, and try as he might, he found it impossible to be rid of that terrible, anguished wailing.

* * *

Allen Sheriff arrived home twenty minutes after he had attacked Carl, and was mildly surprised the old geezer had chased him. It felt good. He felt good. The plan was working smoothly. He went to the garage and sat against the far wall. Next to him was a fingerless leather glove he'd completed earlier that morning. It was large and bulky and fitted perfectly on his right hand. Between the knuckles were five curved stainless steel blades attached by a steel clamp and leather straps. It weighed less than he thought it would. The glove neck reached half way up his forearm with strap ties. He smiled. It was so beautiful.

Putting the glove to one side, he reached over and picked up a machete and sharpening stone. Slowly he drew the stone against the weapons edge and marveled at his reflection shining off the blade. It was long, curved, powerful weapon.

He prayed to God for his vengeance on Dennett to be swift and deadly. The false letter had been sent and he hoped it would fool the pathetic loser. It had to work. He knew James was desperate.

"Tonight," he whispered to the machete. "Tonight, the sheriff's coming to town."

* * *

By midday, James was at the Opera Sands bus stop at the northern end of town. The bus headed for Auckland central was due to have arrived ten minutes ago. It was late as usual. He never fancied catching the bus, they were unreliable and in the long run, expensive, especially for a forty-five minute ride into the city. He waited patiently as all public transport riders do, but this time he didn't mind.

The bus stopped to the right of him. Checking to make sure the voucher was safe and sound in his pocket, James climbed aboard, very audacious about his future as a photographer. This was his one and only chance. He was going for broke. The weight of success or failure weighed heavily on his shoulders.

He was moving to the rear of the bus when the driver pulled out from the bus stop and sped up. James shot forward from the sudden motion and reached out to grab hold of the nearest seat to stop from falling flat on his face.

There was an empty seat right at the back of the bus and James rested his bones from the long walk. He found himself staring out the window, watching cars cruise past, and a large crowd scattered along Owera beach.

The even movement and soft hum of the bus was soothing. His seat was on top of the motor and relaxation took hold of his body.

A 'stop abortion' protest group stood in an even line, each person holding a banner. They started to scream as the bus stopped near the group to pick up a couple of people who'd flagged him down. One of the protesters ran up to the window and held up a sign, which read: **James won't make it**. The banner had a small picture of a camera with a large red X covering it. All the protesters gathered around his window, each holding the same type of banner.

Shocked, James turned away, refusing to believe what he saw. The passengers on the bus turned to face him and started chanting his name, it sounded like thunder inside his head. They were all frowning and pointing at him as if he were a leper covered in open sores or something worse. The two new passengers also held hurtful banners they waved at him.

Then they were on him, all the passengers with banners swinging wildly at him. The banners struck his face, arms and chest. He felt a couple of them slice his face and cut into his hands. He tried to scream but no sound came and there was nowhere for him to hide, he was pushed up hard against the side of the bus. He threw wild kicks and punches but he wasn't able to stop them. He felt the warm blood slide down his face, saw it blotting his shirt, thick clots formed around his collarbone.

Through his tears he saw the bus driver push through the tormentors. They all stopped when they saw him. Was he the leader? They were all quiet, watching the driver. James sunk deeper into the seat. The driver reached across and tapped him on the shoulder; he was smiling, "Last stop, mate."

"Sorry?" James asked sleepily.

"Come on, mate, wake up."

James's tired eyes saw images of Auckland City bus depot. "Thanks. Sorry about that," he replied, rising off the seat. "Do you know how I can get to the university?"

The driver checked his watch. "There's a free bus heads up that way in about five minutes." The driver pointed it out to him, "It's that blue and white one."

Now almost fully awake, James thanked the driver and left. He heard the free bus engine fire up. Worried that he might miss it, James broke into a run and jumped onto the first step. The driver gave him a puzzled look. Smiling through his embarrassment, realizing the driver was only warming up the engine, James asked: "Do you stop at the university?"

The driver nodded.

James took the first available seat. It was a single just behind the driver. He checked his watch. His return bus departed at 3:05 and he would hate to miss it and end up spending the night in Auckland City without a roof over his head. During the day, Auckland was a splendid city with wonderful attractions and all the shops and movie theaters one could ask for, but at night, after 8pm, its personality changed. That was the down side of big cities.

After a few minutes, the bus jerked and slowly rolled forward. The journey took almost seven minutes and James caught himself nodding off twice. The dream was still a vivid nightmare in his memory. It did not fade as most dreams did.

He was a believer in the power of dreams, he knew they usually meant the opposite, but he had a feeling this was not the average run-of-the-mill bad dream. Something was trying to warn him. Stop him even.

The large university entrance loomed into view and James prepared himself.

* * *

Entering the administration building, he felt an academic aura surround him. The hallway was empty; a deathly silence covered the floors, walls and ceiling. He scanned the surroundings, searching for a sign to direct him. Finding none, he walked along the hall feeling deserted as if he were the only person alive on the planet. His memory shot him images of the New Zealand movie 'The Quiet Earth', just to enhance his feeling of lonesomeness. The silence seemed to wrap around his head and squeeze it like a vice.

Straight ahead were a number of doors running down the corridor. On his left, he saw a large sign bolted on its edge to the wall. He realized he must have entered a side door and not the main. It was his first time here. The sign read: Reception.

The soft mutterings of teachers behind classroom doors drifted into the hallway. His sneakers made soft scratching sounds and his uneven breathing seemed to echo. He removed the voucher from his top pocket.

A woman in her mid-forties sat behind a counter-like desk, which spanned from one end of the room to the other. It had a small swinging door at the left end. A large monitor sat on top of the counter and a normal size keyboard sat on a counter below, and beside it was a steaming cup of coffee. The woman swept long black hair from her green eyes. She smiled at James, pleased for the interruption.

"Yes sir, can I help you?"

"Ah, yeah. Miss," he read her name badge, "Laura Finny. I have a voucher for some film and mixing chemicals." He handed her the voucher. His hand shook from the excitement. He was worried something would go wrong.

She frowned. "I've never seen one of these before, but if you go to the photography department, maybe they can help you." She handed back the voucher. "I'm sorry I don't know about any of this."

"No problem," James replied, trying to keep his smile. "Could you tell me where I can find the photography department?"

"Just go straight down the hall, take a left and it's the second door on your right." She smiled again. "You can't miss it."

"Thanks."

"You're welcome," she said and went back to her typing. She looked up a second later to watch him leave.

James nodded goodbye; followed her instructions and was surprised to find it so easily. He listened at the door but couldn't hear any sounds from inside. He knocked quietly and slowly opened the door.

He found the room empty and very white. At the front of the

room, he saw a whiteboard with diagrams and messy written notes in long hand below each picture.

Soft voices came from a door to the far left of the room. He went to it and was about to open the door when he noticed a red light above the doorframe and realized it was a developing room. He knocked and heard: "Wait a minute."

James went back to the whiteboard and sat on the edge of a desk studying the diagrams. It rapidly bored him and he searched for something else to grab his attention and came upon a copy of 'Photography Today'. Flicking through, he mused at the photos used for demonstration although a few gave him some good ideas for Redwoods Forest. Reaching the end of the magazine and being unsure how much time had passed, James rose and knocked on the door a second time.

He received the same reply.

Frustrated and running out of time to catch the last bus to Opera Sands, he said: "Look, I'm in a bit of a hurry and if you don't come out, I'll come in." It was a bluff. He wasn't a threatening type of person and to him it sounded hollow and weak.

But it worked a charm as a young voice said: "Give me thirty seconds, will ya."

Smiling, James went back to the desk and held the voucher in both hands. He looked over it at the developing room where the red light was now turned off. After a moment or two, the door swung open and a man in his late twenties exited wearing a false smile and extending his hand. "Good afternoon, Mr.?"

"Dennett."

"Mr. Dennett. What can I do for you?"

At last! James thought and said: "I have this voucher..." He handed it over.

The young man read it. His face lost some color. "Um, yeah. All right, ah...I remember this now. Hang on a minute." He opened a draw in his desk. "This is for you. You're the last to collect this stuff."

The last! James thought, disappointed.

The young man continued: "In here," he held up a package,

"are two rolls of film, and a newly developed chemical called; Exponpet 2000. We call it: Exo, for short. Now, you need to mix 15 mils of this in your stop bath tray, and use Glacial Acetic acid when developing your film."

That sounded strange.

"Why?" James asked curiously.

"The film in here is Kordarak High Speed Infra Sheet Film 4143. Perfect for haze penetration, adding special effects in commercial architectural and landscape shots, also good for your assignment, and Exponpet will removed all over tinting."

"I've never heard of it."

The young man sighed. "Like I said, it's new. Be careful with Exo, until it is mixed in the second bath it is very acidic and will burn through skin in seconds." His expression was deadly serious.

Worried and more than a little prudent, James asked: "Do I need to wear a mask or anything?"

"Mask? No, there's no smell and harmless if breathed. There are instructions inside and a pair of protective gloves."

He handed the package over. James took it eager to return home. "Thank you." James said.

"No problem."

* * *

The young man watched James leave. When the door closed he said quietly to himself: "Boy, have you pissed off the wrong person." He knew that when Exponpet 2000 was added to the stop bath mix, the chemical reaction would make the Glacial acid bubble and explode, spraying everyone and everything in close range.

He waited a few minutes then went to the public phone in the hallway, inserted his card and dialed. On the seventh ring it was answered. "Yeah, it's done." He waited a bit then said, "Okay, I'll check my account later today." He hung up. Christ, what had he just done? No amount of money would pay off his guilt.

CHAPTER THREE

1573 Scotland

The months passed slowly for Duncan. He lived in a cave on the outside border of his hometown. He fed only when he needed and was careful not to make more like him, but the lonesomeness grew heavier with every passing day. He watched his wife when he could. She too was lonely, people stayed away from her as much as they could. And it was all because of him. What he had done to her. The township knew, even a few outsiders had become privileged of this fact. Tonight they would die. He would rip this town apart.

He hadn't seen his wife in almost six months. Some kids had stumbled into his lair while playing a game. He couldn't bring himself to injure innocent children, so he forced them to secrecy. But children being children had told their folks and so he ran.

Duncan had learned a few months ago that he could change at will. William was the second to learn that lesson, but he didn't give an injury. That alone had gained him some time. Time to run.

Tonight he saw Dr. Shannon with a plump middle-aged lady welcomed into his wife's home. A stranger opened the door. He wondered if she had left town in his six months absence.

The sun was setting. He decided to wait another hour before venturing to the house for some answers.

Duncan paced the outskirts of town crouching in the long grass, his ears tuned to the slightest sound, waiting for nightfall. When it came dark enough, the tension had risen to breaking point and he rushed to the house, throwing caution to the wind.

He heard the screams long before he got there. The screams belonged to his wife, they were high pitched and he felt her pain. With each sound he had to force the change down. But his plan had changed with the screams. He would not peek in the windows and listen at the door as he had intended. No, now he would enter and do what it took to stop her pain. Tonight he planned to destroy this town and he would start with whoever was hurting his wife.

He leapt over the steps, the jump taking him through the front door. It crashed against the fireplace folding in half. Nails falling from the exposed hinges tinkled on the wooden floor.

The doctor opened the bedroom door. "Duncan!"

"What are you doing to me wife," he hissed. Grabbing the doctor by the throat he lifted the heavyset man two feet in the air and carried him into the bedroom.

"Oh my Lord," his wife cried. "Duncan?"

"Aye."

His wife's legs were bent at the knees and parted. Suddenly she screamed again. Duncan released the doctor as the plump lady put her hands between the legs. He stared in awe at the most amazing sight he had ever seen.

Minutes later he heard a slap and the startled cry of a baby. The doctor handed it to Lassie who let it suckle at her breast. She beamed with pride. "It be a boy," she whispered. "Ye son."

"What will be his name?" Duncan asked sitting beside his wife.

She looked down at her wrinkled child, looked into her husband's eyes and said: "Allen. It has a nice sound to it, don't you think?"

"Aye. It's a fine strong name."

"I knew ye weren't dead. Sometimes I felt ye watching over me."

He brushed sweat soaked hair from her face. "Don't talk of such things now. There will be time later."

Duncan heard heavy footsteps in the living room and he realized the doctor and midwife were gone. Two large men entered brandishing swords. They were strangers to him. And they didn't hesitate.

He moved to the foot of the bed. They drew up alongside him. He waited, remained statue still until the feeling to duck came. The two swords swung past his head. Duncan changed.

He leapt at the closest; his jaws clamped on the man's throat and he jerked his head sideways. The man dropped clutching at the blood jetting from his torn veins. His body convulsed. Blood ran into his lungs. He drowned moments later.

The feeling came again, strong - urgent: *Roll.*

And he did, just missing the edge of the sword as it crashed down slicing into the man's dead comrade. He withdrew the sword as Duncan in human form grabbed his head from behind and twisted it a hundred and eighty degrees.

Lassie hadn't moved. She clutched her baby boy protectively to her chest.

Duncan approached her and she shrank away from him. The action stopped him in his tracks. He said: "I understand. Know this: I love you and my son and I will protect ye till the end of me days."

He turned and left. Through the open doorway he saw a large gathering of townspeople grouped at the front of the house. He went to the front porch and faced them.

In a loud voice, he said: "If anyone is disrespectful to my wife or son...I will make them like me, and that is a gift ye wish to not receive."

He stepped off the front steps and walked through the townsfolk who parted as he neared. Duncan smiled. Power and fear, he controlled these emotions; no one could stop him. A new thought emerged and he decided not to destroy this town. His son needed somewhere to grow and develop and call home.

* * *

James arrived home at four thirty. The sun's brightness had dulled over the past hour or so, but the stillness of the air kept these late afternoons warm and dry. He held tight to the package with both hands and walked quickly across the Caravan Park's driveway, almost breaking into a slow jog.

Within sight of his caravan now, he saw something taped to the door. As he reached the caravan he saw it was an envelope attached with duct tape. His name was scribbled on it. James tore it open. The message was from Carl. This was the first time his friend had ever left a note; usually he waited for his return. A bad feeling wrapped around him, like a black cloak.

It read:

My dear friend
I have found the answers I searched for. Sadly though, the demons in my mind have raped me beyond control. I must dispose of them before they take the ones I love.
God has shown me the way. His magnificent light glows within me. This is the only way for me to save myself and destroy the demon seeds Satan has planted in my soul.
Good bye my friend, take care of Martha and the kids in their time of need. Tell them not to worry we will all meet on the other side.
Your friend
Carl

Holy shit! James mind reeled. He folded up the note and placed it in his back pocket and sprinted to the nearest public phone, knowing full well that Mrs. Clemm wouldn't allow him to use hers. The nearest non-vandalized phone was at the opposite end of the park. He could see it in the distance, positioned before a backdrop of pine trees, which marked the boundary. He checked his pocket for change as he neared it.

It looked different somehow. It was almost seven feet high and made of thick plastic, nothing unusual about that. It was the color that was different and he realized the once blue 'coin phone' had changed to a green 'card phone'. His sprint changed into a slow jog. He had never owned a phone card before and never wanted to. Ironically, it was Carl who'd suggested he get a phone card - just in case. That was last year and until now he had no use for one.

Breathless, he reached the phone and lifted the receiver. It was blank - dead, no sound. He looked for a set of instructions as the small screen on the phone printed out 'Please insert phone card'.

Finding the instruction block, he swore and cursed the person who had written with a thick marker: '21/1/95 Joe loves Cathy. 22/1/95 Joe wants to fuck Cathy. 23/1/95 Joe fucked Cathy!' There was also a picture of hearts and a large crudely drawn penis with the words: 'Suck this bitch!' written around the head. These messages covered the instructions.

James punched the numbers 101 and waited. A recorded message answered giving instructions for toll calls, international calls and operator assistance. James pressed: 010 and heard a human voice say: "Good afternoon, tolls. What city please?"

Close to babbling, James said: "I don't have a card but I need to contact some urgently. Can I charge the call to their account?"

"That's up to them sir. Can I have the number please?"

James gave it, and then heard a series of clicks. He felt a shiver run down his spine and shook it off. His fingers twitched nervously, afraid Carl would go through with this bullshit. He was more than worried, because he knew Carl would do it. He didn't want to be a part of this. He didn't need or want this kind of pressure.

"Your name please sir?" the operator asked.

"James Dennett."

"Oh, James, what a pleasant surprise!"

"Martha," he recognized her voice instantly. The soft well-spoken, silk-like words were pleasing to the ear, as was her beauty to the eye. By the pleasantness in her voice, James knew she didn't know of Carl's plan, most likely she didn't know about the kids either.

Martha said: "I'll accept the charges, Miss."

There was a click as the operator switched off.

"James, I haven't heard a word from you in far too long."

"I'm sorry about that. I saw Carl this morning. And he told me about the problem with the kids."

Solemnly, Martha said: "Well, yes. I'm afraid he is not taking it well. He got so mad. Trust me, James. You don't want to see Carl mad."

So, she *did* know, James thought as he heard her sniffle, and that single sound tugged at his heart. "That's why I phoned."

"Yes?" Sniff.

"I, umm..." How was he going to word this? He knew he wasn't being paranoid, but it was still going to sound harsh. He wasn't good at this sort of thing. "I got a note from Carl this afternoon. He taped it to my door when I was out." Now came the hard part. "It basically says he is going to deal with the demon seeds which have taken control of his soul." A pause to let it sink in, then: "Any idea what that could mean?"

The phone was silent for a few moments, then: "Oh no, James, it's against our belief. You don't think he'll do something stupid, do you?"

"Of course not," he lied. He knew damn well that Carl was about to do something fucked up. "Where is he working this month? I'll go and have a chat with him."

"McShingles Island," she sobbed.

"McShingles Island," James repeated, "That's not far from here. What's the company building?"

More sobs, then: "A bridge. It's almost completed. James, Carl's boss phoned not an hour ago asking if Carl was all right, he didn't show up for work this morning."

"He's most likely in church, Martha, I wouldn't worry too much."

James realized the bridge was the perfect place for Carl to kill the demon seeds. Carl couldn't swim and in Carl's mind he would think the demon seeds couldn't swim either. He remembered reading an article in the paper about the government sponsoring the bridge's construction. Many tourists complained about the ferry unable to make it across to the island most days. The sea between McShingles and Orewa could be nasty even on a fine day. So to accommodate the profitable tourist industry, the government had agreed to build a bridge for busses to drive across. This would also mean clearing a large area of the island for a car park and for a bus turn-about as the main attraction to McShingles Island was the trek to the cabins. The tourism board was happy. The general public was not. And James didn't give a shit.

"Martha," he waited for a reply. It came slowly and quietly.

"James."

"I'm going to have a hunt for him. Now, I don't want you to get yourself all worked up. When I find him, I'll call you, all right?"

No reply came.

"All right, Martha? I promise I will call you."

"Fine, James."

With that he hung up. He had never experienced the excitement of terror like this building up within him before and for a second, he almost liked it.

* * *

Clarie's Boat-yard was located at the northern end of Opera Sands. Clary owned the three ferries that took the construction workers, tourists and sightseers to McShingles Island. The yard was old and run down. Clary himself was reaching his thirty-sixth year of ownership. He was praying that once the bridge was completed, that dinky little island would become popular, and then his business might pick up. Sure he'd lose out on the trips to the island (after all, no one would take the ferry when they can drive over?), but people loved to fish and there was money in fish, always had been and always will be.

Clary stared out toward the island, but it wasn't what he was looking at. For a short time he watched the number 2 ferry heading back, struggling to get past a patch of light green motionless ocean. The light patch, in between the mainland and the island looked inviting, soothing and very calm. Too damn calm, considering the rest of the area rocked back and forth producing average sized waves for the surfers farther up the beach.

"Clary!"

He turned to see an exhausted James, running towards him. "Mr. Dennett, nice to see you again. It's been too long. How did our shoot for the posters come out?"

"They're great, Clary." James rested to catch his breath he wasn't as fit as he had thought.

"What's that you're carrying?"

James had forgotten he still held the package from the university, "It's just ... some ... film," a couple of quick breaths, then: "Is that the last ferry?"

"Might be, most of the workers got to go home early today." He scratched his gray stubble and adjusted the cap on his white head of hair.

"What do you mean?"

Clary pointed to the patch of calm water. "See that over there, under the forth support of the bridge?"

James nodded.

"Looks beautiful, doesn't it. Nice and calm and shit."

"Not really."

"Well, that there's a rip, not a normal run of the mill rip either. The MET office gave it some fancy name that I can't recall, but, you know how a rip drags you out and you must swim like a mother to get back?"

"Yeah," James said.

"Well, this one spins you under and out."

James looked at him blankly. "I've never heard of that. What does it actually mean?"

"It's like a whirlpool under there, spinning like a clothes dryer only a hundred times faster." Clary looked back out to see how the ferry was doing.

"What would cause that?"

"Got me, first time I've ever seen one. Heard about 'em though. If you ask me, it's all those digging machines they had out here thirty-something years ago, looking for oil. And now we got construction companies over there digging into the seabed. Mother Nature will only take so much before she gets pissed off and does something about it. Damn, number two is having a hell of a time. Look at her fighting through." He looked back at James. "This morning we hardly noticed it. If it wasn't for the MET office calling up, those workers would be stuck out there all night."

"Clary?"

"The ferries are old, son. The hulls getting a hammering out there and I just hope the old girl can handle it. We've already lost the steering on two ferries, not too hard to fix. Could end up being an all night job. Your trip important?"

"Yes," James said. He didn't want to say too much, Clary was well known to have a wagging tongue.

"Well, we'll see. Is it really that important or could it possibly wait until tomorrow? I don't want to send out the last ferry. Number 2 is coming back now with the last of the workers."

James stood silently waiting for the returning ferry to dock. Time held no meaning any longer, as it seemed to drag on in slow motion. He had a strange feeling that by the end of today his life was going to change.

Two ropes flew from the bow and port as the ferry drew up against the pier. Clary ran over, picked up the ropes and looped them onto two small thick iron clips. He waited until the construction workers exited the boat then began talking to the Maori skipper who wore mirror sunglasses, a pair of dark blue jeans and a long sleeved white shirt hanging open at the third button, reminding James briefly of Mrs. Clemm.

The two men approached him after their short conversation in hushed tones.

"Not looking for that Carl fellow are you?" Clary asked.

James nodded. "Was he aboard?"

"Yep, seemed a tad bit weirder than usual. Started talking about demons and shit and then started preaching to the six campers on board. I swear, if I didn't know Carl any better, I'd say he was freaking out on some bad shit," John, the skipper shook his head. "He says he's gonna walk along the bridge, take the street exit out. Needs to think about something."

"Can you take me there?"

"Sorry mate, not an option. The engine needs a tweak and by the time that's done … It'll be too dark to dock. And besides we ain't yet equipped with flood lights or any kind of lights at all."

James turned to Clary. "Well, do you have a rowboat or something with an outboard motor I could use?"

"With that out there? Don't be a bloody fool." He removed his pipe from the right breast pocket and started puffing on it even though there was no tobacco inside.

"Please, Clary," James pleaded. "There must be something."

Clary silently puffed on his pipe. John looked out at the bridge.

"The rip's that powerful?"

"Aye," Clary mumbled.

James looked skyward wondering if there was a God why would he allow Carl to die? He looked out at McShingles Island and softly said, "Clary?"

"What?"

"How far is the bridge from here?"

"About two kilometers. It starts at the state highway turn off."

Thinking out loud, James said, "I can swim that far, easily."

"Jesus Christ, boy. Haven't you been listening? You go near the thing and you're fucked. How many times do I need to say it?" Clary removed his cap and wiped the sweat from his brow.

"I can swim around it."

"Aye, you can. But tell me how you're gonna get up to the bridge when the ladder leading up there hangs in the middle of that shit?"

"Fuck!"

"Exactly."

James shook his head. All his options were gone because of that damn rip. He figured Carl already knew about it when he decided to kill the demons.

Suddenly, John ran to the center of the pier. Pointing at the bridge he said: "Mr. Dennett, look!"

Straining his eyes to see in the dull light (not sure how John could see with his sunglasses on), James saw a figure of a large man standing on the top railing of the bridge with his arms held out at shoulder height. Even though he couldn't see the person's face he knew who it was. "No Carl," he whispered. "Don't do it. Stop. Please God. Stop."

The figure threw his head back and screamed something unintelligible from this distance, then dived off the bridge. A group of workers with cars on the bridge ran to the edge and looked down.

"Fuck! Fuck! Fuck!" James screamed running to the end of the pier. He could only imagine what was happening to Carl as he entered the water. The powerful surge would take hold of his head, twisting and turning him like a rag doll, spinning him down deeper and deeper, snapping his neck and smashing his bones as he hit the seabed. The natural instinct would force Carl to open his mouth to breathe and only salt water would enter his lungs. Unconsciousness would cover him. Death was around the corner, if it hadn't arrived all ready.

James fell to his knees at the end of the pier. Thoughts flew and spun through his mind, all that he couldn't understand as his eyes searched for a dear friend, whom over the past few years had grown very close to his heart.

The light green patch of ocean remained motionless as if nothing had happened. James dropped to his knees, holding his head in his hands. A few minutes later, the bow of a large white cruiser moved in front of James blocking his view. Looking up, he realized it was the shore patrol, thank God. Someone had the brains to call them. Inside were a couple of fully decked out divers, each with a rope tired around their waist.

James watched as the cruiser moved toward the bridge. "You're too late," he said under his breath. "You're too fucking late." Slowly, with his head low, James rose off his knees and walked away. Tears welled in his eyes.

CHAPTER FOUR

Strolling slowly along the streets lost in past memories and wondering how to break the news to Martha and family, before the police. James walked past their yellow house with the white picket fence three times, circling the large block. He knew the police would get around to telling them fairly soon, if they hadn't already, but James thought it was his duty as a friend to inform them first.

The perfect little god-fearing family, he thought, *strange what happens behind closed doors.*

Dusk had arrived before James, gathering all the courage he could muster, lifted the latch on the white gate and walked, stiff legged to the light gray door. Happy and bright colors, he remembered the first time Carl had invited him over. Bright and happy colors covered any place where wallpaper could not be put.

Martha opened the door before James reached the first green step. "James, come in please. It's so nice to see you." She took a breath and said: "You've heard already?"

James felt embarrassed and ashamed at his earlier reluctance.

He nodded and quietly entered. In the living room, he spotted a new addition to the furniture; it was hard to miss. It was a cross about three feet high with a white plastic effigy of Christ attached to it. It stood against the wall next to a lamp. He felt an overwhelming urge to invert it after today's events, but he successfully suppressed the desire.

He asked, "How are you and the kids handling this?" It seemed the right thing to say as he took a seat on the couch.

"They don't know yet." Martha sat beside him, holding back her tears, "But I'm doing all right."

"Martha," James said, placing the package from Auckland University on the glass coffee table in front of them. He took her hand in his. "I don't know what to say, except that I'm sorry, so god dammed sorry." He tried to sound remorseful but couldn't find anymore inside, he had spent it all before entering this house. "He had a lot on his mind." As soon as he said that he wished he hadn't.

"I know, the kids and their..." Her voice trailed off.

"No, it wasn't just that. Don't blame the kids or yourself."

"The police told me it was an accident. He slipped."

James fished through his pockets until he found Carl's note and handed it to her. "His strong belief in God may have been part of the cause. I think he couldn't tell the difference between what he'd believed his whole life and the guilt he felt. Remember, nothing bad happened at the turn of the century and yet he was so sure it was about to end. God was coming for those to love him. He almost got me believing."

Martha covered her face with her hands and cried. Her body trembled terribly. James offered to make a pot of coffee in the hope that caffeine would calm her nerves a bit, and while he was making it, it would give Martha some time alone.

When James returned with freshly brewed coffee for the both of them, Martha's tears had almost run dry. As they sipped their drinks they talked for almost two hours, their chatter revolving around Carl and the strange ways, which made him special and they laughed at the story of how they had met, even though James had heard the story before. She almost started crying again, so he asked about the large cross, to divert her.

It worked.

She told him, that Carl had bought it at a church auction for a very good price, no one else put in a bid. Carl needed something to help him cope with his children's love for one another. Each night he prayed in front of it. Martha thought he was going overboard, but it didn't appear to be doing any harm, in fact it seemed to be helping and he started talking to the children again. Only a few strained words but at least it was a start.

"And then he stumbled on them last night, as he told you," she finished.

"Then, what about you? How does this affect you?"

She was quiet. Staring into her empty coffee cup, she said: "I've accepted it. A long time ago, I had a feeling about them. I think I gradually grew to except it. Carl on the other hand either didn't see it coming or decided to ignore it."

The cloak of night had fallen, clouds blocked the moon and the stars light, and the night seemed more quiet than usual. The streetlights were on and so were the lights of the neighbors and the home across the street. Martha closed the curtains and turned on a small lamp on a table in the far corner, leaving the room dimly lit. The cross threw its shadow across the floor, and from James's position it was inverted, a terrible representation of its true self, casting an omen of misfortune, which only James saw.

Since he was old enough to understand, his mother had force fed him God's law and when he reached puberty he discovered, through school, that almost all of what the bible claimed could be explained away with rational thought and scientific facts. And that night on the eve of his thirteenth birthday, he had set fire to the family bible. For ten minutes he watched it burn all Halloween orange and chimney red, before his mother caught him. It caused a rift between them that grew with each passing year. He refused to give up his newfound scientific belief and she refused to give up her 'One must have faith' belief. James wondered if Martha was struggling with a similar type of emotion as he had done all those years ago. He doubted it; this woman's faith was strong.

They both sat silently on the couch having run out of stories to tell. The silence in the room was thick enough to cut with a knife. They waited for an interruption, waited for the other to speak first. The telephone buzzed. The sound ripped though the room, causing them both to start. James rose first knowing Martha was in no condition to speak with well meaning friends now.

"Hello?"

"Is that you, James?"

He recognized the voice immediately. "Craig, you and your sister must come home right away, please."

"Why? What's happened?"

"I think I'll leave that to your mother."

"Is it really important? 'Cause..."

"Yes, it is," James said strongly, perhaps a little too bossy.

"Tough shit, it'll have to wait. Me and Suzy are off to a party." He sounded like he was lying. "So, tell mum and dad we'll see them later."

He hung up.

James swore and slammed the receiver into its cradle. Anger at the boy's unruliness engulfed him, but as he saw the sorrowful look that now seemed to be tattooed on Martha's face, he instantly calmed down. He knelt in front of her, again taking her hands in his, "Martha, will you be all right on your own until the kids return home?"

She nodded slowly, hung her head and looked at the floor.

"Perhaps, you should go to bed for a while and rest," he offered.

"That's a good idea, James. Thank you, but maybe later."

"I'm sorry. I have to go but--" He cut his sentence short knowing she wasn't listening any longer. He picked up his parcel and left, unable to stay there any longer. The house was a painful reminder of lost times, which could never be replaced. Flashes of such times came to him as he walked along the empty streets of Orewa, along the state highway, which ran up a steep hill without any lights, past the Redwoods forest entrance until he came to a large wooden sign, which read:

OPERA SANDS
A NICE LITTLE TOWN

There he rested a moment and watched two cars speed past in the cool night. In another ten minutes or so he would be home. Stretching the tightness from his tired body, James headed home.

The park lights illuminated the grounds. His caravan stuck out like a sore thumb but it was still home. James forced the old tin door open, stepped in and lit the kerosene lamp after he had carefully placed the package on the foldaway table.

He knelt on the couch and opened the curtain, staring out into the darkness. Staring up into the almost starless gray cloud studded sky. He realized he might need the water-resistant camera if it rained. He wasn't going to take any chances. There were only two rolls of film. Unable to resist the temptation any longer he tore open the brown paper package. There were no gloves inside like he was told but there were two small black containers and a small frosted glass bottle. Inquisitively, he tore off the plastic seal and twisted off the lid. He peered inside. It looked like ordinary water. Deciding to test it he took a cup from his cabinet and poured a very small amount. He then tore the corner off a piece of paper and dropped it into the glass. Instantly he heard a sizzling sound like water on a hot exhaust pipe, a small stream of smoke rose to the caravans ceiling. He fell back hard against the couch, wide eyed.

How did this not destroy the film, he wondered. The dissolving process ended quickly and just as quickly, James replaced the lid his hand shaking. The small amount in the cup, he threw outside the caravan door, and in the dull light from his lamp he saw the grass it landed on turn brown. The ground was too moist to burn so he wasn't worried about starting a fire.

A business-sized envelope caught his eye. The word: 'Instructions' was printed neatly across its face. James opened it, there were four pages of typed instructions and he sleepily read through them.

Things had changed quite a lot in the past 24 hours. Until the letter arrived, he had started to have second thoughts about photography as a career perhaps he should have stayed with the firm? The old memories depressed him, bad ones surfacing. The worst when Zoe left him, afraid of being without money when his bank balance ran out. He didn't blame her for leaving. She was a woman surrounded by money her whole life and the prospect of facing such hardship certainly wasn't pleasing. And neither was finding the note she had left him. People who he thought were his friends barely spoke to him when they passed on the street. But all this he had been able to block and then accept. He wasn't happy at the firm. Now as a freelance photographer with an assignment, he was happy. Carl's death had depleted the happiness, but James knew life went on and he had to push himself past this, or miss out on an opportunity of a lifetime.

He placed the chemical on the top shelf above the double element stove and went to his room to find the water-resistant camera. He found it under his bed inside his small shoulder strap, canvas bag. He took a jumper in case he was out for a long time, it was getting close to winter and he hated the cold. Although the days were good, early morning was a bitch.

James scooped up both rolls of film off the table and put them with the jumper in the bag. He decided to also take the letter for good luck, this he put in his back pocket and left. The latch didn't hold and the door swayed open. In a nearby caravan a child started crying and somewhere in the night two dogs howled. The clouds above parted allowing moonlight to shine down.

Luck was with me tonight, he thought. *This is going to be great.*

James headed for Redwoods forest and Opera Sands beach looking like a tourist and unknowingly staring destiny right in the eye.

CHAPTER FIVE

James stumbled through the darkness, but found his way to the beach a lot easier once the moon found a larger break in the clouds. Its light illuminated the area. The beach possessed an aura of tranquility and the sounds of the waves washing up onto the cool, dry sand amplified the feeling. He could just see the fluffy white breakers rumbling toward him as he blindly dug through his bag for the camera.

He saw a picnic table on the grassed area and took his bag there, dropping it next to the table instead of on it. He removed the lens cap and pointed it at the rolling waves. He had decided to start at Opera Sands beach first, it was closer than Redwoods forest and his legs were feeling a bit stiff from the day's walking.

He opened the back of the camera and loaded the first roll of film. James fired a few shots at the breakers. He started to turn in circles, taking random shots. Enjoyment filled his heart. The first roll finished quickly, faster than he had expected. He told himself to be more selective. Both these rolls only held 24 shots. Be selective, he repeated, replacing the first roll with the second and last. He returned to the shoreline. *Five shots here and then use the rest on the Redwoods.* That sounded like a good plan.

He heard soft moaning sounds. It was too dark to see any great length so, chuckling to himself, he clicked in the general direction of the lovemaking noises. Without realizing it, his finger fell heavily on the rapid-fire button.

The moans suddenly stopped. There was a loud female gasp, a soft whimper followed by a squelching and cracking noise. It reminded James of biting into a chicken wing. He released his finger as soft drizzle fell. What was that sound?

Thick black clouds moved under the drizzle, which became a steady fall. James became aware of the sudden eerie silence and the rain running down his forehead and neck. He shivered in the sudden coldness as the rain fell heavier, quickly turning into a downpour.

James moved backwards slowly, straining to hear any small sound, straining his eyes to see in the blackness ahead. His heart thumped against his chest. His backward steps increased in speed, until he hit something solid. Something that should not be there, could not be there. He fell sideways to the wet sand. All around deep blackness wrapped the night in a coat of fear. The wet sand clung to his face and clothes. His pulse hammered in his veins.

What the hell was that!

Blindly, James stretched out his arm. It hit the solid object. It was hairy like a dog, had calves the size of videotapes and a long misshapen foot. It growled a horrid ripping sound like sandpaper on concrete. Its stench reached James and he fought the urge to vomit.

The rain stopped dead, a strong wind blew across the beach and sky, blowing the clouds away, and as the moon beamed down once again he saw his worst nightmare come to life. The beast he had dreamed, the beast that visited him as a child, the beast that stood before him, at least seven feet tall with deep red eyes, a head like a deformed dog and a long open jaw showing long sharp gleaming teeth. It threw its head back and howled at the fully visible moon. It echoed across the damp sand and through the wet air, rocketing along the empty beach, rebounding off rock formations, small dunes and the walls of nearby houses.

The beast slowly tilted its head and looked truculently at the trembling James. A long fingered hand with hair on the palms swept through the chilly air. It hit the camera. The long cracked fingernails sliced the strap and the tight plastic camera covering split as it went spinning into the dark night. For a second, James thought he saw moonlight glisten off the beast's fingernails like sunlight hitting a newly polished silver car. The camera ended its flight in the cold water, bobbing twice before a wave crashed on top forcing it against the sand below.

The hand swung again, its claw-like fingernails ripped through James's shirt, tearing the skin below. At first he felt no pain, just a mild tingly sensation, until the beast struck again and again and again. The claws ripped tender flesh from his neck, upper arms and shoulder. Everything moved in slow motion. The claws swept through the air, the blood poured through jagged gaps creating puddles on the wet sand. His sight moved in and out of focus.

The beast growled…

* * *

Tom Dudley awoke with a start. He looked over at his sleeping wife and nudged her until she woke.

She stared at him with sleepy eyes. "What's the matter?"

"Did you hear something?"

"No." She rolled onto her side facing away from him. "Go back to sleep."

"I swear I heard something." He got out of bed, pulling on a bathrobe to cover his pajamas. "Might be those fucking wild dogs again. Tore up our front yard quite nicely, didn't they?" He went to the hallway phone and called John Morale, his next door neighbor and business partner.

John answered on the first ring. "That you, Tom?"

"They're back aren't they?"

"I think so. I've already called the Barker's and the West's place. They're getting dressed as we speak. You do the same and we'll meet out the front."

"Not a problem. Rock and roll," he said and hung up.

Three minutes later, six men gathered outside in the chilly morning air. They all carried a torch and a baseball bat. A howl broke into the cold night air and all six men looked toward the beach, but they couldn't see anything past the grass picnic area. John removed his cell phone from his back pocket. "I'll call the police and see if they can help out."

A scream loud and high-pitched ripped through the night air.

All six men ran towards the beach.

Pain swept through his body and James screamed a second time. The sound broke the slow motion barrier. His shaking slowed. James entered shock as all energy fled his body. His vision blurred and it stayed blurred. He felt lightheaded and wanted to enter unconsciousness or sleep. Rest is what he prayed for, uncaring about what happened now.

New sounds came in the night. Sounds of people shouting with lights darted this way and that. Sweeping across his face, across the beast. The beast looked behind, then back at James. It snorted and ran off on all fours. James' head flicked side to side with considerable force as its hind leg hooked his face and its claws tore his cheek open. James felt the torn meat dangle against his bloody neck, but he no longer cared. All he wanted to do was sleep.

He couldn't comprehend the white beams of light floating up and down his torn body, nor could he comprehend the urgency in the voices behind the light. More lights joined the others and they swayed across the beach like a multi-beamed searchlight. He heard a voice say: "What the fuck's that over there, past the grassed area?" Lights beamed everywhere. The same voice again: "Left of the picnic table over there near the trees." All lights shone in that direction.

Darkness surrounded James. The voices faded, becoming little more than whispers. This is what he had been waiting for. His body was numb. There wasn't any pain. A man was kneeling beside him and a woman was covering his body with towels. The man was saying something but James could only hear a whispered mumble, something about not sleeping. His eyes slowly closed and he welcomed the darkness.

* * *

Tom was the first to see it and he ran up for a closer look, stopping five feet short. He doubled over and vomited. John ran up beside him. "Oh fuck..." he whispered and turned away from two headless bodies stuck together in the art of lovemaking. Joined together by a machete through the boy's back and into the girl below. Blood still dribbled down the boy's back, sliding off his waist and dripping onto the left thigh of the girls parted legs. Their heads sat on top of a sand dune, eyes open giving the illusion of watching the events.

John sat beside Tom and put his arm around the younger man's shoulder, their backs to the sight.

Tom said: "That's Carl Rothsins kids ... Martha's lost her whole family in one day."

They saw others coming up the dunes and warned them away. No one should have to see such a sight.

CHAPTER SIX

He awoke screaming, beads of sweat glistened his forehead and his eyes were wide open in terror. Images of the night hung before him like an ethereal snapshot. A nurse hurried through the door, she called out to the duty nurse for a sedative. James shook violently on the bed. He raised his head and forced it down as hard as possible into the pillow, again and again. The nurse rushed over to him and placed her hands on his shoulders trying to hold him down while at the same time doing her best to keep her hands away from his bandages.

"Calm down. Please sir, relax."

He stopped screaming and realized he was in a hospital bed. The ethereal snapshot vanished. He was breathing hard.

"That's better." She said, closing her eyes, trying to catch her breath. The brief span of panic had jolted the air from her. She had only worked here a month and was struggling to come to grips with the different patients violent outbursts. Working in a prison hospital was a lot different from a normal one and the pay was much better.

The duty nurse entered pushing a trolley. There was a needle and several small bottles stacked neatly in a small steel container. She stopped the trolley at the side of the bed. "He looks calm now," she said.

James was half sitting and half lying on the bed with his head against a pillow that was cocked up against the beds steel railing. His eyes were red and swollen and his jaw hung open. He watched a nurse roll up his pajama sleeve, "This won't hurt a bit." He heard her say. Then to the other nurse: "It's under control now, nurse. You can return to your desk. I'll clean up here."

She inserted the needle into his arm and waited until he was nearly under, before taking a cushion from the plastic visitor chair.

She smiled as she said; "I won't let you identify him, sweetheart. I can't let you take my man away from me."

James lay there, trying to understand her, but the drug was powerful and quick acting. He was drifting closer to sleep with each passing second. A complete numbness was settling over his body. The nurse moved slowly to the bed. The visitor's chair seemed miles away. She held the cushion out in front of her like a shield. Reaching the bed she took a deep breath and forced the pillow down. Smothering James with all the power she had.

* * *

Dr. Keith de Grassol strolled passed the desk nurse, stopping at the side of the reception desk. He gazed at her beauty while adjusting the glasses on the bridge of his nose. Her long dark hair tied into a bun; perfect lined teeth, button nose and full not fat figure.

"Can I help you, Dr. de Grassol?" She said.

Pulling his eyes from her figure, he replied in an embarrassed tone. "I heard Nurse Manny call for a sedative. Is our patient up and running then?"

"He was having another attack."

He frowned, "I'd better go to check on him." He looked down the hall, "Where are the guards?"

"I don't know Dr., they weren't here when I came on duty two hours ago."

"That's a first. In the seven years I have worked here..." He let the sentence drift off, and made his way down the hall. The patients' door was ajar and he spotted nurse Manny Richmond holding a pillow against his patient's face. To the desk nurse he said, "Call security, now!"

He barged through the door. Nurse Manny turned, a surprised look on her face, she still clutched the pillow. He reached her from behind and grabbed her in a bear hug, lifting her slight frame off the floor. She kicked and screamed, but he held on and carried her to the door as the elevator doors across the hall opened and two large security guards rushed over.

"Take her." de Grassol said and quickly returned to the room.

He grabbed the pillow and threw it across the room. He checked all vital signs. Apart from his patient's shallow breathing, everything seemed fine. He stood there for another five minutes before being confident the patient was safe from danger. Then he went to the security office where he knew nurse Manny and the security officers were waiting.

* * *

The next three days were a blur to James as he popped in and out of consciousness, his body filled with drugs. Every few hours a nurse had to wake him up to get him to talk to her for at least five minutes, this proved difficult for both parties but they managed and on the fourth day, James awoke on his own. He was tired and had no energy. He stared at the ceiling. There were no sounds. If it weren't for his aching muscles, he would have thought he was dead.

The door opened and a doctor with a bright and happy smile entered. He looked in his late thirties with a thin moustache, deep set eyes with dark rings of tiredness around them, thick eyebrows, short light brown hair and a solid build. He was very photogenic and looked vaguely familiar.

The doctor asked, "How are you this morning?"

James didn't reply he was too tired for idle chitchat.

The doctor went around to the side of the bed and felt his pulse. "I'm Dr. de Grasssol. I hope you don't mind if I call you John Doe? You have not told us your name yet..." He waited for an answer, none came, so he continued, "I guess you must be feeling a little disoriented, don't worry, that will pass. Any pain?"

"How long..." James rubbed his bandaged throat. It hurt when he spoke and his voice was rough.

"Ah, you will be needing a glass of water," de Grassol pushed the call button, "And you won't be needing these." He nodded at the intravenous line taped to his forearm. Carefully, he removed them.

The doctor's name registered in James and he said, "Have I read about ... you ... in ... a ... magazine?" God that hurt.

"Are you interested in medical journals?"

The door opened and a young nurse said, "Yes, doctor?"

"It seems our patient is in need of a glass of water, nurse."

She nodded, "Yes, doctor," and left.

"Your nervous system took quite a beating."

James closed his eyes as the nurse returned with a tall glass of water. The doctor took it from her, to James he said, "Come on." He helped James into a sitting position, "Sip it slowly." He cautioned.

James took only a few sips before shaking his head at the glass. The doctor pushed the incline button and the top half of the bed rose. "How long have I been here?"

"Seven days in all."

"When can I leave?"

The doctor sighed, "Not for a while, I'm afraid, Mr.-"

"Dennett," James finished for him, "James Dennett. Two 'N's and two 'T's."

Dr. de Grassol went to the end of the bed and corrected the progress report sheet, "The police will want to speak to you soon," he said, "and because of the other day, there is an officer outside your door twenty four seven."

"Twenty four seven?" James asked, his throat felt a lot better now.

"Twenty four hours a day, seven days a week."

A thin line of sweat glistened on James' forehead. The room got hotter, "Can I have some fresh air in here, please?" He wiped sweat from his head and sat upright in bed and inhaled deeply. His strength was returning slowly.

"Of course," Dr. de Grassol said and went to the curtained window, pulled them apart and opened the window inwards. James saw thick iron bars set in the brick frame. The light shone in sending shadows of them across the room. He squinted at the light waiting for his eyes to adjust, "Why do the police want to talk to me?"

The doctor went to the door, opened it and said, "I shall leave that in their hands. I'll send them in a few minutes."

James wondered why he was not in a regular hospital. What was he doing in a prison hospital? He hadn't done anything wrong, had he? He tried to think back, to recall the night on the beach. It wasn't working, he could only remember taking photos, what did he shoot? Panic shot through him. Did they think he was a killer? No, that was impossible. No one got killed. He was still alive and he was the only one to get attacked.

Then he remembered hearing the lovers and then the ... oh God, someone did die.

Two police officers entered without knocking. One was in uniform, and the other a young man in his mid twenties who had very short hair. His name badge read: Pollic. The other wore plain clothes, a suit. He introduced himself as Detective David Kerrs. He was slightly over weight and in his mid forties. His face looked hard, as if he had seen too much of the bad side of people.

"Mr. Dennett, feeling better I hope?" His voice was deep and rough.

"I have had better days." He replied waiting for them to accuse him of something. He knew they were going to. Why else would he be in a hospital with bars? He saw the young officer Pollic remove a pad and pencil from his breast pocket.

"You don't mind if we ask you a few questions, do you?" It wasn't really a question.

James shook his head, "I don't remember much."

Pollic snorted. David glared at him.

"Well, perhaps you could start by telling us what you do remember."

James closed his eyes and thought for a moment, trying to recall the events six days past, trying to picture the time at the beach, "I went to Opera Sands to take some night time photos." The scenes started to return, clearing the more he thought about it. He was surprised to remember so much under such pressure. He continued, "I had just replaced my first roll of film with the second when I heard noises. I thought it was two lovers so I shot in their direction."

Pollic said, "Do you always take candid photos, Mr. Dennett?"

He ignored officer Pollic's remark, and said, "That's when I heard..." He was lost for words and fell quiet. He didn't want to say what the sound reminded him of. Flashes of the past came to him. James squeezed his eyes shut trying to block the images, but they continued projected on the back of his eyelids. He rubbed vigorously against his eyes in an attempt to crush the slightly blurred images and send them back to his subconscious where they could be locked behind some door and never come out again, unless he wished it.

"Are you all right," Detective Kerrs asked, "Would you like us to come back later?"

"I'm sorry, but everything escapes me at the moment."

Kerrs nodded, "Understandable." He said, "We'll continue this some other time." He turned to leave and said as an after thought, "Perhaps you'd like to talk to someone about the attack?"

James frowned, "A head shrink?"

"I would advise it." Kerrs said.

"Am I under arrest?"

Kerrs faced him, "Should you be?"

James pointed at the bars on the window. Detective Kerrs nodded.

He said, "No, Mr. Dennett. You are here for your own protection."

James closed his eyes. He needed rest.

Detective Kerrs said, "I'll send someone around to have a chat with you. You'll like her. She's a nice lady." He waited for James to agree to the meeting, but the patient wasn't moving and seemed asleep. To Pollic he said, "Let him get some rest. Let's go."

Once outside, Pollic said, "Do you think he's covering?"

Detective Kerrs shook his head. "He's had a lot of emotional strain recently, Christ, you saw his face. Would you cover for someone who ripped you apart like that?"

* * *

James slept for half an hour. He had not intended to sleep he hoped only to fool the police so they would leave. He did not want to remember that night. He was successful at pushing the visions away, but for how long? If they had stayed, he might have panicked, and that would not have looked good. He expected them to play 'Good cop' 'Bad cop', but they were very straightforward, that must only be for the movies, he thought.

Slowly, he climbed out of bed. His legs lacked energy but he had to get them moving. As he stood up, pain shot through his chest and upper back. He couldn't breathe and fell back onto the bed in a sitting position. He inhaled deeply and slowly. When the pain subsided he tried again, and was successful. He opened the top two buttons of his pajama top and saw his upper body completely covered in one large bandage. There were pink patches where his blood had seeped through.

He walked slowly to the window. A gentle breeze ruffled his hair. Outside he saw a large gate standing at least seven feet high. Between the gate and the hospital, the ground was barren. A concrete driveway led to a parking area. He expected barbwire fences and guards with weapons, but all he saw were security cameras. Past the gate was another world filled with trees and animals and to the left was a large green paddock with cows. He heard the sound of cars passing but couldn't see them from his window. Opposite the driveway, which led to the gate, James could just make out some children playing on swings in a park, their parents keeping a watchful eye.

This wasn't what he expected when he first learned he was in a prison hospital. He had thought he was in prison grounds and outside he would see large tattooed men lifting weights. He guessed he wasn't in a prison but in a hospital separate, perhaps the prison was on the other side? He knew prisons had their private hospitals, but a lot of things were becoming privately owned lately. Maybe this was a normal hospital with only this wing to hold prisoners? James decided he would ask Dr. de Grassol when he next saw him.

Outside, he saw a dark blue Mercedes Benz pull up to the gate. A slender hand came out of the window holding a card, which was pushed into a console on a stand. The card was then held up to the camera. A moment later the gate slid open. The car eased into the parking area, stopping under the hospital ledge blocking James's view. He swore quietly, this was the only interesting thing to happen today.

He turned and faced the door. Sunlight bounced off the glossy white finish. He went to the door and gently turned the knob. He pushed without success then tried pulling it open. It didn't budge. Locked. Perhaps this was a prison after all.

Disappointed and tired he went to the bathroom. He made for the small door and caught a glimpse of something horrid in the mirror leading to the bathroom as he passed it. He stopped dead in his tracks and spun around to look at his reflection. Dark gray rings circled his eyes, the left cheek and side of his forehead was bruised and swollen. He slowly moved closer to the mirror and turned his head to see the other side. He had a feeling it was going to be worse.

His eyes widened in horror and disgust. Three deep gashes in a downward slope were open. The flesh on the inside was dry. He saw little pinpricks lining the scars, obviously they had stitched the rips the best they could. Faint outlines of yellow puss were still evident in the open scars.

He had never seen anything this repulsive before, only in horror movies had he seen worst, yet he knew they were faked, his reflection was not. He felt his stomach tear then he doubled over and vomited in the sink. He came up for air and that sour taste filled him again and he vomited a second time. Tears welled in his eyes.

He washed his mouth and splashed water on his face, forcing back the tears. He looked again in the mirror. Bright light flashed as if lightning had erupted between the glass and the silver/brown paint at the back. Instantly the mirror turned dark, rain fell and two figures struggled in the background. One human, but the other? It was something else. At first James thought it was a bear, but it was too thin and agile and New Zealand didn't have wild bears. The thing's large paws slashed down across the human's chest. The animal's head turned. It looked directly in the mirror--

There was a loud knocking at the door and a female voice asked, "May I come in?"

The scene vanished as quickly as it had started. James ignored the knocking and opened his pajama shirt, fearful of what he might find. He unhooked the bandage and slowly unrolled it, suddenly wishing he hadn't. He wondered how he had survived. The gashes in his face were mild compared with his chest. There were several long gashes some reaching his belly button. All these had been stitched together, joining the skin. The stitches remained. He looked like a rag doll, which had been sewn together after going ten rounds with a blender.

"Ladies and gentlemen, marvel at the man with barely a face or body," he said angrily at the mirror. His fists clenched tightly and he banged them down on the sink, "Mother fucker!" He hissed. He could no longer pretend he was fine and happy, a 'go with the flow' type of guy, as they say. No. He was hurt, angry and felt like shit. His reflection was how others would see him the rest of his days, how they would judge him. This was too much, first Carl and now him.

He wanted a razor blade.

He stared at his reflection for a long time. "You're an ugly piece of-"

"I hope you aren't talking about me."

He spun around, shocked to hear someone else in the room. The woman stood five feet nine inches high, without her high heels she'd probably lose three or four inches. Long dark hair rolled over her shoulders. She wore a red jacket over a white blouse and a light blue miniskirt. Her light green eyes showed compunction as she stared at him. She didn't look offended or surprised. Maybe she had been forewarned. Smooth face and crystal clear complexion illuminated her beauty and James realized what Detective Kerrs had meant when he had said, 'You'll like her.' And James did, realizing that his anger had subsided for the time being.

"I'm Doctor Stephens, Carol Stephens," she held out her hand.

James shook it and felt a tingle run through his body. He suddenly felt nervous and knew why she was here. She got here pretty quickly, he thought.

"Mr. Dennett, I don't believe you are supposed to be up and about. And I'm positive you're not supposed to remove any bandages."

"I had to take a leak." He lied. She tilted her head slightly to the left and smiled. James thought she knew he was lying so he added, "And I need some exercise. I don't want to stay here forever."

"Perhaps you should sit on the bed, you look tired. I saw you look out the window earlier," she was avoiding mentioning the outburst she had heard. She had seen him staring in the mirror as if watching something inside it.

She turned and walked away from the bathroom entrance, taking a seat next to the bed. She hadn't looked back knowing that James would follow if he wanted to talk, whether he knew it consciously or not. She smiled again as she watched James ease himself onto the bed. He had done up his pajama shirt for which she was thankful. She asked, "Do you have anyone I should contact, let them know you're here?"

"No," James replied. The only person he could think of was Martha, and he didn't want her to see him like this.

"No one, not even a dog?"

"No pets allowed where I live. Besides, I don't feel comfortable around dogs."

"Really, why is that?"

"Don't really know. Never owned one, my mum doesn't like them."

"Do you know why?"

Reluctantly, James said, "Yeah, 'cause my dad was killed saving me from a dog attack."

"I'm sorry to hear that. How old were you?"

"I don't remember." He wanted to change the subject. "So where am I?"

"Orewa hospital. It is privately owned by Dr. Kennon."

James frowned, "I don't recall a private hospital around here."

"You're about five miles out of town. There's a beach just around the corner and a family trekking area, which you probably saw from the window."

"Hang on, the only place around there is a..."

"Mental facility," she finished for him, "Which explains the bars on your windows."

"Why am I here?"

"It's the best place to treat you and you're safe here. You saw the security, when I arrived, and they have known me for five years. And," she added, "it is the best place for recovery. The view outside is so tranquil."

"I feel fine," he added, "Did they catch the animal that attacked me?"

"Animal?"

James closed his eyes, "It was a wolf, large and black." He whispered.

"James," she said softly, smoothly, "it wasn't an animal that attacked you."

He opened his eyes and looked at her coldly, "I'm not lying, that *is* what attacked me."

"Six people witnessed the attack, it was they who drove the attacker away. They saw a man running away from you, down the beach. He was too far away for anyone to get a good look. You're the only person who knows what he looks like."

James shook his head; "They are mistaken. I know what I fucking saw!"

"And it's my job to help you clarify what you actually saw."

"It was a wolf, damn it. I am not blind. Its face was inches from mine. I smelt its breath. I felt its anger. Look what it did to me. Are you telling me a man can do this? Those claws were..." His voice trailed off remembering the moonlight shine off them like a newly polished car. The way light shone against shiny steel objects. Was it really a man? The memories seemed distant, but they were returning and he didn't want them to. A large drumming sound thumped against his ears and the back of his eyes. The veins in the temple throbbed in sequence to the drumming and James vigorously rubbed the irritating areas with his forefingers.

"Headache?"

The drumming faded, "No, I'm fine."

"Good." Carol opened her briefcase and removed a silver pen, which when the light hit it, glittered an array of rainbow colors. James took a deep breath and relaxed. He watched her closely.

"Would you agree to some hypnotic therapy?"

James shrugged. "Whatever."

"I do require a verbal 'Yes' or 'No'."

"Yes," he said, "if it'll prove to you that what I saw was an animal, not a man."

"Of course." She smiled, and in a calm voice she said. "Watch the pen, please."

The pen waved back and forth slowly several times before stopping and easing slower than before, closer to his nose. She spoke softly and slowly, mouthing each word perfectly. The array of colors the pen gave off sprayed across the room coloring the dull walls. The soft and gentle voice of Carol Stephens made James's eyelids heavy they fluttered for a moment before falling closed.

James was asleep but his subconscious was wide-awake. He looked peaceful and at ease with the world and the cruel ways of fate. Surprised that he had gone under so quickly, Carol asked, "James, can you hear me?"

"Hmmm" His breathing was slow and even.

He seemed willing to convey his knowledge of the other night a week ago, but there seemed to be something there, holding him back. His eyelids fluttered and his rapid eye movement was in full speed. Something didn't want him there - they did not want the doctor or James to probe the past.

"James, how are you feeling?"

"Hmmm. Fine. I feel fine."

"I would like to take you back to the night you were taking photos of 'Opera sands'"

James shook his head, "No, I don't want to go there."

"Why not? You can help us catch the person who did this to you."

"No, I'm scared. Don't make me go there. Please."

The room's door swung open slowly as detective Kerrs entered and saw James laying on the bed with his hands twitching and eyes closed. Dr. Stephens sat on a plastic seat holding a clipboard and a small voice activated tape recorder. She turned around and saw him. She put her finger to her lips. He had to be quiet. He pretended to tiptoe to her and she smiled. God, how he loved that smile. She was a truly blessed counselor, she had the gift, could make anyone relax and talk.

He whispered in her ear, "Good work. He's under already. That was quick."

"Something is holding him back. I think he has a lot of repressed memories. But you didn't hear me tell you that, okay?"

"Oh." Kerrs said, yet he didn't understand how some memories would stop a man from talking about his own attack at the beach, especially when it would mean catching the killer. Unless, Dennett did not want the killer caught. Perhaps Dennett had his own form of revenge planned. He knew Carol would dig it out, so he said. "I'll let you get on with it then, shall I?"

"Many thanks." She answered.

"Let me know if he spills any names."

"I'll do whatever's in my power to help you, detective. But we both know it's up to James to tell you, I can't, I can only lead him in that direction."

"Anything would be appreciated."

Carol smiled, "You're not asking me to break the rules, are you?"

He smiled in return and left quietly. James looked asleep, but his R.E.M. said otherwise.

Carol put the tape recorder on the cabinet next to the bed. She moved a half-full glass of water out of the recorder's way. She picked up where she had left off, "You say you are scared. What is it that makes you feel this way?" She watched the tape slowly spin when she spoke.

"I've seen it before." James said quietly.

"A murder?"

"No," he sighed heavily, "A werewolf."

"At the beach?" She was intrigued. This was the first werewolf case she'd had. She had read a few cases based in England and Paris, but they were rare. Nobody believed in werewolves anymore. The vampire cases had showed its face a few times in the seventies and eighties, but only once in the past seven years though. Even people who needed help didn't drink blood these days, too dangerous. Most cases involved God or the devil giving instructions.

Carol rose from her seat, she thought better when standing and went to the window. She leaned against the sill and said, "There was no werewolf, James, not even a dog."

"Yes there was." His voice was firm. His eyes opened. "There are werewolves." He said.

Carol moved to the side of the bed. James's eyes were open but he didn't see the room. He saw something totally different.

"What do you see, James? Describe it to me."

Not looking in her direction he said. "Are you fucking blind?"

She didn't answer.

"Shh, It's coming through the growth now."

Carol tried to see where his eyes were directed, but they darted about a lot. She was slowly growing tense, this could easily get out of hand, and she had lost control once before when she first started out on her own. The patient destroyed part of her office trying to hide from someone, a gang member if she remembered correctly. She didn't want the same thing to happen to James, so she said, "James, listen to me. Whatever it is, it can't see you and it can't hurt you. There are no such things as werewolves."

"Oh yeah." He said. "Then what the fuck is that!" He pointed at the door leading to the bathroom.

"James, it's not real." Her voice was as calm as she could make it. Time to wake him up, she thought, this is too long. Keep everything under ten minutes, do it in stages. It was her rule. Today, she had broken it. "James, look at me."

He stared wide-eyed at the wall.

"James." Her voice more authoritative, "I'm going to count to three..."

"It's seen me! Oh my God!" James jumped from the bed knocking over the cabinet the tape recorder and glass fell to the floor. The glass shattered on impact, water and shards scattered around the bed, which was standing crooked from his kick out. He ran to the closest corner and shrank to his knees, holding his arms crossed in front of his face as a shield.

Frightened, but trying to remain calm, Carol said. "Listen to me, James, whatever it is that you can see is not real."

"Liar!" He screamed. The veins in his temple throbbed. The drumming returned.

"Please listen to me, James," fear had reached her, fear for her safety. The plastic chair began to shake. "When I count to three, you will be calm and the werewolf image will be replaced by the person who attacked you and killed the two teenagers. One..."

"It attacked me, and them."

The barrier was too strong she'll have to go back further next time. Whatever it was it was buried deep and locked behind steel doors.

"Two..."

The chair rose off the ground, it hovered above the bed. Carol froze. The chair wobbled then flew directly at her, like a strong arm had thrown it. She managed to duck just it time. It skimmed the top of her head, and then crashed into the wall, missing the window by a couple of inches. It fell to the floor the back split open and the seat twisted.

Quickly regaining her thoughts, Carol said. "Three."

James fell from his crouching position and quivered on the floor. His body shook violently. His expression held shock and fear. The shaking of his body calmed quickly and he stared at the door leading to the bathroom.

"What do you see, James?"

"You did it. It's staring at me, growling but it won't come closer. It knows you're here."

"Is that what it's saying to you?"

"It just knows."

It had to end now. He still saw the werewolf. Something terrible had happened long ago; she had to find it.

"James, I am going to count to fifteen. When I reach fifteen, you will be in bed and you'll sleep until morning. I want you to try to remember an event from the past, if you do, it cannot harm you or scare you. Do you understand?"

"Yes." He rose off the floor.

"I want you to contact me with every detail of the incident, leave nothing out no matter how small. Do you understand this?"

"Yes." He said. He reached the bed and stopped in front of the broken glass even though he wasn't looking down. Carol went to his side, gently took his arm and led him around to the other side of the bed. She kicked the chair out of her path. It skidded to the bathroom door. James's eyes followed the sound. "He's gone."

"He?" she asked helping him gently him into bed.

"The werewolf. He's gone. I'm safe for now. Thank you."

"One last instruction James. When you awake, you will remember nothing of what happened today, except that our talk went fine. Do you understand this?"

"Yes." He pulled the covers up to his chin and curled into a fetal position and fell asleep.

Carol wondered why he would see a werewolf of all things. She had decided not to allow him to recall the recent events for fear it would scare him off. She knew it would resurface very soon. She wanted to be there when it happened, so he wouldn't be taken by surprise. And she wouldn't be either the next time. She was formulating a plan already.

She went to her tape recorder, scooped it up and checked it for damage, "Do you still work?" she spoke. The tape slowly turned. Good. She ejected the tape and left quietly, looking back once to check James was sleeping. The suggestions she had given were weak, and she doubted if he would comply. He would, if he wanted to. She could only suggest.

In the hallway she saw detective Kerrs leaning against the wall near the nurse's station, he straightened up when he saw her, "Almost ran in a few times when I heard the shouting, but I figured you'd call out if you needed help."

"You were right." She smiled.

"So," he asked, "any names?"

"Sorry."

"A description?"

"Sorry, we weren't able to get that far," she shrugged her shoulders, "Maybe next time."

Kerrs closed his eyes, rubbed them and sighed, "What do you suggest?" He asked, already knowing the answer.

"Continued counseling, but not until he is released from here."

"The doctor said he could leave in about a week, depending on how well he heals."

"Good." She said heading for the elevator, "Do be sure to give him my number when he is released."

"Already given it to the sign out desk. Hey doc, I want you to help him. I need to know how he is involved in this mess, what he knows, or if he was an innocent bystander at the wrong place at the wrong time."

She nodded to him as the elevator doors opened. Her next stop was the library to brush up on her telekinesis knowledge.

CHAPTER SEVEN

James tossed and turned in his sleep. He was dreaming. He knew it was a dream, but it was also real. This was his past, a past he had forgotten until now. It was coming back to him, but he didn't want to remember it. He tried to wake himself but couldn't.

He watched a three-year old boy kick a soccer ball around a messy backyard, filled with old rusty car parts, spanners, a collapsed swimming pool and odds and ends. The child grew tired of the game since there was no one else to play with him. He could hear the television set in the living room of his house. Dad was in there.

Kicking the ball away, he ran through the open French sliding doors, along the hallway with five doors that led to bedrooms and another that led to the toilet, passed the staircase leading to the upstairs rooms. The boy's mother would often be in the sewing room upstairs and his father in the weight room.

The television was on loud, which meant the boy's father had finished training and was now drinking. He liked the television loud when he drank. On the television an old Jimmy Stewart movie played, 'The man who knew too much'. The boy ran to his father and tugged on the man's shirtsleeve. The large, stubble faced man turned to him and growled, "What!"

Suddenly the past memory came flooding back to James. He knew this scene well. His father had been a fisherman who was laid off due to a bad back, drinking while on the boat and fistfights with the crew. Most afternoons, his father would sit at home drinking.

This was one of them.

Three years old James stared at the man with large arms and oversized rough hands. He knew what he wanted to say, but couldn't. He wanted to play soccer with his father like they used to before Dad lost his job.

"What the hell do you want?"

James backed away, his eyes wide.

"You interrupted the movie, got my attention so what the hell do you want?" He leaned close to James the smell of whiskey was strong. Cal grabbed James by the collar of his shirt.

"I want to play, Daddy." James whimpered.

"Cal!" His mother screamed, entering the room, she was carrying a new jacket she had made for James, "Don't you dare hit my son."

"Or what? What will you do bitch?"

"No, Daddy, please."

Cal lifted James off the floor. The fear in the boy was his power and the tears rolling off his boy's cheeks were his reason.

"Cal, let him go."

"I'll make him a man if the last god damn thing I do." He tossed James across the floor. His head hit the wooden floor hard and he burst into tears. He stayed on the floor crying softly, if he made a big fuss his father would get off the chair and really give him something to cry about.

His mother ran to him, scooped him up and hugged him tightly. She rubbed his head gently, whispering soothing words.

"Oh, for fuck sake, woman. Will you stop treating him like he is still a baby? He has to learn to be a man sometime."

"I don't see a man around here to teach him." She looked coldly at Cal.

Quick as lightning he jumped up from his seat, his hand drew back ready to strike her. Instead he spun around and kicked the television, its two back legs snapped and it toppled backwards, crashing against the wall and landing on its side. It still worked but the screen grew darker.

"I've had it up to here with the two of you!"

"Get out." His mother said softly.

"Fuck you."

"Get out!" She screamed, "Get out! Get out! Get out!"

"Fine, I'm out of here." He said with clenched teeth. He stormed to the front door, flipping over the dinner table as he passed, "Fucking bitch." He spat, slamming the front door shut.

His mother sat on the floor still holding him. "Don't worry," she said, "it's all over now." And she started to cry.

Then James heard another voice, distant. Slowly growing louder, clearer. This voice wasn't meant to be here. As the words became understandable, the dream faded. White light broke into the darkness and he saw a figure in front of him. His vision was blurry.

"Mr. Dennett."

James's vision cleared. Dr. de Grassol stood over him, "Doctor?" He said.

"You've been asleep for almost two days. How do you feel?"

"Apart from sleepy, I feel fine." He stretched out on the bed and suddenly squeezed his eyes shut as a bolt of pain shot across his back.

The doctor frowned, "I'll make sure you get some painkillers for that."

"I can leave?"

"Sure can, if you feel up to it. I do however recommend another night and of course you will have to return in two or three weeks to have those stitches removed. They aren't dissolvable. Your injuries were too wide to risk them opening."

"I'd like to stay another night."

"That's fine," De Grassol said, "Have a good nights sleep." He left.

James wanted to stay forever, hidden away from the outside world. He feared returning to the Caravan Park. Back to Mrs. Clemm and her open dress. His friends or strangers, he wondered how would they react when they saw him? His face was scared. His chest was worse. James curled up in the blankets, best not to think about that yet.

He had dreamt of his natural father. A person he had forgotten. A memory he wished had not surfaced. It was a painful part of the past he had blocked, and now it returned. Maybe his attack had brought it back, maybe not. He hoped that no more would resurface.

When his father had left, they waited a week for him to return, but he never did. James was glad. His mother found a good job, new friends and a new dad for him. Cal's name was never mentioned again and Richard replaced him as his father. For several years, his life had been good. Then the dog killed Richard.

* * *

Carol Stephens left the library. She had planned to go there two days ago but had been sidetracked when her beeper beeped. The next day she had been too busy with paperwork to leave her office (which doubled as her home). But finally, today she had made it.

Unfortunately she didn't find anything she didn't already know, so   she was returning home after only thirty minutes.

She pulled into her driveway between two lines of trees and parked her car in the garage, which was more of a carport with a rollaway door than a garage.

The house was built to resemble a log cabin. Several pine trees in a semi-circle secluded it. Carol unlocked the oak door and stepped inside. A red flashing light caught her eye. She automatically reached up and turned off the alarm, before going into the living room, where a large bookshelf stood against the far wall, reaching almost to the ceiling. Running her finger along the spines of books thick enough to take months to read. She scanned the titles and found a new, unread book. She remembered buying it six years ago when she passed her final exam, just in case she came across such a case. And finally Carol had good reason to use it.

Throwing her red jacket on the leather couch next to her kitten, Carol slumped down in her recliner with the hard cover book on her lap and reached for the remote on the glass table beside the chair.

Newspaper cuttings of UFO sightings or other strange stuff hung on her wall covered in protective plastic. She found them amusing and displayed them for visitors to muse over, but she had yet to have a visitor, especially of the male kind. Her office was at the side of the house, an extension she had built four years ago. Two Van Gogh copies hung above a large screen television. To the right, two large thick black curtains covered large windows concealing a picturesque view of a well-kept garden with a birdbath fountain.

Carol found the remote and turned on the television although she had no intention of watching it she only wanted some background noise. She stretched out on the chair and opened the book to a table of contents. She turned to the page number listed under telekinesis and read the opening paragraph:

'Telekinesis is the ability to move objects or to cause change within objects solely by the force of the mind.

The phenomenon has often and most reliably been reported in times of crisis or in severe stress situations.

It has been mistaken as the work of poltergeists at times.'

A second entry read:

'A form of psychokinesis, which involves moving objects with the mind without ever physically coming in contact with them. Telekinesis is essentially the ability to move an object on the physical plane using only physic power.

Some people think this is an occult practice. 'TK' works by energy fields or by 'waves' of energy to repel or draw an object to or from you.

Most people's encounter with TK is accidental and comes at times of intense stress. We all have the ability to harness this power of the mind.'

A seven-step process of improving your telekinesis and the difference between movement and telekinesis followed this. Carol didn't read it. She knew she could find more information on the Internet and was about to go to her computer when a two minute news break on the television began, giving the viewer a slight foretaste of the nights main news. Her ears picked up something about a wave of dog attacks. She looked at the screen only to see and hear the anchorperson say: "That's later tonight at six."

She searched for today's newspaper. It wasn't on the shoe case in the hallway near the door where she usually put it. Then she remembered that she had left it in the mailbox this morning in her rush to the hospital.

Carol ran down the driveway to fetch it. On the way back she searched for an article. She wasn't entirely sure what she was looking for at first, but then she found an article titled "Photographer attacked after lovers murder". She quickly read the story, finishing it as she reached her front door. At least they had not mentioned James's name, although there was a small inserted photograph of his caravan. She felt a tinge of sorrow or was it pity, for James. He had no one and nothing to return to. At least she had her kitten. James needed something to come home to. It would be good therapy for him.

She decided to go against her better judgment and get a puppy for him. Doctor de Grassol had phoned her earlier on her cell phone. He had given James her card and he would be leaving sometime tomorrow morning.

She opened the front door, tossed the newspaper onto the shoe case and went into the living room to get her car keys. She went to her jacket. The kitten was playing a game of the hunter and the hunted. Carol's jacket was the hunted. It was diving in and out of the sleeves, digging its claws into the back and flipping itself all over the place.

"Come on, kitty," she said, lifting it off and putting it gently on the floor, "Sorry, I have to go now. Back later."

The kitten watched her leave and jumped onto the windowsill and watched Carol drive away. It pawed the window and mewed softly.

* * *

He was there, searching James's caravan for the film of his time at the beach. It was a hopeless search, he knew James had not been back to the caravan yet as he was still in hospital. Worse yet, he was still alive. That pissed him off more than anything did. The guy just didn't know when to die. His girlfriend Manny had failed to find the camera or film, and she had been stupid to try to do his job and now she was in jail. He didn't need her anyway. She was getting too attached. At least he didn't have to worry about her spilling anything especially his name.

He saw the bottle of Exonpet on the shelf above a double element stove. He smiled. Searching the caravan did not take long. It was small. No way could he live in one of these. He'd spent the last ten minutes looking here in the last light of the day.

Where the hell is it!

He didn't know what happened to it after he had struck it with his special glove. He saw the camera fly off, but after the beach had calmed down and the police and ambulance had left, he went to look for the camera but to no avail. Perhaps it was lost, or the police had found it. He didn't know anyone in the police department who could help him.

Too long had been spent in here. It was time to go. He decided to leave James a little hello note when a car's headlights shone into the caravan. Quickly he ducked out of the light. He moved cautiously to the window and parted the curtain enough to peek outside. He hoped James hadn't returned he was not prepared for a confrontation.

A dark blue Mercedes rolled to a halt beside the tin caravan. Allen moved quickly into the bedroom and squeezed out of the small window. He fell to the ground and rubbed his shoulders and side, he was sure he had lost some skin off his left shoulder. He moved to the side of the caravan and watched from the corner.

An attractive dark haired woman, who looked familiar (yet he could not place her), removed a small box from the back seat of her car. She talked to it like a child and he wondered what she was doing, until she turned, carrying it to the caravan. He saw a cute golden Labrador puppy with its head and front paws on the top edge of the box. The puppy sure looked happy.

"Miss Stephens." Mrs. Clemm called, running from her office, "Excuse me, Miss Stephens." She waved her hands trying to catch the doctor's attention. Her voice was very loud.

Allen couldn't see any point for Ethel to be waving her arms when she was behind the doctor.

Now he remembered the woman.

Carol Stephens turned around wearing a false smile.

"When will Mr. Dennett be returning?"

"Tomorrow morning, I believe." Carol shifted her weight and balanced the box better in her arms.

"I don't much care for dogs." She looked harshly at the puppy, it whimpered and hid in its box. "And he's also more than a week late with the rent."

You charge rent for that tin box? She thought but said. "Mrs. Clemm, I am James's doctor and what he really needs right now is to have something to come home to."

"I read about his attack in the paper, is it really that serious?"

Carol stared at the woman.

"The paper didn't say his name but I put two and two together."

"How much is his rent?"

"He owes me $168. That's for two weeks."

Carol sighed, "I'll make you a deal, Mrs. Clemm. I'll pay the rent he owes with a little extra. You tell him you decided to forget the rent for the past two weeks and not complain about the puppy. And."

"What?" Ethel Clemm asked slowly.

"If James doesn't return by tomorrow afternoon, you'll feed the puppy and let him run around for a bit."

"I don't think so. I don't like dogs."

Carol put the box on the ground next to Mrs. Clemms feet, which quickly moved away. The puppy looked up at her expectantly.

Carol opened her car door and pulled out her checkbook. She scribbled on it and showed Mrs. Clemm the amount.

Mrs. Clemm took the check and said, "I'm not taking any responsibility for that thing." She turned and headed back in the direction of the office.

* * *

Allen watched Carol bend down and pet the puppy. "I just broke all the rules I know of, for you. I'm supposed to stay separate. But you'll like him when you meet him."

Just like you? Allen thought.

He watched quietly as the lady entered the caravan and a few minutes later returned to her car without the box. She looked sad. She drove off as the tin door swung open. A few minutes later the puppy started to whine.

He entered.

The man lifted it out of the box and gently patted it. He spotted a business size envelope on the table. He picked it up and sat on the couch with the puppy on his lap.

"Carol Stephens." He whispered. The thought of her brought back painful memories. Memories of useless sessions trying to overcome (as she put it) his inferiority complex that he didn't know he had until she told him. Apparently, his father gave it to him. Mostly she wanted to talk about his feelings about his father. He tried to hate his father but couldn't. The man was his dad, his blood. They had the same DNA. He tried but could not hate him.

Allen had to admit that since he was seventeen and had stood up to his father, their relationship had grown close. The last ten years were great. It seemed that the doctor didn't want to hear about that.

She questioned him, all the questions having the same meaning and an answer he didn't have: Why do you still hate your half brother? What would happen if you met and introduced yourselves? Are you worried about a meeting? Do you feel the hatred might leave? What drives you Allen? What one thing apart from hatred really motivates you?

After a year he gave up the sessions with the sexy doctor, even after a year he lost interest in looking at her legs. She was professionally detached. Why was it different with James? Was she willing to risk her profession for him? Perhaps she felt a slight *thing* for him? He would put an end to that.

His anger rose. Why did people choose his half brother's side all the time?

He opened the letter. It read:

This small gift is for you James, call me to set up an appointment. If you prefer another person, I can arrange that.

Carol.

Short and sweet, he thought.

Hate.

An emotion he felt almost daily since his father's death. He felt it growing stronger everyday within him. He felt the heat of hatred burning inside him, and he liked it. It made him feel stronger than any other man. It gave him a great deal of pleasure. Sometimes, he felt like an animal that had gained human intelligence but lived on instinct, an animal that could change identities at will, kind one moment, vicious the next. He considered himself a Human-Beast. Its over-riding emotion was hatred.

Meanness was in his blood he knew it, got it from his father's side of the family.

He put the letter back in the envelope and placed it gently on the table. The puppy wriggled and looked up at him. Holding it before him and looking into its innocent eyes, he said. "James doesn't deserve a present." His voice went cold, "Not after what he made my dad do to me. That bastard doesn't deserve shit!"

Cuddling the puppy in his arm and gently rubbing his chin against its tiny head, he went to the kitchen area. A long bone handle knife rested against the cold-water tap. Moonlight glistened off the steel blade. He liked it. He saw more power in the strength of steel.

The puppy reached up his chest and licked his cheek. The man plunged the knife into the puppy. The knife passed right through, and pierced his stomach. The puppy yelped in pain and its legs tried to push it away from the pain. It looked to the man for help it's eyes showing pain and pleading.

Allen removed the knife and dropped the puppy on the floor. It tried to get up and walk around but couldn't. He couldn't understand why he had done that. He hated violence to animals because they didn't deserve it, except cats - the keepers of the dead, purely Satan's pet.

He watched the puppy crawl around on the floor, its side covered in blood. It's whimpering its pain. For the first time he felt sorry for his actions.

"Fuck you, James," he hissed, "Look what you made me do."

He sat on the couch and watched the puppy slowly bleed to death. He couldn't bring himself to put it out of its misery.

PART TWO

There is no life,
except death
There is no vision
except by faith.
- Frank (The Enforcer)
Nitti's epitaph.

CHAPTER EIGHT

Mrs. Clemms apartment was located next to the office. Actually, it was connected to it on the side but the connecting door was locked and the key, never found. If someone arrived sometime late at night, Mrs. Clemm was always quick off the mark. Long time residents thought she lived looking out the window.

Her apartment was compact with two bedrooms, a small bathroom and kitchen. The walls were covered with white (yellow stained) wallpaper with thorn colored flower patterns, some patches of smoke stained wallpaper ruined the once nice design. White carpet, which had lost its bounce and fluffiness years ago, covered the floor. A television played in the corner, opposite the front door.

Ethel was seated in an old cloth covered chair next to a three-seat couch and another chair. No one sat in the spare chair; it was her later husbands. It was all she and her late husband had needed, no children were ever planned but one came by surprise, just before her thirty-eighth birthday. She hadn't seen him in years. When his father died, he disappeared. If he were still alive he would be 27 years old now.

She only partially read the romance novel sitting open in her lap. She had other things on her mind. Like, what had happened to James? That silly woman of a doctor had not told her much, in fact hadn't told her anything she could pass onto her friends at the bridge club. She now wished she hadn't walked away from the doctor. A little prodding was all that was required, Ethel told herself, and you're getting soft in your old age woman. Now, she would just have to wait for Mr. Dennett to return.

She looked over in the direction of James's caravan, even though she couldn't see it, with a sour look. She had rented him the worst caravan in the park, she had tried to sell it, even inquired about the price of dumping it, but James came along and accepted it with its high rent, like the fool he is. There's one born every minute, she thought quietly laughing to herself.

A distant and soft whining broke through her thoughts. The doctor had left only a moment ago and already that puppy was lonely and crying for company. The doctor said it was a quiet pup. It seemed obvious that Dr. Stephens had lied. Ethel knew it. Everyone lied. Her parents, her husband who had said he loved her, and then died even her brothers and sisters who were too busy to call or visit. She discovered them all. None of them were prim or proper; none had the skill of knowing what was the right or wrong way of acting in life and public. She distanced herself from them all.

The puppy yelped in pain.

"Fallen out of your box, have you?" Ethel laughed and turned her attention back to the novel.

Reading about a character slowly lifting the heroine's dress to her waist, Ethel heard something scratch the door. Single scratches sounding like slowly torn cardboard. At first she thought it was children playing around - but only one couple had children and they were too old to play baby games. Then, she remembered hearing the puppy fall out of the box. Was that what was damaging her door? The little prick had found its way to her door. She will teach it a lesson it will never forget.

Ethel hurried to the door and waited for another sound. When none came she frowned in disappointment. Slowly she reached out and pushed down the door handle. Pulling the door from the jamb, she cautiously and easily let the door open wide just in case the puppy was crazed and tried to bite her. She hated dogs and they hated her, she did her best to keep away from them and hoped they would keep away from her. All dogs were potentially vicious, she knew that, had known that since she was sixteen.

The evening was unusually warm. The air surged in and filled her lungs. It tasted different, dull even, it lacked the tangy taste of the countryside. It seemed almost city-like. It was very uncommon this close to the beach. The wind was still. Tree leafs hung limply from branches. Blades of grass, bent touching the ground. Caravan windows were open. The loud sound of televisions blared across the grounds and laughter coming from inside.

Laughter...

Flashing lights of the school ball she attended at sixteen, dancing on the floor with Ted, the man she wanted to marry, Ted, the kick boxer. A man, who would protect her, she'd thought, until he got too fresh after the dance and she had slapped his face and stormed off home, paying no attention to the German shepherd roaming along her street...

She snapped out of the 38 years old memory. That was something she didn't want to remember. Yet, so many things brought it back, everyday little things and she had to divert her attention forcefully. She did her best to block out the laughter and gave the grounds one final sweep with her eyes in search of the puppy. She felt too tired to go looking, so she closed the door and went back to her novel. The words fuzzed and blurred, until her eyes finally closed and she slept.

* * *

Allen didn't leave the Caravan Park. Instead he took up a position near the tress and watched Mrs. Clemms house. He sat there for hours, unmoving. He hated the bitch. All the years of self-righteous crap he had to listen too. And what did his father do about it, nothing. He was pussy whipped. The power didn't start to change until he was in his late teens and his father was no longer as interested in sex as before. Their bond grew tight once his father hit the ripe old age of fifty. Things were changing now his father was dead. He would make sure of that.

Dennett.

The thought of his name made his blood boil. The beatings his father gave him when James succeeded in school and he didn't. His report card showing B's and C's - then the belt came off. His father's leatherwork glove was the worst. The belt made the most noise but the glove fucking hurt. And the worst part was he did try, he gave school the best shot he could, for all those years until he decided enough was enough and dropped out. The first time he stood up to his father. The first and only time they came to blows. Allen wasn't ashamed to admit he lost, and quickly too. His father was a real man built from the old stock, strong and hard.

Thinking back, coming to blows was the best thing for the both of them. It proved that Allen was his own person. Things changed. He and his father talked more grew close over the years and James was never mentioned again. But Allen's hatred persisted.

Dennett was going to die. He would make it happen.

A rustling came from the forest behind him; he turned to see two yellow eyes staring at him. In the darkness he could just make out the animals fangs.

The dog approached, slowly and cautiously. It was alone. Allen smiled.

"Come here," he said gently.

The dog froze in its tracks, its body tense.

Allen clicked his fingers, "Come on. I won't hurt you."

Slowly the animal approached. Allen held out his hand. The dog sniffed it.

Allen reached into his pocket and removed a packet of cigarettes. He lit one. The dog growled, its top lip curled up. He stared at the dog. He felt no fear. He didn't think the animal would attack him after all they were almost the same. The dog was a plain animal, he was a Human-Beast, and he was the master. He stared the dog down. After a few minutes, it sat next to him. He stroked its massive head. The animal was completely relaxed with Allen.

"I need your help, my friend."

It stared up at him.

"It's too early. Let's wait a few hours," Allen leaned against a tree and closed his eyes. The dog rested its head on his lap.

* * *

Ethel jumped awake by the sudden noise of television static. The air inside the room was cold. The romance novel was face down on the floor some of its pages scrunched by the fall. Rubbing her eyes, she rose off the chair. Her back felt stiff. She felt like having a cigarette but was too tired and besides there wasn't anyone else around and she considered herself a social smoker. She went to the television and checked all five stations for something to watch even infomercials would do something to help put her to sleep again. But all the channels showed static, which was strange as all five now ran 24 hours a day. She wriggled the antenna connection at the back to no avail. She switched it off.

The small digital clock on the top of the television read: 1:50am.

A dog barked loudly outside, somewhere in the direction of the beach. She had read news reports in the paper of wild dogs in the area, roaming the beach, knocking over rubbish bins looking for food. Dogs that had gone for a walk without their owners and become lost or were dumped as puppies, too many for the local ranger to catch/collect. There were bound to be a few desperate ones. Some people had killed for food, hunger was powerful it made people do things they could never have dreamed of before. So it came as no surprise when Ethel read about a little girl attacked, playing on the beach. Local residents did what they could to hunt it down, but the animal had yet to be caught. It had taken off her arm with its strong jaws. Parts of it were found later as the little girl lay dying in hospital. Two days later, Ethel read about the girl's death.

Ignoring the barking dog, she turned on a light to do some reading. She had read this novel three times before and it was still good, a nice little book by a crafty writer. Ethel had hundreds of romance novels; her bedroom littered with them, some she had read more than once. She had read so many she believed she could write one or two, but the idea never flourished, she was far to busy for such nonsense. She was a reader, not a writer and quite happy to fork over good money for a good book. Sometimes she would buy discounted books by unknowns, just in case she came across a jewel. Which had happened a few times.

Taking a seat on the couch (good places to stretch out and sleep when she grew tired) Ethel straightened the crushed pages. She started to read the last pages of 'A school girls dream', when a set of headlights shone into the room, glaring against the sidewall and bouncing off the television screen as the car passed.

Curiously, she went to the window and parted the curtain. She saw a well-dressed man in his forties climb out the front door of a dark BMW, and an attractive lady a few years younger exit from the passenger side. They both looked very tired. Ethel heard a child hidden in the back seat ask, "Are we there yet, mummy?" The father shook his head and said something quietly to the child. He headed towards the office. Ethel waited. A few moments later she heard the electronic buzz of the attention bell as it rang in her apartment.

Taking her time she went to the coat rack and grabbed a warm jacket.

The gentleman greeted her outside. He was looking in the direction of her house. "Sorry to disturb you so late." He smiled, but he was tired and it didn't last long.

"Are you lost or looking for a place to stay the night?"

The young lady joined her husband. He slipped his arm around her. "We're in need of a room for the night, if it is possible." The smile returned.

"I'm sorry but we-"

"Please," the young lady said, "We have been driving all day."

"I'm quite happy to pay twice the going rate, for disturbing you at such an hour."

Damn money driven men, Ethel thought. She should have known it from the start. The BMW, good clothes - more likely brand names. She assessed the diamond ring on her right hand, gold on her left, the pearl necklace at her throat. The sterling silver with dotted diamond wristband - it all emulated money. Ethel thought she could live happily on just the woman's jewelry. She liked what rich people achieved but hated the attitude most of them had, thinking money could buy anything.

"We only have caravans here."

"Caravans?" the man said his voice carrying a hint of distaste.

"Like the sign says outside the gate, this is a caravan park."

"Could you suggest some place?" the woman said.

"Well..." Ethel started, but the man cut her off.

"I thought caravan parks had cabins?"

She was growing tired of these people and the night was colder than she thought, she pulled the coat tight around her, "We only have caravans. There are some empty as the summer season's finished. If you'd like..."

"I will not subject my family to that." The man spat. "Bloody small towns."

"I'm sorry to have bothered you," the woman said, "We'll keep looking. Thank you for your time."

The man had returned to the car. "Liz, get in the damn car now!"

She headed back to the car after shaking hands with Ethel, "Don't yell at me, Thorn, please."

"Just get in the fucking car." His face was reddening with anger. Ethel watched them drive off, Poor woman, she thought. Funny how holidays were meant to relax when if fact they usually caused more stress than the demands of work. She waited for the car lights to fade into the night before heading back to her couch and novel.

A deep growling froze her in mid-stride. Her mind flashed back recalling her ordeal at sixteen. Slowly she turned. She tried to block the memory, but it was too strong, the sound of the animal too near. Almost directly behind her it stood about twenty feet from her near the trees. For a second she thought she saw a person duck behind a tree, but it was too dark to tell for sure. The dog stepped closer. White foam oozed from its mouth. The top lip curled back. Its fangs flashed in the moonlight.

Ethel's body filled with terror.

Her heart pounded in her chest like a sledgehammer.

Her breath caught and throat locked.

The pulse thundered in her veins.

Ethel struggled for breath.

Ethel wet herself.

The animal growled, spurred on by the smell and the woman's fear. Its head dipped down, eyes never leaving the prey. Shaking violently, Ethel found the strength to move ever so slowly towards her house. She couldn't move her eyes from the animal's cold stare. The yellow eyes boring deep into her rooted her. Terrified and unable to restrain herself, she turned and ran as fast as she could for her door.

The dog followed slowly - snarling.

Ethel made it to her door. Breathing hard and with tears in her eyes, she turned to see how close the animal was. She could not run fast, at her age. Maybe she shouldn't have stayed outside and watched the couple drive away. She felt sure that if she had returned to her apartment as soon as they had climbed into their car, she would now be safe. It was obvious that the animal had watched and waited for the car to leave. As it was watching her now, watching intensely.

She entered her house and slammed the door behind her.

The dog watched her disappear behind the door. It heard a series of clicks, then a soft tinkling of something being slid along part of the door. It knew that sound, it was the sound of a chain. Then it heard dragging sounds. What was the woman doing?

It ran headfirst into the door.

The door was solid.

It howled.

Inside, Ethel tried to scream, but couldn't. She ran to the wall opposite the door and the open curtain. With her back hard against it she slid down to the floor, weeping.

The dog charged three more times. It howled in frustration.

Silence.

The animal stopped.

Not a sound, inside or out. No night animals moved or called out like usual. Everything was still.

Ethel drew her knees up to her chest and hugged herself. Why didn't the residents call the police? They must have heard the animal.

The crashing against the door surely would have awoken some people. Not all residents had a phone, but there must be something they could do to help? Maybe they already were, which is why the dog had stopped. In her fear she had not heard them.

Her heartbeat slowed in the quietude.

The eerie thick silence seemed to continue forever. Ethel's mind raced, trying to think of what to do. When she was sixteen a neighbor saved her by charging at the German Shepherd with a baseball bat. She could not hold back the memory. The night was perfectly clear, just like tonight. The memories so clear, so picture perfect. The German Shepherd jumped at her tore her gown. Its teeth bit into her side. The blood, oh god, the blood splattered on the pavement. She didn't even try to fight off the animal. She lay still until the neighbor came...

Ethel stared at the television and set of drawers pushed up against the door. The couch and two chairs were pushed up against them. If she had moved them so easily she doubted if it would take much on the part of the dog to nudge them aside. She cuddled herself with her head resting against her knees; tears streamed from the corner of her eyes. Her body trembled but not as badly as before. This was adrenaline charged shaking, not fear, that had subsided. She remembered the newspaper stories about the dogs there had been a special number to call if any of the animals had been spotted. Bugger, she couldn't remember the number and yet she usually had a good head for numbers. She slowly rose to her feet, her legs trembled but she managed to walk quickly to the phone. It was an old dial phone, thick black and heavy and almost as extinct as some reptiles from the Mesozoic age. The sound of an open line pleased her. She didn't know why she thought it would be dead.

It was not an ax murder out there, only a dog. A big fucking foam dribbling dog nonetheless.

Ethel dialed the emergency number.

The operator responded after the fourth ring. It was a recorded voice, "If you have a touch tone phone, please push 1 for the police, 2 for the fire department and 3 for the hospital. If you are unsure which service you require, please push 0 or hold ... Your call is being connected now."

Ethel waited. She stared at the front door.

A live operator answered, "What service, please."

Ethel wasn't quite sure. She stared at the door thinking she heard a sound.

"Which service do you require?"

There was a scrape against the door and Ethel gasped, almost dropping the phone.

"I'll put you through to the police. Please wait."

A series of clicks, then: "Owera Police station, Officer Pollic speaking."

"Oh, officer," she found her voice, "this is... This is Mrs. Clemm of Opera Sand Caravan Park."

"Yes, Mrs. Clemm, how may I be of assistance?"

"A dog just tried to attack me." Her breathing hard and fast, "I think it's still out there. It ran into my door three times!"

"Calm down, Mrs. Clemm. Are you inside now?"

"Of course," she said, "Where do you think I'm calling from?"

Officer Pollic sighed. "I'll put you through to the ranger."

"No wait, " A couple of deep breaths, "It has some white foam-like stuff around its mouth. It could have rabbis or something."

The line was silent for a moment. Ethel could hear officer Pollic's breathing. Then. "Is the dog still outside?"

"I don't know."

"Would you mind going to the window and having a look?"

"Do I mind?" She replied. After what she had been through, he now expected her to search for the animal. What was he thinking? It was his job to serve and protect, why wasn't he speeding here right now? She said, "Yes, I bloody well do mind. What if it sees me at the window?"

"It is very important, Mrs. Clemm. I have to let the ranger know if the dog's still there."

"I'm scared."

"It's all right to be scared. I have the ranger on the line now and he's headed your way. He needs to know what to expect."

"Oh, very well." She said reluctantly. It probably was important. Ethel only hoped they would hurry. She had a feeling that the dog wouldn't just leave after only three attempts. "Wait a second." Her voice trembled.

The phone's receiver fell from her hands, dangling by its cord. It gently tapped the wall as it swayed to and fro. Ethel's heartbeat quickened with each step closer to the window, as she got closer it gathered speed. Her breath came in short bursts. She moved around the couch, using its arm for support. She leaned toward the window and peeked out the crack in the curtains. Her nerves twitched and danced on broken glass through her body. She knew what she would find but she looked anyway.

Ethel swallowed hard.

The dog was there, as she had suspected. It was staring at the door probably wondering what to make of it, or what to do with it. The animal was motionless. Cold eyes fixed firmly on the door, waiting for it to open most likely. The animal's lips were curled back, but it wasn't snarling. Froth rolled down both sides of its jaw. It was hungry and could smell the woman's fear. It knew better than to leave.

Ethel quickly returned to the phone, "It's still there. It's waiting for me!" Her voice filled with high-strung terror.

"Mrs. Clemm, please calm yourself. The less noise you make the better."

"You must come, now!"

"The ranger's on his way try to relax."

"Will he be armed?"

DING DING DING DING - DONG DONG DONG DONG - BONNNNGGG BONNNNGGG.

"What the hell was that?" Pollic asked.

"Chime clock, it just turned two."

A loud snarl came from outside. Death seemed to ooze over it.

"I'll inform the ranger. Please hold on," Pollic said hearing the viciousness of the snarl and hoping the entire Caravan Park wouldn't wake up and go outside to check the noise. This lady was serious. That dog sounded out of control. He was glad he wasn't a ranger.

Ethel moved away from the phone. The receiver dropped from her hand. The clock must have snapped the dog out of its trance making it remember its objective - Me! Ethel stumbled backwards. The dog head butted the door again. The force of the strike knocked the television off the set of drawers, the screen exploded. The chest moved forward slightly, its wooden legs jammed into the carpet. The back of the couch lunged forward but it fell back again.

Ethel's back shoulders slammed into the wall. She groaned in pain and scurried up against it. She stared at the door, knowing the next strike could very well break it open.

Silence.

Ethel's heavy breathing.

Sound.

Loud, scattering, painful.

The window exploded inwards. Glass sprayed the floor as the dog landed inside on all fours.

Ethel screamed the sound was blood curdling.

The dog crouched forward with its full weight on its front paws. Teeth bared eyes in close. Jagged pieces of glass remained firmly imbedded in its joints, yet the animal seemed not to notice the pain. Cuts covered the head and legs. It looked like a wolf of ancient times.

Ethel tried to scream again but no sound would come.

* * *

Michael Fratscure sped along State Highway 1. He had been at the local vet office in Wellsford City, putting down one wild dog he had captured earlier that day. The local vet administered the shot, and afterwards they had a couple of beers and a good chat. Lucy Agrave was the nicest person he had ever met, and she was damn good at her job. He found he could talk to her for hours and never run out of things to say. But, sadly, she only wanted to be friends. He could live with that and ... who knew, maybe one day...?

He thought today was that day but Pollic had called him on his cell phone just as he was getting ready to make his play. Another bloody wild dog! This was crazy. In his fifteen years as a ranger, this was the first time he'd come across six wild dogs in under a week.

He had taken to carrying a rifle with him, he had a dart pistol, which is what he mainly used, but the last two dogs did not go down easily and he could only fire one dart at a time. The rifle was only a .303 but it would do the trick. He didn't like high-powered weapons he saw no point in them. The rifle was padlocked under the dash and the dart pistol was in the locked glove compartment as per regulations.

Pollic was following standard procedure but Michael was not impressed, especially when Lucy seemed ready to cave in. He knew Pollic had the lady on another line and asked him to patch it through so they both could listen. Then he climbed into his Rav4 and headed to Opera Sands Caravan Park. He wondered how long it would take one of the dogs to get there. They had been roaming the beach the past couple of days. In fact, didn't someone get attacked out there? Oh yeah it wasn't a dog though, it was some weird fuckwit. Like wild dogs there seemed to be too many of them around these days also.

He asked Pollic to get the lady to check and see if the animal was still hanging around.

It was.

Michael slammed the brakes. The Rav4 slid to a stop and he turned around, cursing himself for not paying attention and missing the turn off that lead to the Caravan Park. He wiped all thoughts from his mind and focused his entire attention on getting there as quickly as possible.

DING DING DING DING - DONG DONG DONG DONG - BONNNNGGG BONNNNGGG.

What the fuck...?

He heard the lady tell officer Pollic it was her chime clock.

Then he heard the snarl. He fumbled in his pocket for the key to unlock the rifle and the dart pistol. He didn't like the sound of that snarl. He knew it would be a big dog he was about to face. Then he heard Pollic say to him, "Mike, I think she's left the phone. How far away are you?"

"About five minutes," he said, then heard the sound of breaking glass, "Make that two," He pushed the accelerator to the floor.

* * *

Ethel tried to move away but her back was against the wall.

Her eyes were locked with the dogs.

The dog howled and leapt.

Its teeth pierced her aged skin with little effort. Her housedress tore. Ethel swung her arms to and fro trying to defend herself against the wolf like animal. It was nothing like her sixteen years old terror. It's jaws snapped on her hand and it swung its head viciously.

Her voice returned with the excruciating pain. It excited the dog as part of her hand and little finger tore free. Blood spewed over the beast. It dropped the prize.

Instinctively, she covered the hand with her other and squeezed it against her chest. Her vision blurred. Unconsciousness was coming and she welcomed it with open arms.

The dog's claws dug into her stomach as she fell to her knees. The buttons of her housedress gave way to the constant tugging and flew off, spinning madly on the floor between her and the dog. The dress already having been ripped slipped from her body and got tangled in the dog's paws. It fell on its side, kicking and struggling with the garment trying to free itself.

Ethel saw her chance to escape or at least try to. She was dizzy and pain shot through her naked body. She forced herself to look down and then wished she hadn't. Her stomach was torn open.

Blood oozed from the gap, it did not spray out like in the movies.

Her heartbeat throbbed painfully against her chest. A piece of gray intestine showed itself amongst the torn flesh. A squeezing tightness took hold of her chest. She knew there was no escape.

The dog freed itself. Got to its feet.

Ethel's lungs tightened. It was nearly impossible for her to breathe. The room blurred and began to spin. The squeezing tightness of her chest increased. She now knew what it felt like to be a worm squashed in the hand of a youngster.

The dog tilted its head, confused at the woman's actions. Suddenly a set of headlights shone against the far wall opposite the attack. The animal turned away from its prey that was clutching her chest and rolling on the floor. The dog sensed danger.

* * *

Michael pulled into the Caravan Park and slammed on his breaks. The Rav4 fishtailed on the dirt driveway. He saw a large group of people standing around numerous caravans all of them staring at a large broken window and listening to the sounds coming from the house. At least they weren't stupid and gone for a closer look.

He rolled down his window and said, "Everyone, get back in your homes now!"

Slowly and as quietly as he could he approached the window. He went to the side of the house and slid along the wall until he reached the frame. Shards of glass remained in the putty. He carefully leaned forward and looked. From his angle he could only see a lady in her mid to late fifties lying on the floor. Her stomach and hand were torn apart. Her face was gray and lips blue. He heard a deep breathing and stepped in front of the smashed window.

The dog faced him, sniffing the air. It knew he was there but was waiting for a look. It bared its teeth a piece of flesh was wedged between its front fangs. It wasted no time in charging at the window.

"Fuck!" Michael screamed and ran towards his Rav4. He heard the dog scrambling through the window after him, its claws scraping the window frame and breaking what little glass remained. He reached his car and jumped in, not once looking behind, that would have slowed him down. He looked to the window. The dog was gone. He scanned the area but couldn't see it. It was a black dog and could hide easily in the darkness.

He took a quick breath and followed that with a long inhale and one very slow exhale. His heart slowed. This was the bloodiest night of his career. He lifted the CB mike off its cradle, "Station, this is Michael Fratscure. I require an ambulance out here at Opera Sands Caravan Park. There has been a dog attack, the victim has serious wounds to her body and has most likely suffered a heart attack. The dog is rabid."

A low rumbling growl.

He dropped the mike. The dog was facing his door. It charged.

"Shit!" He scrambled across the seat as the dog hit headfirst. He heard the door crumple inwards. The dog walked away from the vehicle, turned and jogged back towards it. Its yellow eyes rose in the air as it leapt onto the bonnet. The windscreen cracked from the force of the strike from the animal's head. The safety glass webbed white.

He reached for the rifle, praying it had been loaded. He fumbled the safety switch to the off position. He knew he had only one shot before the dog was in the cab tearing him apart. He lay across the seat, rifle pointed at the window. He would wait for the dog to push the glass in before he fired hopefully he would have enough time to get a line on it.

It pushed at the glass just as the sound of an ambulance became audible screaming through the night.

The webbed glass fell in on Michael and, his eyes squeezed tightly closed, he screamed and blindly fired. He waited for the unavoidable pain and thought of his missed chance with Lucy. Seconds passed. Nothing happened. No growls, no pain.

Nothing. He opened his eyes. The dog was gone. He sat upright in his seat and saw the dog limping into the forest. He had hit the dog. Only its leg but it would slow the animal down. It would be caught very soon.

People were coming out of their caravans again, but Michael thought it would be safe for the time being. He turned on the loud speakers on the roof of his car. "This is Ranger Michael Fratscure. Please remain in or near your caravans until further notice. Thank you."

Carrying his rifle, Michael opened the passenger side door and went to the smashed window. He saw the lady motionless and climbed through the window. He checked her pulse. No beat could be felt. Her skin was cold. He rolled her onto her back and performed CPR but when he pushed down on her chest, blood shot out of her mouth.

"Shit," he whispered. He sat by her side and hung his head.

There was nothing to do now, except wait for the ambulance. It wasn't far away he heard its siren growing louder by the second.

Ethel Clemm was dead.

Caravan owners gathered around the smashed window.

"Oh my god!" A lady cried. There were gasps of shock among others.

A few minutes later the ambulance arrived. Medics jumped out of the back carrying a stretcher. In the commotion no one noticed a darkly dressed young man look through the window and leave a few minutes later headed the same way as the dog. No one heard him mumble, "Good bye, mother."

CHAPTER NINE

James couldn't sleep. He tried to force the memory of the attack from his subconscious to his conscious mind. No matter how hard he tried, they refused to surface. The thought of being attacked by a myth scared the hell out of him. He feared the idea of a werewolf - in fact it terrified him. In a last ditch attempt and not knowing where else to turn, he reached above the bed to a small contact panel and pushed the red button next to the radio with a set of headphones hanging on a hook.

After a few minutes, the duty nurse entered. Her dark gray streaked hair was tied into a tight bun. She didn't look very pleased to be called away from her desk, but she managed a smile.

She said, "Mr. Dennett that button is for emergencies only."

"Sorry," he replied, even thought he wasn't, "but I was wondering if you had any old newspapers, about a week old?"

The nurse's smile grew. "Do you want to read about yourself?"

"Just what the papers know about..."

"Well, I'll see what I can do." The nurse replied tiredly and then added. "You're name was kept out of the papers."

"Dr. de Grassol said no one knew my name at that time."

Her smile faded, "I'll have a look. There might be one or two lying around."

"Thanks a lot."

A long time passed and he wondered if she had forgotten. He remembered the scene in the mirror and wanted to know if it had any resemblance to the papers. Why couldn't he recall that night? It was only a week ago. James drew the covers up to his neck, even though the room was warm. He had almost drifted off to sleep when the duty nurse returned with one newspaper and one magazine. She dropped it on the end of the bed and left without saying a word.

"Thank you." He called out as the door closed.

James sat upright and scooped it onto his lap. He checked the front cover of the magazine: More news about the royal family, Presidential elections stuff, oh, lose weight while eating junk food; find love and happiness in the stars; make millions by staying at home; Myths - Have they returned? Are they real? Exclusive interview inside.

Shocked, James re-read the headline. It was not one of the most respected magazines, but the writers got their information from somewhere. Had someone else been attacked? Did this person also have the same delusions, as Dr. Stephens would think? More than anything, James wondered why he saw a myth. It wasn't possible to see a myth, was it? If it wasn't, what exactly had he seen? What the hell was happening to him?

Many questions posed but no answers were immediately available. He needed some solid help, not wacko head shrinking stuff. Maybe this 'trash' magazine held a few answers. He turned the cover and looked down the table of contents for the article but he couldn't see it. Like other magazines they had given it a different title than that on the cover. He turned the pages a few at a time until he found it. It was the same old dross. He read about a man who claimed to be James' best friend.

Apparently, he was staying over the night and they had decided to go for a walk along the beach, when they heard a man screaming in pain. They went to investigate and found a transformation in progress. It went on to describe that the change from man to beast, even had a blurry picture.

"What a load of fucking horse shit!" James threw the magazine across the room. One question entered his mind: Who had told them it was a werewolf attack? No real newspaper would carry that. He picked up the newspaper. The headline was simple: Couple found dead - witness attacked.

As he read through, the article contained nothing about animals, roaming dogs or likewise. Reading carefully, he wasn't so sure his subconscious had told Dr. Stephens everything about that night. He knew she had asked him, but he didn't know what had been said. Even though he knew this, he had the nagging thought that they had just talked and everything went well. It was strange and he wondered what had happened or what they had spoken about. Surely he would remember something - anything about their conversation. But no! He drew a blank there and decided to give up.

His head was a mess. And tomorrow night he was leaving. That worried him more. Part of his face and neck were fucked up and he knew people would stare and children would call him names, if they had the guts. He could live with it, possibly. It would take time to learn to ignore the stares and whispered remarks. He wished the werewolf had finished him off. He was disfigured now, a freak. And if that's how he saw himself then he knew that is how others would see him.

A freak.

He lay down and covered his eyes with his forearm. Self-pity sucks, he thought and drifted off to sleep.

* * *

He found her place easily enough. It looked the same as he remembered it. The grounds were neat and orderly. He hid in the shadows of the trees. It was almost 3am. He crept around to the side of her house and saw a colored glow sparkle between the gaps of the thick curtains. Dr. Stephens must be watching late night television, he told himself. Why wasn't she asleep at this late hour? He didn't care. He remembered where he could gain entry undetected, where the alarm was not correctly wired. He remembered where the connection points weren't screwed in properly and had stuck together. It had not worked when he was her patient. He hoped it was still undiscovered.

There were a lot of small animals about, which would make for many excuses for any sounds he mistakenly made. The bright eyes of a possum watched as he shimmied up the drainpipe and scrambled over guttering. The noise he had sounded ten fold in the quietness of the night, he hoped Carol Stephens would think it was a small animal making its way to the nearest tree.

He wanted to have some fun, to test his luck. He found a pinecone lying in the gutter, lifted it out, cursing at the dark thick slime that covered the bottom, leaned over the side of the house and dropped it. It struck the window frame. Coincidental as it hit a possum leapt from a tree in front of the window and scurried after it.

Bright light blazed below. He knew she was scanning the darkness, unable to see where he was. He spotted the possum running from the light. They were quick little buggers.

He looked towards the area where the light didn't quite reach. It was at a point where it faded and was blocked by bush coverage. His heart skipped a beat. The breath froze in his lungs. Something was out there. Something was out there and it was watching *him*. Not a possum or other small creature he could easily crush in his hands but something big, something strong. He had an uneasy feeling, which urged him to hurry.

The bright light was cut as the curtains closed and darkness returned. The beast dashed to its left. Allen recognized it. A mild breeze blew through the bush sending a shiver through his body. The sounds of nightlife animals thundered in his head. He covered his ears but it did little to help. Perhaps he shouldn't be here, but it had seemed like a good idea at the time.

His mother was dead at long last. This pleased him and he never laid a finger on her. Only James was left. He knew he should not have chosen the beach. Not that it was he who had chosen it. James was an unexpected surprise. The plan was to get rid of the Rothsins' kids, they were brother and sister and the acts they performed were not permitted under the law of God. The plan was to take them out and a few days later, once James had grown to accept the fate of his best friend and kids, then take him out in Redwoods forest where they would not be disturbed. Who would have thought that James was so cold hearted and self-centered as to leave his friend's wife in her time of need for his own selfish wants? He sat there for fifteen minutes before he convinced himself this was the right course of action.

Concentrating he was able to block most sounds and with his mind refocused, he leaned over the roof once more this time lying on his stomach, at the side of the house where a window seemed to call to him. The gutter clamps poked into his skin. Blood rushed to his head as he hung half off the roof.

He strained, trying to force the window frame slightly from its hinges, pop out of alignment and flick open. Doing it this way was harder than he thought. The wood creaked. It sounded like thunder to him. Reaching to the bottom of the window, he managed to squeeze three of his fingers under the opening and found it easy to flick the black plastic hook to the side, leaving it unlocked. Three minutes later he was inside.

The house was silent, which meant no alarm had been triggered.

That pleased him. He headed for Dr. Stephens's bedroom on tiptoe even though the floor was carpeted. Once she saw him, her immediate thought would probably be that he was going to rape her, but he was not that type of person. He was too smart and too godly to fall for pleasures of the flesh in that way.

He passed the hall mirror and checked his reflection. Something was wrong, missing. He stared at his reflection for several moments and suddenly realized what it was. Quietly as he could he sneaked into the kitchen. He could hear the television in the living room.

Under the counter he found two bottles of whiskey and several soft drinks. Dr. Stephens obviously hadn't changed routines since his departure, either that or she had completely forgotten about the drinks.

Perhaps, with a drink in his hand, she might remember him, which is what he prayed for, then he could deal with her straight away and then James Dennett wouldn't have the good doctor telling him what was real or not and that would make him easier prey.

Allen mixed himself a whiskey and coke.

He moved silently to the adjoining doors. They were connected and on rollers so when the door was pushed open, it opened in a W style folding in on itself. Gently, he gave it a soft push. It opened a crack. He could just see the television showing an infomercial and the back of an easy chair and a sofa. He looked in the opposite direction. She wasn't in here - unless she had fallen asleep on the sofa. He eased the doors open and entered. He moved cautiously to the back of the sofa. He could see from where he now stood that she wasn't there. He took a sip from his drink. Where are you?

The only place he could think of was her bedroom, but why had she left the television on? Maybe she was too tired to turn it off. It didn't really matter; if she was in her room asleep he would continue according to his hasty made plan; if she wasn't, then he was out of here with nothing to show except wasted time.

He made his way to her room. It was easy to find. If he hadn't remembered the drink and turned down the hallway, he would have walked right into her room. He boldly opened the door. She was asleep, tucked snugly in bed. He watched her for a moment. Carol Stephens moaned in her sleep. His chest felt like it was in a vice being squeezed and his nerves were sliced open with a jagged piece of glass. His stomach turned as butterflies flew madly in all directions. He knew why he was nervous. This lady knew most of his inner secrets and she was a head shrink so she could possibly turn his words around on him, make him feel guilty, make him think he was doing something wrong. He had to play it cool. Watch his words and be weary of hers.

Allen reached out and flicked on the light. The ice in his drink chinked quietly against the glass and he had to remind himself to remain as cool as that ice, no matter what happens.

The florescent light flickered into life. The room filled with a blinding white light.

There was no reaction from Dr. Stephens. She slept peacefully.

"Fine," he mumbled, quietly going to her side of the bed, where, against the sidewall under a window was a small table. On it was a radio/clock alarm, a small desk lamp, an empty coffee mug and an ashtray with a packet of unopened cigarettes next to it that had a fine layer of dust on the plastic coating and the brand was the same since he was last here. She was out when he last broke in, all he wanted then was to read his file, see what she had written about him. He ended up touring the house before leaving. He knew Dr. Stephens didn't smoke and he always wondered why she kept a packet of cigarettes and an ashtray but no lighter or matches. And why they were now in her bedroom and not the office as they had been.

Also on the table was a light brown folder with a tab reading: James Dennett. He opened it. Inside was a single sheet of A4 typed page. He read about her first meeting with James and about a plastic chair flying across the room. She had scribbled a footnote in pen,

'Highly vulnerable at this time. Must not be pressured take slowly step by step.'

Carol stirred and murmured in her sleep. She rolled onto her side, slowly opening her eyes in the bright light.

Allen sat on the edge of the desk; he was sipping the drink and reading the Dennett file when he noticed her looking at him.

He saw the panic in her eyes but she did not jump from the bed or anything like he had thought. Instead she drew the blankets up to her chin and slid up to the headboard. She watched him closely as he placed the sheet of paper back into the folder.

"Your hand writing isn't very neat," he said placing the file behind him, "Tell me, " he added, "How did the chair fly across the room? You didn't explain that in your notes."

In an uneasy voice, she asked, "Do I know you?"

He smiled, "It hasn't been that long doc." She didn't recognize him, he decided to give her some time, and he doubted if James would be out of hospital for at least another week. If Manny hadn't fucked up he would have the answers he required. He asked, "When does James get released?"

Her eyes watered, "What do you want?"

He reached behind him and picked up the file. He waved it at her. "I want him."

"What do you want?" She repeated.

Allen realized she was looking at the glass when she spoke. Say my name, he wished, say my name bitch, say it God damn it! He should have shaved and worn different clothes, he realized a little late. He had a two-day stubble, it was almost a beard it grew so fast and he used always to wear slacks and a business shirt.

He sighed loudly and said. "To play a game."

"Game?"

He nodded and smiled and picked up the alarm clock. It read: 3:48am. He had to be quick. The sun would be rising in just over an hour. "That's right," he said, putting the clock back.

"Who are you?"

"That's the game." He smiled. "You know me, doc. As a bear shits in the woods, you know me." He paused, looked at the floor then back at her, "You have two days. Exactly 48 hours, " he looked at his watch, "Starting from now."

"Why?"

"Why not?"

"A game?" Carol said. Realization dawned on her face. Allen smiled. She said, "You're the one who-"

He cut her sentence short. "I am the one," he said.

"Why me?" She asked.

The man smiled, "'Cause you're the bitch who wants to help him. I really can't allow that." He brushed his hair back with the palm of his hand. "Those kids on the beach - the ones I set right, they were brother and sister. Incest is not God's law. The path of the Lord is hard to follow but that doesn't mean we shouldn't walk it. James coming to the beach at the same time," he sighed, "ah that was the icing on the cake. I would have achieved my goal if the neighbors had not heard his girly screams."

He watched her closely. Allen knew to be wary of this woman, he knew that only too well even if she looked scared, her mind was most likely running through a million escape possibilities. He had to be fast and let her know the limits before she acted on any of her thoughts. If he saw himself about to lose control, he would kill her right here and now, but then she would not know who he was and he wanted her to know his name. He wanted her to remember him.

"Don't bother with the cops. I'll be watching you. Cancel all your appointments. If you fuck up." He threw the folder at her and it hit her forehead. Carol didn't try to block it.

Allen rose off the desk, knelt on the bed and leaned in close to her. Her eyes showed the fear, and her hand trembled. He held a clenched fist close to her face and said, "If you fuck up, I will bring the wrath of God upon you. I'll be watching and you'll know as much."

"How do you expect me to find your name? Is it Simon?"

Here we go, he thought, she's trying something.

"Paul? Michael? Jan? There are a million names I can choose, don't you see? I need a clue."

Allen pointed to the folder; "You failed me when I needed you. I had a..." Shit he almost told her to check her files which would not be so bad then he could finish her tonight, but where would be the fun in that? He smiled as he rose off the bed and added. "You'll remember me. I'm like a cop in the old western movies." He winked and headed for the door. He looked back at her, she hadn't moved. He laughed. In forty-eight hours, it would all be over.

* * *

Carol watched him leave. Watched him slam the bedroom door. She waited a few minutes, listening but didn't hear him leave.

He could still be outside her door, but she didn't think so. Unable to control it any longer, tears streamed down her face. She felt lucky not to have been touched. The man looked familiar but she could not place him. Something about his eyes and strangely, the drink he was holding. She realized he hadn't worn gloves and had taken the glass with him. She hugged the blankets closer. There would be no more sleep tonight and she sure as hell wasn't about to leave her bedroom just yet.

She would have to play his game for the time being. What was the clue he had given her? Something about failing him? A western cop? What on earth was he talking about? She decided she would have to call the police but that could wait a bit.

He seemed determined to let her find his name. Was it his ego talking? No confidence? No, he had a lot of confidence to break in here like that.

Damn it! He had invaded her house, her bedroom, and her life. Son of a bitch!

* * *

He was out of her house quickly and quietly the same way he had entered. He wondered what she was doing now? Crying, most likely. Calling the cops? That was doubtful. Most likely she was still lying in her bed, afraid to move. He laughed at the thought. The night air was cold and he was a bundle of nerves. He knew not why. He had killed before and found it was easy. Carl Rothsins' kids deserved to die. They were disgusting slime. Plunging the machete through them while they fucked (he couldn't call it making love, not between brother and sister), passing it through their black souls had been bliss. He felt like it was the first time he had done that was truly worthy of God's love. He remembered the saying as he pushed his way through dense bush towards an unpaved road, which was a short cut to his house.

Revenge is mine, said the Lord. God's love burned in his heart now.

God will grant him his revenge.

He didn't feel like going home, there was nothing there for him. A new day was beginning, starting with the orange glow of the sun scraping the Earth's crust. Energy pulsed through his veins, he felt like he could do anything. The power of doing right surged through his body, electrifying his soul. It was the most erotic thing he had ever felt, yet he had fucked up and he knew it.

Part one of his plan had collided with the second. He had been too eager with Dr. Stephens. James's heart had to be broken first. James had to feel emotional pain, not only physical. This had to be achieved before Dr. Stephens became as involved as she was now.

Sure, Carl had died and it caused some emotional pain but obviously not enough to stop James from going to the beach. Allen shook his head. He remembered now. He was weak. When he saw James at the beach he couldn't control himself he felt an uncontrollable urge to end his life there and then. But he had plans for everyone who had fucked with him. No one would escape his wrath like James had.

He consoled himself. James wasn't part of the plan that night. It was okay to have missed.

Something moved in the dense growth of the bush. He was not alarmed or shocked for nothing truly scared him these days. He saw yellow eyes peer at him twenty meters away. He laughed quietly. It was the dog, which had watched him enter the doctor's house. The animal was perhaps a gift from God, and he wondered how a dog could possibly help him. What was he going to do with a dog? It growled, a deep trembling sound vibrating from the pit of its lungs.

It bared its fangs as the man moved closer.

The dark coated dog, semi-hidden by the low hanging branches and dense bush growth, refused to move. Its yellow eyes glistened in the ending dusk, gleaming at Allen, showing only hatred. Its eerie growls grew deeper as if it were from the pits of Hell itself.

Now, Allen felt a prickle of fear, and he looked skyward for help, asking God if he should continue. He felt something he hadn't felt in years. He hated the feeling of fear. Fear was for the weak.

Was this a test from the Lord? He wondered, after all God tested humanity everyday with wars, hunger, and violence in movies and in the streets. Violence was all right while it served a purpose for the Lord, but mindless violence, what use was that?

Yes. This was a test from God. The beast would not hurt him. This is a test of his faith, to see if he was worthy of His love and for revenge on those who broke His law. It is a long and hard path to the pearly gates.

It moved suddenly and quickly, turning away from Allen. It ran towards the edge of the bush land, south of his destination, stopping a few yards away. Its eyes called to him called him to follow. They no longer looked evil or eerie or threatening but Allen could still see a hint of poison. The way its eyes commanded him to follow spoke to him stronger than anything he had ever felt before did. It was hard to resist such a force. He found himself being pulled toward the beast.

It drew him to the edge of the forest.

Allen somehow knew he had to walk out onto the dirt road, which connected with his road home two hundred yards or so down the line. He headed to it. The beast growled and foam bubbled between its teeth and lips. Its cold eyes stared at him, watching every move he made. It crouched down like a Black Panther stalking its prey. He wondered what was going on. What did God want him to do? He reached the dirt road having full trust in his savior. The beast rose onto its hind legs and howled at the rising sun. The cry sent a shiver down Allen's back. Then he saw what he feared. But he would not move. God was with him.

White ivory horns grew from the sides of the beast's head. Five inches long thick claws grew from its paws. The fangs became longer. Eyes changed from yellow to green with a black slit across its width. It grew taller, larger.

Allen stood his ground.

His knees trembled.

He stared coldly at the beast from Hell.

God was with him.

The beast smelled the man's fear.

It howled.

This was not a creature of Gods creation.

It moved like lightning, streaking onto the dirt road towards the man whose smell of fear suddenly vanished.

* * *

William Bonny pushed his car to the max. The motor roared like a lion, he considered himself the king of speed in his custom Escort Mark II. The party William was returning from had been wild, not only was he considerably drunk but luckily stoned as well and the highlight of the night was scoring with Sharon - twice. One of the best parties he had been to in a long time. At seventeen, he was king of the dirt roads, or so he thought. The thrill when the car slid and spun around a corner was the greatest rush of all. Anything could be coming in the other direction. One never knew. It was wild, great and this morning was the same as all the others.

Dust spewed up from the tires as he neared the second to last corner before hitting the intersection. Suddenly he slowed down. Easing his foot off the accelerator the speed dropped from 115 km/h to 80 km/h. why had he done that? The speed needle bounced between 80 and 85. The corner appeared to approach in slow motion. Starting the turn, William swore at himself. What was he doing? This was the best corner of them all. It stared wide and cut inwards and tight. Five times he had gone off the road and into the ditch. Fuck slowing down. He planted his foot...

* * *

Headlights shone on Allen but he didn't notice. His concentration was focused on the beast as it charged at him. Its jaws open...

* * *

William saw the man standing in the middle of the road, in direct line with his car. He felt the back slide out, knew it was wrong but slammed both feet hard on the brake pedal...

* * *

The horned beast, its green black slit lizard eyes narrowing, leapt...

* * *

The Escort's brake pedal hit the floor with no resistance. The brakes were gone. Too intoxicated to think of a counter, William tried to turn the steering wheel but his hands slipped. He was seconds away from hitting and no doubt killing the idiot on the road...

* * *

The beast hit Allen. Its jaws, wide and open, inches away from his throat...

* * *

The Escort struck with the force of a thunderbolt. The car rose as it bumped over the victim, landing hard on the road. Suddenly the brakes worked. Deep tracks followed the locked tires as the Escort slid across the road from side to side. It finally stopped, inches away from the ditch and bank.

William inhaled deeply trying to catch his breath. He felt stone cold sober and sat motionless in the bucket seat with his eyes closed calming himself.

What the fuck am I going to do? It's fucking Manslaughter at the least! I'm truly fucked. Goddamn idiots everywhere. Hang on, he told himself, No one's around. I'm the only witness and I'm not about to rat on myself, am I?

"Yes," he nearly screamed, "you fucking beauty, William." He pounded his fists against the steering wheel several times. "It's only right for me to see the mess I made." He climbed out of the car. His legs were rubbery.

He saw the crumpled heap a couple of meters up the road. The head was crushed open, the body all twisted and torn. He eased closer, taking a good look, "Oh, thank Christ," he mumbled, "It's only a big fucking dog. I thought it was ... Shit, what the fuck did I smoke?" He grabbed the animal's legs and pulled it to the side of the road. With that done, he returned to his car and drove off. Much slower this time, just in case. From this day forward he would step down as king of the dirt road and take things a tad easier. Just in case.

* * *

Standing deep in the bush, hidden by the trees and the darkness they offered. Allen watched the young man drive away. He stared at the dog lying in the ditch, its horns and fangs and claws gone. He crossed himself, wondering how he got here a spilt second before the car struck. He smiled. God had saved him from Satan's pet. He was in one piece. Yet, something was different. His eyes hurt from the morning light streaming through the tree branches. His eyes were different.

Looking back deeper into the forest, he noticed the change.

He could see clearly in the dark like a cat or dog. He saw the black insects running about their business. He went closer for a better look. They ignored him as if he didn't exist. Ignored him like a night shadow.

CHAPTER TEN

James Dennett dressed quietly and slowly in the hospital room. Dr. de Grassol had given him a final check out twenty minutes earlier. The tender flesh around his scars was healing well and as long as they weren't aggravated the scarring should be minimal although they would always be visible.

James was reluctant to leave. He feared the taunting and stares that were surely to come. The humiliation would kill him inside. He told himself to be strong but did not believe he could be strong enough, long enough. He asked the doctor for bandages or something to cover the marks of an attack he will never forget but the doctor refused his request. The wounds needed to dry out. Reluctantly James nodded as he brushed his clothes free of lint.

The hospital corridors were cold, empty and silent. He felt like he was walking through a graveyard or in a movie where the hero walked away on his own moments before the credits rolled. He tried to put on a 'Who cares, I can handle it' attitude so he would be ready for it when he reached the main street in Orewa. He couldn't hide from people forever. He wondered about the reaction at the Caravan Park. He could imagine Mrs. Clemms look and comments; she wouldn't laugh until he was out of earshot. It felt just as bad knowing that she was going to.

He didn't fancy such a long walk home. All the cars that would pass him and all the stares he was bound to notice. Then again, he thought, maybe I'm over reacting? He would not laugh at a disfigured person, instead he would stare at the ground until they had passed or stop to look at something in the opposite direction. Was it cold to ignore these people? Was he going to feel this coldness?

The decision was made. He was not about to walk home. Well at least not during the daylight hours. He remembered Dr. Carol Stephens; maybe she would give him a lift. He searched his pockets for her card and found it in his front left. In the back pocket he found the letter with the assignment of photographing Redwoods forest and Opera Sands. He didn't recall putting it in his pocket usually he placed such important items in the shoebox under his bed. Yet, here it was the letter, which had landed him in the animal's presence.

The company's phone number was printed at the top. He decided to call and apologize for failing his assignment. He hoped they'd give him another chance at something else. Once he explained what had happened, then it was likely to happen.

He walked with his head down after leaving the hospital grounds, fearful of what he might see and hear. He reached a blue striped coin phone not far from the hospital gates. Normally James would have seen this as a good sign, but he had now given up on looking for good or bad signs in everyday happenings, especially after the attack. Damn the animal that had disfigured his face and chest. Why had it not been caught yet, or if it had, why hadn't he been told?

He realized he feared another attack. It could or would happen anywhere, anytime. He could never feel safe with it still roaming the streets at night. People only changed into werewolves at night.

James didn't believe it had to be a full moon for that to happen. Movies were not always accurate. It wasn't a full moon when he saw the werewolf for the first time, all those years ago. Why had it not taken him then? Why wait until last week? These were questions James had no answer for and he sure as hell did not want to meet it again. Twice in his life was enough.

James saw children in the playground across from the hospital in a field not far away, but far enough for them and their parents to not be able to see his face clearly. After all, he couldn't make out their features, why should they be able to make out his? He remembered Dr. de Grassol had said it would take awhile before he found the confidence to walk the streets with his head held high oblivious to reactions around him. It would take courage and time - something James felt he had little of.

He pushed open the full-length door made of hard plastic. He dropped a 50 cents coin into the machine and dialed the number displayed in the letterhead. A 'no such number' tone followed. He hung up and dialed again. The same repeated. He called directory service. A quiet spoken woman gave him a number, which was very different from that in the letter. He punched in the new number and this time there was a ringing tone and an answer.

"Good afternoon, I C Corp. publishing."

"Hi, my name's James Dennett," he told the young female voice at the other end, "Could I speak to the editor please?"

"Which editor would that be, sir?"

Wow, big magazine, he thought, how many editors did they have?

"The magazine editor." He replied.

"We have three editors in that department. Could you be more specific?"

"Um. How about the photography department?"

"That would be Mr. Percy. One moment."

James heard a series of clicks, then elevator music. He waited.

"Hello, Robert Percy executive editor, how may I help you?" His voice was rough and he sounded tired.

"Mr. Percy, I'm James Dennett. Sorry to bother you, but I was unable to return the night time shots as you requested, but you see..."

"Dennett?" Robert interrupted, "There's no one on my staff named Dennett."

"Sir," James said, "I'm not on your staff," he held the letter in front of him. He had a terrible feeling. "You sent me a letter requesting infrared shots of Redwoods forest and Opera Sands beach." Rain stared to fall, softly at first growing steadily harder and James frowned at it. He saw parents and children running to their cars. A cold wind started and he knew a storm was on its way.

"Opera Sands, where the hell is that? What's your name again?"

"Dennett, James Dennett. You sent me a-"

"Dennett. Is that with two T's?"

"Yes," James heard Robert Percy tapping away on a computer keyboard.

"I'm sorry, Mr. Dennett. Your name isn't on our computer. You say we wanted infrared shots?"

"That's correct sir, of Operas Sands and Redwoods forest."

"I see," Robert paused and his voice tone changed to that of a person growing annoyed, "Mr. Dennett, do you know what kind of magazine it is that we publish?"

James thought for a minute. He had never heard of the company, and said, "No," his voice flat. Something was happening here that he didn't like.

"We publish 'Inside Homes' and 'Reconstruction', House magazines, Mr. Dennett. I am a busy man, so if you'll excuse me-"

"But-"

"Good bye, Mr. Dennett." It was final. He hung up.

The storm broke. Heavy rain pelted down. It thundered against the ground, forming puddles, and pounded the plastic cover of the phone box.

Stunned, James slowly hung up. Looking down at the letter he felt all hope of his dream becoming a reality slipping away. His one real chance and it was gone. A great emptiness engulfed his heart. Standing in the coin box, he felt a cloak of loneliness wrap around him and in anger he screwed up the letter and threw it outside, it soaked quickly and was washed into the gutter. He slammed the door closed keeping the rain outside. The anger was a tight knot inside, his hands clenched into fists and he punched the phone repeatedly. Stopping when his knuckles bled. Tears welled up in his eyes, but not from the pain of the punches he noticed.

He slid to the floor of the booth. Everything seemed against him, even his own life. He checked his hands. Destiny and Lady Luck had spat in his face. James held his head and cried as the wind and rain found its way through gaps and ran down on the inside of the box. The occasional drop fell on his shoulder.

He hadn't called Dr. Stephens. James had felt like walking after the rain eased off. It took three hours to reach his home. The storm ended, although the sky remained dark, as he walked along the driveway. He hadn't bothered trying to hitchhike. There was no point in it. He doubted if anyone would have stopped for him, all torn, disfigured and wet through.

* * *

The female lycanthrope followed James as Duncan had ordered her to. It wasn't easy and a few times she had thought about returning and getting her clothes but feared losing him. She had watched him in the telephone booth from the opposite side of the park and she had heard the conversation. The editor was very rude; people seldom acted like that in her day. She saw him break down and cry and she pitied him.

She felt an attraction to this man from what Duncan had said; James was the man who'd bring the lycanthropes back to their rightful place as leaders of this world. Back to a time when lycanthropes ruled, a time when man worshiped them and a time when man feared them.

Whatever happened to change those times she wasn't sure about or if what she had heard was only a myth. But one thing was for sure: If James had the power to bring their lost glory back, then she was bound by her blood and her want to make it happen and to protect James with her life.

She wasn't entirely sure she was up to this kind of responsibility, but Duncan had ordered this and it proved that he finally trusted her again after all the mistakes she had made that put their lives in danger.

Duncan was away with the other male, Phillip. There were times when a special thirst had to be quenched. It was a thirst only males felt. She was the only female among them for the past hundred years. She serviced their needs in human or lycanthrope form, it was a special privilege but being the only female it didn't hold any special meaning. If only Duncan would give her another female to create, then she would be truly happy.

James rounded a corner and she lost sight of him again, but this time she didn't worry, she knew where he was headed: Home.

* * *

The Caravan Park looked desolate. He cut across the grounds avoiding the park's office and Mrs. Clemm. He needed something to hide his face but the only thing he had was a WCW sports cap. He hurried toward his home, which he considered a sweltering tin box even on cooler days. He almost reached it when he spotted Nick, coming his way, carrying a can of beer.

"James," he called.

"Hey Nick," he called in return holding both hands above his eyes as if the sun was too strong, in a vain attempt to hide the scars from his old friend. "What's up?" He called. "I'm kind of tired. Would like to get some sleep."

"Some bad shit's gone down since you've been away." Nick's breathing was uneven, he was overweight, unfit, balding but happy go lucky in his approach to life."

"I've been in hospital." James offered.

"Yeah, I know. I heard Mrs. Clemm and some sexy bitch saying you was her patient." He grinned, "You lucky dog. That your doctor, aye?" He pulled a face. "You scored a nice piece of meat there!"

James laughed and dropped his guard. His hands fell from his face exposing his scars to his friend. He quickly replaced them. But he was too late.

His friend pulled his hands away and said, "Fuck me..." He looked closely at the injuries, "Man, I heard you got hurt but...fuck! What happened?"

"Long story, which I'd rather not tell. I don't feel too much like talking if you don't mind." James replaced his hands. He had felt like he was being inspected like a parcel going through customs, "I'd like to get some rest before talking to Mrs. Clemm.

I don't really want to, but she'll throw me out if I don't get the rent to her soon."

Nick looked at the ground. "Um," he said before taking a long swallow on his can. "Ah, you can't stay here anymore, no one can."

"What?"

Taking a deep breath, Nick said, "You see, Mrs. Clemm was ... um..."

"Spit it out," James said.

"Well, there was this fucking rabid dog here last night, and well, Mrs. Clemm's gone to join her husband."

At first, James didn't understand, then everything clicked, her husband was dead and so was she.

Nick was still talking, "I don't think there's anyone willing to take over this dump. Everyone's packing up their caravans, shit some are even claiming the rented ones are theirs." He laughed but it sounded forced. "You gonna take yours?"

James smiled, "Where's everyone going?"

"No idea. Most have been asking to use my phone. Had to tell 'em all to fuck off and use the public one." He smiled, "Some are a bit pissed with me."

"Why are you still here?"

"Waiting for my sister to arrive from Christchurch. Should he here tomorrow. Do you have anywhere to go?"

James shrugged his shoulders. "I'll find somewhere."

"You're quite welcome to come and stay with me and my sister. There are a lot of jobs down there. Shit, you could even start your own photography business instead of doing this freelance stuff. Hey," he added, "everyone loves the portraits you do."

"Thanks for the complement, but I think I'll pass on the offer. I like living around here." Yet, Nick did have a point about starting up his own business and he had received complements about his family shots. Running his own business wouldn't be that hard, after all, he had done many people and family shots to make ends meet for a while now. But his dream was as a freelance photography and not a party clicker.

He left Nick standing there and went to his caravan. He felt no emotions about Mrs. Clemm. In fact he was glad she'd brought the farm. It was a shame he had to move, he had nowhere to go. He'd check the yellow pages later. He would continue to live in his caravan as long as possible. He could always move into one of the nicer ones. Fuck it. He'd sleep until tomorrow and then deal with life's troubles.

The tin door was ajar as usual. He looked back at one of the largest unoccupied caravans in the park. It was a deep red color with very little rust. It looked inviting. James decided to move in tomorrow. He was too tired to do anything for the rest of the day.

He swung the door open. Something dangled from the roof. The shock threw him backward off the concrete steps and he hit the moist grass, landing on his side. He groaned and opened his eyes. He saw Nick rushing to him.

"Jesus, you all right?"

James pointed to his door. Nick turned and saw it to. His face lost color, "Mother fucker," he whispered.

He saw the puppy, gutted and hanging from the roof by its large intestine, which was wrapped around its tiny body. A pool of blood splattered below it with the edges dried and crusty. Pinned to the side of the puppy, on the open flesh was a bloodstained note. The sight reminded him of his scars.

It was the note Carol had written.

A force field of fear encased James. He couldn't move, could no longer find the energy. Someone had invaded his home, his castle and slaughtered a poor animal, which had once looked very cute but now looked ... simply gutted. Its dead eyes looked at James and he wondered who would have done such a cruel act. It had to be the werewolf in its human form. Only a person without a heart or soul could have done this. This was ... He couldn't find the words for it. He tried to turn away from the puppy's eyes, the sorrow and pain, the questioning look of 'why'. He could imagine its confusion, from the look on its face, in its eyes. It penetrated his heart.

James found the strength to move into a kneeling position. He thought he was about to disgorge and tightly clutched his stomach, forgetting about the scars. He wondered how Nick was holding up. Nick's reaction on the other hand, James realized, was quite the opposite. He doubted if this sort of thing bothered his friend. Nick was a horror fan and had seen too many movies to be affected in any way, style or form. He was a horror fanatic since the early eighties. The 'Decade of gore', he called it, had hardened his mind and feelings.

Although this was real, it sure as hell didn't feel like it.

Seeing the note, James's friend moved into the caravan. His face scrunched up at the smell. His nostrils were burning by the time he had pulled off the note. The blood had blotted the paper making it hard to read. All he could make out was; A gift and the letter C. the rest was coated in a brownish dried blood.

He looked at James and said, "I'll call the cops."

As he turned to leave, there was a loud thump behind and they both looked at the fallen puppy. It had landed with considerable force in the pool of its blood. James cupped over and vomited, unable to hold back the rushing liquid. The falling puppy made it seem all that more real. It brought the reality crashing home. James realized the werewolf wanted him. For some reason it had chosen this point in his life. It felt like having two different people after him, the werewolf and the man. There was no way he could run from it, it would always find him. He was fucked. Last week was only a taste of its powers. How strong was it really?

Nick knelt next to his mate and said, "There are some sick fucks out there." He placed his large hands under James' arms and help him to his feet, "Come on. Let's head over to my caravan. What do ya think?"

James didn't reply. He kept his eyes on the ground and watched his feet shuffle forward.

In due time the police arrived and explained that there wasn't a whole lot they could do, most of the neighbors had packed up and were in the process of moving on. None that they had spoken to had seen or heard anything. The options were limited, but there were options, but the best thing James could do was to pack his bags and move on to another location. They'll take care of the puppy. It was under control.

Officer Hobbs sat on the comfortable built in couch of Nick's caravan, explaining the situation to them. He suggested to James to gather his belongings now or arrange a time in which the lab boys would be finished or he could be supervised. They didn't have much to work with but what they did have they wished it not to be disturbed.

James had listened as he tried to shake the image of the puppy's eyes. Everywhere he looked he saw them crying out for help. The coffee cup shook gently in his hands as he nodded in agreement with everything the officer said, although he didn't really hear or understand half of it. He knew it would all sink in later.

Hobbs' partner, officer Pawman entered the caravan after a quick knock on the door and whispered something in Hobbs' ear. He looked querulously at his partner and said, "Really? You're yanking my chain."

Officer Pawman shook his head and handed the printout to Hobbs who slowly read it. Pawman said, "Hot off the computer."

Officer Hobbs looked at James and said, "It says here that you are involved with a double homicide investigation."

James nodded.

"Shit," Nick exclaimed, "What the hell has happened, James? What did you walk into?"

"I don't know, Nick. I really don't know."

"Do you know a Martha Rothsins?" Hobbs asked but he already knew the answer to this.

"Carl's wife for many years," James paused and looked Nick in the eye, "Carl's also gone."

Nick stared blankly at him.

"There was an accident at work," James lied.

"Last night," Hobbs said, reading off the printout, "A body washed up onto Opera Sands, matching the description of Mr. Rothsins. His wife is too upset to view the body on her own and has requested your presence for the identification."

"Sure," James replied, wondering why her children couldn't help out. Surely they must know by now. He didn't voice this question, he was sure he could ask them himself when he next saw them. He rose off the seat, placed his cup in the sink and wondered how much more of this he could handle. How much longer before he started to lose it? When would he break? He felt very near to that point now. How much time is left? He thought as he followed the police officers to their vehicle.

He wanted to vanish. Live where no one and no beast would ever find him. There had to be a place and he would have to leave in secret, start a new life with a new name and all. He could never take another picture in his life. God, he felt empty just thinking about that other life. James knew he could never manage it. He would rather die, instead of giving everything up. He would face what had to be done. And if the strain got too much and he cracked then ... fuck it.

* * *

Martha thought she had passed the crying stage, but when she saw Carl's flour white complexion and rock hard and bloated body lying on a steel slab all the tears and memories flooded back in full force. It was the second time she'd been here in the last week. She had no one left no family. God was punishing her. For what, she had no idea.

The police had told her that James had just been released from hospital and that he had fought with the man who killed her children. But he was blocking it for some reason he didn't even know. She was asked not to push him, and if she could, could she not mention it for the time being. The person who took her children away would be caught, and James's mind was a mess right now and he needed help to get it in order. And it was highly likely that he was unaware that it was her children's passing that he had witnessed.

"Murder." She had told detective Kerrs, "You can say it. I am a grown woman. I can handle..." Her voice trailed off, tears lined her eyes. "I won't pressure him," she promised when she saw

James lead towards her by two other police officers. "James!" she cried out when he entered the room, and they hugged tightly. And now, here they were looking down at Carl's corpse. Yes, she could use that word because Carl wasn't in there any longer.

James held her for support, and she felt better having him with her. She could never have done this alone or with her church friends who were all two-dimensional. They would say the right things at the right times but she doubted if she'd receive any comfort from them. James was the obvious choice, he was a good friend and also very close to Carl. She looked up at him but was unable to read his face. It held no expression. What was he thinking?

Detective Kerrs lead them out a few minutes later. Martha had to sign some papers. Kerrs thanked her and expressed his sorrow. Although he sounded uncomfortable, he was very professional.

James had sat outside the office on a wooden bench. His eyes were closed but she knew he wasn't sleeping. She went to him and said. "I heard about Mrs. Clemm." She said it quietly.

James opened his eyes they were puffy and blood shot. He reached into his jacket pocket and removed some pills Dr. de Grassol had given him. The paper packet was wet from the rain earlier but the box inside seemed fine.

"Do you have somewhere to stay?" She queried taking a seat beside him.

He shook his head: No. Then got up and went to the water machine and poured a cup of cold water. He swallowed two pills, checked the instructions on the box then took another two.

Martha ignored his coldness. He'd be his old self, soon enough.

"You're more than welcome to stay at my house." She said, watching his every movement.

"I don't want to get you involved."

Martha sighed. She stood up and took the box of pills away. She read the box but had no idea what they are for. She said,

"Your body can heal itself. Don't take too many of these, just enough to dull the pain."

He smiled, "Yes nurse." He said.

"How about it James? There's plenty of room."

"I don't want to get you involved." He repeated.

"I am involved, dear." She was going to tell him even though she told herself not to, not yet. Wrong time, wrong place. She saw Detective Kerrs open the door to his office. She looked at the floor. "The same person who attacked you also took my babies away." James could only stare at her stunned.

* * *

Carol Stephens awoke that afternoon. Amazed to discover that she had in fact gone to sleep. The alarm clock read: 3:30pm in bright red numbers. She must have been more tired that she thought. Climbing out of bed, she opened the curtains. It was a dark day outside. Everything was so quiet. She caught herself searching the trees and bushes for last night's visitor. I'll be watching, he'd said. She found nothing. It might have been an empty threat, but she was taking it seriously.

The man was serious in what he said and what he did. She would have to call the police soon. There were coded messages for times like these but they were usually used when the person was with you. That didn't matter. This man was dangerous. She only hoped that whoever answered the phone knew the code, she'd be asking for trouble if she requested Kerrs, or someone she was certain knew the code.

For a brief time she thought it was a dream. How could someone get past her alarms? They were wired all over the house. She remembered checking them when she felt sure he had left and all alarms read: Ready.

She slipped on a robe and went into the hallway to check them again. She shook her head. It couldn't have been a dream, could it? It was too real. If it was a dream what did it mean? Dreams have a screwed up way of passing on important information. She knew sometimes people were in a dream understood that they were dreaming and when they awoke it was quickly forgotten, but then there were the other types. Dreams that were too real and when you woke up you believed it had happened, but there was always that nagging feeling that it could have been a dream and Carol didn't have that nagging feeling.

She headed to the kitchen and turned on the jug. She rubbed sleep from her eyes and yawned. She hadn't slept much. The sliding doors were open, giving a full view of the living room. It was a mess.

Newspapers were open and spread over the floor, old case files stacked on the coffee table. Textbooks were scattered about. A dirty coffee cup lay on its side (her kitten must have knocked it over) and two video cases were open in front of the television set. Had she believed the dream so much as to start looking for a name? No wonder she was tired.

Carol yawned again. She was going to have to start cleaning up and then go through them methodically, make sure all was still in order. "Kitty, come her girl. Do you want some milk?" She looked around for her kitten. It usually slept on the bed with her or on the windowsill. Where was it hiding this morning? She called again. She'll turn up when she gets hungry, Carol thought.

The jug whistled.

Carol pulled the plug. On the dinner table was her appointment book, she flicked through it to Monday's page and saw she had two clients penciled in for evening sessions. Today was Saturday. It was always free time including Sunday, unless something urgent came up, like last Sunday when she had visited James.

Holding the book in one hand she scooped sugar and instant coffee into a cup, then poured in the hot water. Going to the fridge, she noticed a weird odor, unpleasant. Something had gone off in the fridge. She opened the door and pulled out the carton of milk. There was no coldness from the fridge. No wonder some food had gone off, the fridge is broken, she thought. The carton of milk was also warm. As she closed the door, she noticed something in the corner.

Oh, God no please.

She slowly opened the door. Stuffed in the corner, wrapped into a ball was her kitten. A scream erupted from the deep regions of her lungs. The appointment book slipped from her hand, a second later the carton of milk followed. The book landed face up with the heavy leather cover open. The carton of milk thumped beside it, landing on it side. From the open nozzle pink milk poured out. The pages of the appointment book blotted with the bloody milk.

Carol covered her mouth with her hands and forced herself not to vomit. She reached out for something to hold onto for support. The fridge door was within reach. She rested her weight on it but the door opened more with her weight on it and she lost balance. She crashed to the floor, felt her wrist twist as she automatically placed her hands in front of her to break the short fall. Her eyes filled with water.

The door gently swung to close and came to a stop against her head. She pushed it away and, breathing hard with tears streaming down her cheeks she saw the message written where the egg rack had been. It was written in the kitten's blood. It read: No dream doc. No dream. The clock is ticking.

He knew what she was thinking. And she knew he had returned after she gave up on the file search. This proved the man was real and was indeed watching her. And, he had access to her house, whenever he pleased.

Chapter Eleven

James entered his caravan, he could still smell the puppy's blood, could still see the stain on the floor. He tried not to look at it, but found his eyes continually drawn to it. Entering the bedroom, he pulled his duffel bag from under the bed and haphazardly tossed his clothes inside. He fastened the straps, laid it on the bed and pulled out his shoebox. Quickly he rummaged through the box, decided he did not require any of the papers inside, he replaced the lid and put it under the bed again. He took one last look at his old home.

Three years seemed like a long time but it passed so fast. He hadn't achieved anything in this place. The time in this caravan would soon become an old bad memory.

He picked up his duffel bag, slung it over his left shoulder, and winced in pain. It was heavier than he thought and his flesh was still too tender for heavy weight. Instead he grabbed it by the top flap where the frame was and carried it that way. He took it to the front door and dropped it onto the grass behind the concrete steps. He glanced over at the patrol car idling, waiting for him. Holding up a hand he indicated 'One more minute' and disappeared inside the caravan once again.

Stacked under the table were some old photography magazines. He grabbed the four most recent, and placed them on the table. He was careful of his steps making sure he stepped over the bloodstain. He reached up and grabbed the bottle of Exonpet 2000 he didn't think he would ever use it now. The camera with the infrared film was gone. The police had not found it and he was in no condition to go looking. James doubted it he had caught anything useful. As far as he was concerned it was a waste of time. It was a set-up and he knew that now. The beast had come for him and failed. It would not be the last time either.

And staying at Martha's place was putting her in danger.

He snatched the bottle of Exonpet 2000 off the shelf above the stove and carried it and the magazines outside. Detective Kerrs and Martha were sitting in the car silently waiting for him. He thought Kerrs would at least help him with the duffel bag. But the detective only watched him. As James reached the trunk, its lid automatically popped open, triggered from inside. He tossed in the bag and magazines but opted to hold the bottle, just in case it spilt.

Why had he brought the bottle with him? James had no idea. It was useless now. There seemed to be no point in wasting his energy to carry it, but for reasons he did not understand, he felt compelled to bring it. It rested between his legs as he sat next to Martha in the back seat. His new landlord, although only temporary, sat silently. No sounds escaped her even her breathing was thin, shallow and soundless.

Detective Kerrs tried to start up a conversation but failed when no one answered him. Depression hung heavily inside the patrol car. It didn't surprise him, not after the events his two passengers had faced. He felt for them, he really did, which is why he offered to drive them home, only to discover James was moving into Martha's house for a while. He'd gone from volunteer taxi driver to volunteer house mover in the space of five minutes when James had asked if he could pick up some things on the way to Martha's. He was a police detective not a taxi driver or house mover. He knew he should have stayed in his office, held a cold heart, remained only as an observer to the happenings outside his office, but he hadn't and that was that. At least he wasn't required to help James in the moving process. That would have really pissed him off if James had asked for a hand.

The patrol car pulled onto the side street, leading to Martha's little, empty house.

* * *

The police scanner whispered in the back of the room. Mostly he heard only static but there would come a brief splattering of orders to two or more cars. It was daylight, a time when things were usually quiet. But he had to listen.

His eyes hurt from the sunlight and he had to wear dark sunglasses to keep the pain at bay. He was bored and lost for anything useful to do. He hated waiting. Time ticked by slowly when you were forced to wait. Perhaps he would not have to wait for long. Maybe, Dr. Stephens would come across his name by accident. Then again, maybe not. It didn't matter; she was going to die, any way he looked at it. And he had to assume she also knew this.

He was fired up. Wanted - needed to do something. Anything would suffice.

He had to break the slow time spell.

Allen was surprised not feeling anything after seeing or perhaps ordering his mother's death. He thought he would feel something, emptiness, relief, bitterness, something at least. But he felt nothing, not a single bloody thing, not even happiness about it. All the years of dreaming of her death had dulled his senses, would it be the same with James? God, Allen hoped not.

He paced back and forth across his living room floor, finally heading to the fireplace. It was an old style set up with large bricks, big enough to step inside, easy enough to shuffle up the chimney to the roof, if someone wanted to. Dead coals lay in a pile and he gently patted them down into the tray below. For a moment or two, he aimlessly stared at his work. No thoughts ran through his head, no ideas, nothing.

On the mantle above the chimney was a photo of his parents.

His dad, big, rough and looking as strong as a horse stood next to a slight woman with a large chest. The woman was slightly older than the man was. Allen took the picture off the mantle and studied the photo of his mother. It was taken before Allen was born, before they moved into the Caravan Park. She was very attractive with beautiful ocean blue eyes and long luxurious silky dark hair. It was hard to picture this woman as the woman he grew up with.

Had she completely let herself go, after her marriage? Did she think there was no going back once the vows very exchanged? What happened to chance his once beautiful mother into what she had ended as? That was one question he would never have the answer to. It no longer mattered now that she was gone. Earlier than he had planned but it seemed that all his plans were jumping ahead of schedule. This didn't bother him, much. It only proved his plans were working and that God was on his side.

Staring at the photo, he remembered how, after years of being compared to James, he discovered who this James Dennett was.

His father had ordered him to clean out the attic; they needed room to store old furniture. They had recently received their first credit card and dad decided it was time to use it for some new goods. These were a television, one of those fancy colored ones, a new bed, dining table with chairs, a couch and some odds and ends. They left Allen to clean up the attic as they went shopping. He had pleaded with them to bring him along, said he would be good and not ask for a single thing.

"Get up to that attic now, boy, before I take my belt to you!" His father boomed and Allen knew that when his father used that tone in his voice, all discussion was over. Disappointed, he ascended the attic steps.

There was more room up here. More than anyone thought. There was a pile of big boxes, a dressmaker's dummy, a typewriter, an old National radio and some newspapers. What was he supposed to do with this junk? He was not told. In the end he decided to move it all to the back wall and stack it as high as he could.

He struggled with the large boxes, they were heavy for a nine-year-old and he realized there was no way he could stack them on top of one another. Instead he lined the large ones side by side and smaller boxes he could lift were placed on top of the big boxes. The newspapers were stacked on top of the boxes in a neat pile and the old radio was jammed between the roof and a box.

It took almost an hour to do this and he sat down with his back leaning against the wall. He looked at his work and felt proud. Dad will be happy, he thought. He was about to close his eyes for a rest when he saw a small shoebox in the furthermost corner from him. He hadn't noticed it before. It was lying on its side. Most likely having tumbled out of a large box unnoticed until now.

Getting to his feet, he stretched, deciding to collect the box, threw it on top of the rest and be done with it. Afterwards he would go down have a glass of orange juice and maybe read his adventure book. Dragging his feet, he went to the shoebox and picked it up. A pile of photos and letters fell out. Swearing, he kneeled in front of them and started to put them back where they belonged. He looked at the photos they were of his father and some other woman. They were very young. Must have been around seventeen years old. This was the only photo he had seen of his father in his young days. This lady was also pretty, but not in the same way as his mother. She had shoulder length hair, blue eyes and was pencil thin. Scribbled on the back of the photo was a date only: 1947. Some of the other photos were of this woman only and others of this woman and a child. He could see wrinkles around the woman's eyes and mouth in the photos with the child. They were color photos but not good quality. This must have been the sixties. He checked the date for the back. It read: James at 2yrs.

Is this the James my father keeps talking about?

He looked through the papers some had yellowed with age.

There he found a marriage certificate and birth certificate. With the words: Child: James Dennett. Father: Cal Dennett. He stopped reading. Dennett? His dad's name was Cal Sheriff. He didn't understand any of this, but at least he knew who James was. And instantly he hated him. James was his brother only by half, but a brother nonetheless. He put all the photos and papers back in the shoebox and put it inside one of the larger boxes. He didn't want his father to know he had seen it. He knew what would happen if he did, and Allen did not want to suffer that pain.

Now, nearing his twenty fifth birthday and with years of hatred built up into a burning obsession, he had followed James. And at least he struck. It felt good, like sex, it was a brilliant release.

He put the photo back on the mantle and went to the fridge for a beer. He pulled a stubby bottle and twisted off its cap. The memories had shaken him and he felt tight, a wounded up 'jack-in-the-box'. He doubted the beer would sooth him. He emptied the bottle in three long swigs. The cool liquid flowed easily down his throat. He put the empty bottle on the table. He had been right the beer had done nothing.

He wondered what was happening at Opera Sands Caravan Park. Would they close the place down? He hoped not, it would make finding James harder but not impossible. Where could he go in two days? He would leave Opera Sands, it was his hometown and Allen knew he wouldn't hitchhike, with those scars.

Oh God! He was so tense. His muscles were tight and bunched. There was only one way to get rid of this and that was to run it off.

Dressed in jeans and a tee shirt, he ran out the front door. Heading in the opposite direction of Orewa center he ran towards Opera Sands. He jumped fences and ran through farms, dogging cows and sheep. In his mind, Allen did not see the animals, or farmhouses, and he didn't feel the tar seal as he ran across the roads. He pictured himself running through fields of another time. Wheat fields as far as the eye could see. Felt the crop crushing under his feet. A time from long ago when things were simple and people married for life. This was the time he wished for. He could see the clear blue sky, could feel the warm autumn breeze and the cool soil under his feet. He felt the sharp stalks crushing under his bare feet. He was free here, and he ran, ran with all his might.

* * *

Carol Stephens searched her files. It was the only clue that man had given. Something nagged at her but she could not place it. Something about the man himself, the way he stood and his drink. Where had he gotten that? Surely he didn't bring it with him.

Whatever it was she couldn't place it, so she stared on her files again, not knowing what she was looking for, but hoping she would know it when she saw it. She slowly flicked through her files, one by one, reading parts of the cases. Skim reading most of it. The most frustrating thing was she recalled most of these files.

She had combed through thirty files by now and none held any pattern or any resemblance to the man last night or to what she had found in the fridge. She had buried kitty in the garden without a marker. She cleaned away the blood and scrubbed the floor before settling down to this job. It would have been impossible to concentrate knowing kitty was still in the fridge. Knowing that kitty was gone was hard but at the moment she forced herself to tune it out. Her own life was at stake now. She would let her emotions get to her later.

It would be nice, or convenient if she had a habit of photographing each patient and attaching it to the file, but she had never heard of any doctor doing this and she didn't want to be the first. She knew why it wasn't done, hell she could break the rules, but all her patients were weekly and she remembered their faces until they stopped coming, then they vanished from her memory.

She heard a noise outside and froze. She stared at the window.

Was that him?

Is he watching me?

She moved slowly to the window, parted the curtain and gazed out. Nothing. There was nothing out there that she could see. She shivered involuntarily. Paranoia was getting to her and she tried to shake it off. She had to concentrate. He gave her forty-eight hours, and from what she had read and studied at school, most people of this man's disposition kept their word regarding times. There were cases where this had not happened, but she felt sure the man last night was one of them who did keep his word. And that scared her even more.

There were more than seventy files, mostly long term, which meant three months or longer. These files took most of her time, there were some, which she instantly dismissed: women.

Some of the files held tape recorded sessions, and pages of typed work. These she quickly scanned like the others. Carol would only listen to the tapes if she thought she had found something. Twice she had listened to tapes, but realized she was on the wrong track after a few minutes.

She considered leaving the long-term files and concentrating on the short term ones which were only a few pages thick, she would be able to shoot through these faster and eliminate them if necessary, but something told her to eliminate them without bothering to read them. The man was too confident to have been a short timer. Stick with the large files, she told herself and sighed deeply. She felt tired and needed a break.

She went to her garden, to the small mound of freshly turned earth.

"I'm sorry, kitty." She whispered.

CHAPTER TWELVE

The golden wheat fields slowly blurred into a giant haze and vanished. Replaced by modern day roads and telephone poles. He could feel the hard tar seal once again under his feet. For the past half an hour he had ran as fast as he could to burn up the excess adrenaline. It had worked, and he slowed down to a jog when he saw the turn off sign for Opera Sands Caravan Park. He doubted if James would still be there, but there had to be someone still about with some information. If not there might be some clues. He could only hope.

Breathing hard, sweating hard, but not physically tired. He entered the Caravan Park. The grounds were barren save the caravans, which were owned by the park and had been left behind, abandoned. Left to rot and swelter in the summer heat and rust in the cold, wet, winter.

He spotted James's caravan and realized the park and contents would soon be government property if no one claimed it. And he had no intention of doing that. He wondered when the police would visit him to say his mother was dead and this park was his, if he wanted it? They had to find him first and when they did, his plan would be finished. James would be dead, the doctor too. Perhaps then, he could settle down, and owning a caravan park suddenly sounded like a good idea. After all, he had no other plans.

The caravan was half shaded by a large Oak tree a few yards from the rear of it. The same tree he had watched Dr. Carol Stephens talk to Mrs. Clemm, and place the puppy inside. A gift (slightly altered by him) that James should have found by now with some bits here or a bit there.

He laughed quietly to himself. It was a sad memory but at least he could look back on it and laugh. He wondered what James' reaction was.

The tin door of the caravan was ajar. He pulled it open.

The puppy was gone, but the bloodstains and smell were evident. He saw a faint white dust covering most of the caravan. Dusting the sink, doorframe, table edges, cups, drawer and the window and frame. The lab boys had obviously been here recently and he suddenly remembered he had not worn gloves or wiped his prints away when he last visited. Fuck, you fucking idiot, he cursed, how could I have been so stupid? I completely fucked up. Are my prints on record? He didn't think so. He had never been arrested, so how could they have them? It was too late to worry about that now. What is done is done.

Entering the caravan, he went to the dusted window for a closer look. The dust was smooth, it showed no prints, yet he remembered clearly pushing that window open, pressing his whole hand against the glass. He had probably left some skin on the window. Had this place been cleaned? Who would have cleaned it with a gutted puppy dripping blood onto the floor?

He checked the other dusted areas. There weren't any prints (of anyone's) anywhere. No prints to be seen. No prints to be taken. Nothing found. This time he was in the clear. He had been lucky and was not about to take that chance again. He reminded himself to wipe down Dr. Stephens' house after his next visit. Yes, he must remember to do that.

"Can I help you with anything?"

He spun around, surprised to hear another voice in the caravan.

Nick stared at the man coldly, "What are you doing here? This is not your caravan."

"Looking for James Dennett." He spoke softly and calmly as he sized the other man up and realized he could take him easily. "He lives here doesn't he?"

"He used to. This place has been closed down."

"I wondered why the place looked dead. Why are you still here?"

"That has nothing to do with you. Like I said, no one lives here anymore. So, why don't you leave?"

Fuck you, sinner, he thought, but said. "You don't know where I could find him, do you?"

"No, I certainly do not. He gathered his belongings and left with the police."

"The police, he's not in any trouble is he?"

Nick said. "In case he does return for some reason, who shall I say called by?"

"Tell him, his brother called by to pay a visit." Allen smiled.

"I didn't know he had a brother."

Allen wiped sweat from his face. "I'm his half brother. He doesn't know about me yet. I hoped to surprise him, after all it took me over a year to track him down."

Allen could see the man studying him. Perhaps he looked a little like James, a slightly younger version, but he had never seen any resemblance. The man said. "Wish I could help you. I am sorry I can't."

Allen smiled, "That's all right. It's going to take me a little bit longer to find him, that's all." He started to leave and then added. "Thanks for you help."

* * *

Nick didn't watch him leave. Instead he walked around the caravan, checking the windows, making sure they were closed. He wished his sister would hurry up. There was no one here to talk to anymore, and he wasn't a television freak. He couldn't wait to get out of here. This place had always been a dump, but with him as the only person left here, the place looked worse, if that was possible. He wandered around to the front door of James's caravan and slammed the door shut. He watched it a moment just to be sure it didn't pop open. It had a habit of doing that. It didn't seen to bother James but it would worry him. Too many fucked up people in the world today.

Lost in his thoughts, Nick did not hear the fast paced footsteps behind him, until it was too late. A hunting knife drew across his throat, twisted and then drew down to his chest. Allen held him just long enough to pull out the knife and then released him. Nick fell to the ground.

He gagged and clutched at his throat, his eyes wide and bulging at the pain. Shocked, Nick watched the man squat down next to him and wipe the hunting knife clean on his pants. He coughed up blood and felt it rolling down his cheek and dripping on to his ear.

The last thing Nick heard was: "I found this in your caravan, over there. It's very nice. I love the bone handle. May I keep it?" Allen laughed. "I can't let you live. I'm sorry about that. But if you do know where James is and told him about me." He sighed. "Well, I can't have that. Not yet. My plan will not fail." His voice rose and his face scrunched up in anger. "I will not let a fat slob cunt like you ruin my plan!"

The last thing Nick saw was the knife being raised.

The last thing he felt was it plunging deep into his cut chest.

Nick's eyes slowly closed.

Complete darkness.

Complete silence.

Death. Completely.

CHAPTER THIRTEEN

Wow, Allen thought as he entered Nick's caravan, this place is fit for a king. He searched the caravan for a shower and found one. It was small and cramped, but he needed to wash the blood off him and his clothes. He had dragged Nick's heavy body into the woods and left it there for the dogs and other animals to chew on. This caravan had been set up nicely. It was large, clean and had a homey feel about it. There were two recliners, and the complimentary built in couch. A large well-stocked fridge and a beer fridge, half full, Allen helped himself to a beer. He was hot and sweaty from his exercise. Nick had weighed a ton. Plenty for the animals, he thought.

He sat down on the couch, slowly sipping at the beer when he spied the note. The writing was messy but readable. It read: Sister, Sunday around 7pm.

Checking his watch, he smiled. He had around four hours to get cleaned up. He wondered how much hot water this caravan had. He preferred long hot showers but he could make do under any circumstance. Finishing the beer, he got up and went looking for a towel. He found one in the bedroom along with a double waterbed.

Allen stripped off his clothes and threw them in the shower, turning on the hot water at the same time. A fan, hidden by plastic coating, automatically started. Steam vanished into the ceiling. He was impressed. It was like being in one of them five star hotels, or a top of the line motor home.

He stepped into the shower, hot water pounded against his body. It felt great. He felt alive. Pink water ran down the drain as the water cleaned him and his clothes. He stomped on his clothes several times and then held them up for inspection checking they were free of blood. He smiled and turned off the shower. He had no intention of using Nick's shampoo or other toiletries. Wringing out his clothes, he wondered where the dryer was located. He had not given it a thought until just now.

"Shit," he whispered, then remembered his mother's house.

The power was still on at this place so he gathered it must still be on at her place. The same generator fed all the power. How it was sectioned off for each caravan, he had no idea and didn't give it a second thought as he toweled himself and went looking for something to cover his body with for his walk to his mothers'.

He didn't need more than the towel because nobody lived here anymore, but he was modest, and found a long oilskin raincoat in the closet. It was nice and heavy and decided he would keep it.

With his shoes on and the raincoat covering his entire body, save his shoes, Allen made his way to mother's house. He had never been in this place. Ethel took over the manager's position a week after Cal died. She hadn't bothered to mourn his passing for a respectable time. What was her excuse? Oh, yeah. "Your father would understand." And with that she moved out offering him a room at her new place. "It's not as big as this place but it's cozy."

He moved out that night found his own apartment after spending a week at his friend's parent's house. And that was that. He never saw his mother again until the night she died. He was surprised they had never bumped into each other in town he always kept an eye out - just in case. He had read in the paper how she had bought the Caravan Park, almost three years ago. Cal had left some money in his will to her. Allen received two thousand but his mother also got the money from the sale of the house. It took two years to sell, and she received a good price.

He entered through the unlocked front door he did not want to chance getting cut on the smashed window.

Her house felt cold, not chilly cold, just cold. It had no heart, no aura, and no feel. When he rented his first apartment, it had a feel to it, and it felt right for him to move in there. Manny's car, when he helped her buy it, had a feel to it. It also felt right, and she'd never had a problem with it. But this place didn't have any kind of feel just like a newly built house. Allen hated it instantly.

He wanted to be back at his house, listening to the police scanner. Waiting for Carol to call them. He would know when he heard a car being directed there. Cops weren't a problem. They never stayed long.

The clothes dryer was at the back of the house. He tossed his clothes in and set the timer for one hour. There was nothing else to do so he explored the place. It was not what he expected. It sure was cozy. It sure was a dump, like most old people houses. The two bedrooms were side by side. The first door he opened was Ethel's bedroom. It stank of lavender and talcum powder. He quickly closed the door.

The second room was dusty; it housed his father's lazy boy chair. Allen turned on the light. This room like his mother's room faced the forest and sunlight didn't reach very far into the rooms.

He made his way to the chair. Using his hand, he brushed off as much dust as he could and sat down. This chair had a feel to it. This chair felt like his father. He extended the leg rest and tilted the chair back. He waited and rested waiting to hear the buzzer of the dryer.

He drifted off to sleep.

* * *

He was nine today, school had finished and he was rushing home. A big cake was waiting for him. A chocolate cake mum always made a chocolate cake. Today's was the greatest day. Not only was it his birthday, but he had his report card. A's and B's, unfortunately, there was one C. Dad would not get angry over one C, especially when it regarded sports. Allen was terrible at sports, any sports. He hoped his test results were better than someone named James. Since he could remember, his father pushed him to be better than James, a person he had never met and was almost four years his senior. They did not even attend the same school.

Allen barged through the front door, "I'm home." He shouted at the top of his lungs.

"I'm in the kitchen." His mother called.

Allen ran there. He stopped outside the kitchen door, he knew better than to go running in there. There would be no birthday and no presents if that happened, like it had, two years ago. "Can I come in?"

"Sure."

He eased the swinging doors open. "Where's dad?" He stared at the empty mixing bowl, wanting to lick the unused cake mix.

"Your father will be back at six. That's when we sit down for dinner." She checked the oven. Watching the cake rise, she said. "I have some bad news, honey."

His mother only used 'Honey' when the bad news was for him, "What is it?"

Still not looking at him, she said. "I had some calls today from your friend's parents," she moved to the sink to wash her hands. "I'm afraid they all can't make it."

Allen said nothing. Tears welled in his eyes he always went to his friend's party.

"I'm so sorry, honey," she still had her back to him, "but that's all right, it'll be a family party. How does that sound?"

"Great." He replied trying to sound happy about it. He found out later that his mother hadn't invited anyone. She had actually called up his friend's parents and informed them there wasn't a party. She did this every year until he turned thirteen and he had by his own choice decided not to celebrate his birthday.

He sat at the table exactly at six, with his mother and they waited two hours for his father to return home. For the first time and not the last, Allen saw his father drunk. He stumbled into the house, he saw his family sitting at the table and said, "What are you two looking at?"

"I thought you stopped drinking?" Ethel said.

"So did I," a grumbled reply. His eyes were half closed and he stared at Allen. "Get your report card?"

"Today's my birthday, dad."

"No shit? Where's your fucking report card?"

"In my school bag," Allen replied. "In my room." He wanted to cry, but knew not to do it in front of his father. He pushed his chair out and ran into his room. Inside he took a few deep breaths to get his emotions under control and returned to the dinner table five minutes later. He handed his report card to his father.

Unable to focus properly on the small writing, he handed it to Ethel and said, "You read it."

Ethel did as she was told. Allen thought she looked scared.

"Well, let's see, um, Math B+. That's good." Her voice quivered.

Allen pretended not to notice, his father sure hadn't. Ethel continued, "English A-. P.E slash Sports C, and-"

His father broke in, "C?"

"Yes, but all the rest are A's and B's"

"Hmm, what does the comment say about sports?"

Ethel read it quietly, and then said, "Allen needs to apply himself more."

Cal said. "That is fucking disgraceful. Get to your room. That better not be a tear I see. Are they tears? Boys never cry!"

Allen ran to his room and slammed the door shut. Why couldn't his father be happy with his other grades? He tried very hard. He was not meant to play sports. God had a plan for everybody, and sports were not on His list for Allen.

His parents started arguing. He heard them clearly. James was mentioned a few times. Allen felt hatred for that person. He wished him dead. He heard a slap and his mother screamed. He heard empty dinner plates pushed off the table. Something hit the wall hard enough for Allen to feel the vibration in his room. More slaps and then the sound of clothes tearing. His mother gasping, and then crying.

Sometime Allen fell asleep. He had not slept long when his father shook him awake. His father stood before him in his underwear; "You need some learning, boy. How many times have I told you to be better than James? How many more times must I tell you?" For the first time, Cal used his hands to administer some learning to Allen.

For the following two weeks, Allen couldn't go to school or church. On Sundays he stayed at home with his mother, while Cal tended for them both. He seldom drank after that night, which pleased Allen. His father was a different person when he drank. It was also from this time that his mother started to gain weight.

* * *

A buzzing sound woke him. His neck was stiff. He climbed off the chair and stretched. The dream lingered but he knew where he was he knew that memory was over. Why didn't he ever dream of the happier times? That would be nice, he thought as he went to the clothes dryer and, after flicking his clothes free of lint, got dressed.

About to open the front door and leave, he stopped when he heard a car coming down the driveway. He moved to the window and saw it heading to Nick's caravan. He checked his watch. Sister was early, very early. Except for the dream he was glad that that caravan didn't have a dryer, if it did, he would be in a very awkward position about now.

He watched her knock on the door, then enter only to exit a minute later, "Nick!" She called, "Nick, where are you?"

Allen decided it was time to leave. He watched her enter the forest, still calling Nick's name. It was time to leave quickly. Allen ran to the main road and walked from there. Ten minutes later he heard the distant wail of sirens, police sirens. They were faint but growing louder by the second. He crossed the road, jumped the wire fence and ran hard across the field.

CHAPTER FOURTEEN

James thanked Detective Kerrs for his help and followed Martha inside. For the first time he was nervous entering her house. What would he do? Say? Act? He would have to find his own place soon, but he would wait until Martha was feeling better. Once inside the house he immediately realized something was missing. The bright and happy colors were evident, as always. The house looked the same but it didn't have the warm and happy aura anymore that it used to possess. It felt somber. Lonely. Empty.

Still, James had the feeling something was missing. Martha's large warm smile was not the only thing gone. He couldn't pin it down, but whatever it was it used to play a big part in the family's life and seemed out of place not being here.

Martha offered him her son's room. It was painted a bright blue, almost sky like. The white ceiling appeared to be a lost cloud stuck amongst a beautiful sky with no wind to push it away. The double bed was stuck in the right hand corner. There was a stereo beside it, a chest of drawers and a dresser with a large mirror. On the other side was a bookcase filled with horror and suspense novels from such masters as Stephen King, Richard Laymon, David Martin and John Saul. There were other authors he had never head of before.

James wasn't the type of person who enjoyed these kinds of books or movies. When he was young, a kid in fact, he loved horror, couldn't get enough of it but now he preferred dramas or suspense, nothing too graphic. He had enough graphic images in his life already. But, if he found himself lost for something to occupy his time, then perhaps he might have a look but only if he was dead bored.

There was also a stack of magazines leaning against the legs of the bookcase they were the usual teenage pop magazines. Pinned to the closet wall was a poster of 'Meatloaf - Bat out of Hell 2' and a RTR pin up of 'Motorhead'. He considered taking down the posters, but decided against it. He was only a guest even though Martha had told him to stay as long as he liked.

James felt something was wrong when he put his clothes in Craig's drawer and hung his coat and pants in the closet. They were already empty. In the closet he found two suitcases full of clothes. He opened one to find it full of teenage clothes. The second contained female clothes and dresses. Had Martha already packed their clothes away or were the kids planning something? He wouldn't voice this question, it was best left unanswered and the cases untouched. He pushed them against the wall of the closet and shut its door. He placed his photography equipment on top of the dresser for the time being. He didn't plan on living here for long.

He began to doubt his true reasons for being here. Could he truly be of any help to Martha in her time of need? Maybe there were other underlying motives? Did he want to help Martha or help himself to her?

What the hell are you thinking! He screamed at himself. Shit, there's no way I can stay here, he decided, it was best for him to leave and he repacked his duffel bag.

He had his speech all worked out by the time he finished packing: "Martha," he would say, "I'm sorry, but I can't stay here. It doesn't seem right for me to be here at the moment." He would then take her soft hand in his and say. "Please don't think harshly of me, we both have problems we need to face, alone, before we can feel good about ourselves. You know that I'm not a religious man, but I do believe that your God will help and solace you through this rough period. Whereas I have to take care of things my own way."

He would then look deeply into her eyes and end with. "I think it is better this way, for the both of us." And before she had a chance to protest, if she was inclined to do so, he would he heading for the door. And he would not look back he didn't want to see the look on her face as he left most likely never to return. It was cruel, but at least it was the right thing to do. After all he did have feelings for Martha and when Carl and the kids were around there was no temptation, now it was just the two of them. If he stayed he would be fighting that want endlessly. He had to leave.

Halfway down the hall, carrying his repacked duffel bag, he paused at Martha's bedroom. The door was ajar and he could hear soft sobs inside. Gently he eased the door open, wide enough so he could see in. James saw Martha, spread out on the bed, one leg dangling towards the floor, holding a photo tightly to her breast. Her lips trembled and tears ran a torrent down her face. She looked like a six-year-old child who'd just lost her kitten.

James quietly closed the door, afraid to be spotted. This was a personal and very private moment. It was seeing Martha like that that he knew he was going to stay, for a while at least.

He went back to the room and unpacked his bag. He needed a shower. In the hospital all he had was sponge baths, and although he was quite happy to have them, showers were by far better in every way. He always felt better after taking a shower and couldn't get used to having a bath. Why people wanted to relax in a film of their daily filth, was beyond him. He showered from the age of eight, and hadn't had a bath since then, even though his mother told him baths were better and you could stay in them longer. The thought was not appealing. He was a shower man.

He locked the bathroom door and turned on the water. He waited patiently for the water to heat up before entering the cubicle.

The hot gushing water from the showerhead felt marvelous. His hair clung to the side of his head, and he noticed how quickly it had grown since its last cut two months ago. He decided to grow it long for a while. He'd had long hair since he was six years old until he was 24 then he was offered a job at the law firm, on the condition he cut his hair. For six years he'd carried it short. Time for a change, he thought, considering growing a beard as well.

He remembered his mother offering to trim his hair to just below shoulder length, as she did every six weeks. He recalled the first cut after his father had died at the hands of the dog. He was seated in the kitchen. Her mother was getting the scissors from the kitchen cupboard, when she stated. "James honey, I swear your hair is growing too fast these days for me to keep it under control."

"It's not my fault."

"I know it isn't." She bent down and kissed him on the cheek.

"Yuck." He made a face and rubbed it off.

"Not the least bit disappointed but trying to sound it, his mother replied. "And what is yucky about a mother giving her son a kiss?"

"Because." He explained. "It's for babies."

"You're my little baby, and always will be." She cuddled him from behind.

"Not any more, I'm not. I'm the man of the house now, since daddy..." His voice trailed off.

James remembered turning in his chair and looking at his mother for confirmation, she looked so small and lost at that moment and he wished he hadn't mentioned it. The color drained from her face but quickly returned as she said. "That's right dear, you're the man of the family now."

The shower water suddenly turned cold. The sudden shock brought him out of the vivid memory, for which he was thankful.

That was the night his cat Spot was killed. He whispered. "And the night I made my toys fly, and met..." He hesitated to mention it, "And met the beast for the first time."

The hot water returned. Martha must have used the kitchen water, not knowing he was in here.

James had never been as terrified as that night until two weeks ago at Opera Sands. He felt a headache building, softly pounding against his temples. It increased intensity fast. He squeezed his eyes shut to block out the pain. For some reason an image of the bar of soap came to mind. The drumming sound echoed in his ears. It was time to get out of the shower.

Something hard and wet hit the center of his forehead, then dropped to the metal floor.

"What the fuck?" James rubbed his forehead, looking down between his feet.

Resting on the floor was the bar of soap, shower water bounced off its surface. Reaching down to retrieve it, the shower water thundering off the back of his head decreased the pain of the headache. Quickly it vanished. James picked up the soap and studied it. The thought that he had made it hit him quickly entered and then left his thoughts. He could not do that any more. When he tried he failed, but this time he had not even tried. So, he wondered, what happened? He was positive he left it sitting in its holder to the right of the showerhead.

He shook his head and replaced it.

"Crazy thoughts." He said, "Crazy thoughts."

James turned off the shower and dried himself. With the towel around his waist, he returned to his room and dressed. A thick curtain of tiredness pressed against his eyes. The day's events had stolen a great deal of energy from him. He was not yet fully recovered so his energy levels were already low. Even though the shower had rejuvenated him, he thought he should take a quick nap before facing Martha in this new situation and deciding what had to be done next.

He analyzed the incident in the shower but couldn't find any answers. He lay down on the bed, only the towel covering him, and thought, what the hell's going on here?

He quickly dropped off to sleep.

* * *

Carol read the material carefully. The case file was very interesting containing elements of aggressive behavior brought about by schizophrenia. Reading the last page of the fourth session, she came across an analysis she had written almost two years ago:

The possible schizophrenia is triggered by self-righteous morals, which were somehow forced upon him in early childhood. A person he meets or learns about with conflicting views brings the change in personality. Whether it is another persona or only his anger getting the better of him, I have yet to decide.

He has mentioned working on plans to help him be a better person, or at least feel better. I have not yet learned of these plans, but I worry about them.

His father has been successful in installing hatred.

Allen has a very low image of himself. He dreams of being a better person, but feels this can only be achieved if his plans work.

He is walking a thin line between the Ying and Yang.

Reading the note and knowing more now than she did then, especially about herself, she thought the note was melodramatic, if only a little. But then again, maybe it wasn't. The man she met last night had a way about him, which Allen didn't show or have during the sessions. Had he developed another persona?

CHAPTER FIFTEEN

Martha came out the next morning. It was a very late start for her: 10:30am. She had cried most of the night and her eyes felt puffy. The depression was very deep and strong. Her entire family was gone. Murdered. How could she go on living? What was left for her? There seemed to be no point. Then late last night, after her tears had dried, she ordered herself to put a stop to the self-pity and adapt to the newfound emptiness. She still had a life to run and was determined not to lose that by giving up. She felt one hundred percent certain that the police would catch the person responsible. She would not let a single person to destroy her life as well.

Were they selfish thoughts? If so, then she was entitled to them. She would fight to keep it no matter how empty it was. She had a lot of friends from church and social functions they would help fill the gap.

Although, she dreaded the inevitable *"I'm so sorry"*, comments that were sure to come. First Carl disappeared and all she heard was: "He'll be found safe and sound holding his bible, you'll see." Then her poor children were next. The phone calls had taken an even greater toll on her emotions to the point where she unplugged the phone. It sat on the table dead and silent, only made of plastic, yet she was so relieved by the simple act of silencing it that she relaxed. And now, Carl had been found dead, swelled and bloated by the ocean.

A new life had forced itself upon her. God had given her a fresh start, but she didn't want it. If there was a choice between an afterlife in Hell or having her family back, Martha knew she would quickly sign on the dotted line with her blood.

Her feet shuffled along the carpet hallway and into the living room. Her sight was sleep blurred and she rubbed her eyes as she passed James sleeping on the couch, unnoticed and entered the kitchen. The linoleum in the kitchen was cold and felt refreshing on the soles of her feet. She went to the jug and plugged it in.

Waiting for the jug to boil, she stared out the kitchen window.

The street was busy this morning filled with people coming and going. Leading personal lives oblivious to the pain she felt. For an instant she hated them all. A memory loomed into view of Carl and the kids returning from a day out fishing. The children were only seven at that time. Carl with a big, silly and proud grin on his face, holding up five fish the children would later claim they caught. The sight was so very vivid, so real, Martha caught herself heading to the side door to run around and greet them. She stopped herself knowing it was only a memory, not real, regardless of her feelings. She quietly released the door handle as the jug beeped and automatically turned itself off.

She made her coffee and headed to the living room to relax and after her morning drink she would take a shower and then decide what she would do today. She desperately needed something to keep her occupied, take her mind off things for a while, to fill the deep emptiness inside.

She wore a long white tee shirt, which reached half way down her thighs with long sleeves. She didn't remember putting it on. Most of what she could remember from last night was lying on her bed grieving.

Carrying the cup carefully, it was filled to the brim she headed to the couch and unexpectedly found James asleep on the couch. The sight startled her and she gave out a quick cry of surprise. It jolted her and the cup of coffee tilted. Hot coffee jumped out of the cup, splattering the lower part of her tee shirt.

The sound awoke James and he rubbed his eyes.

"I'm sorry." Martha said holding the wet part of the shirt away from her legs. She noticed him staring at her and said. "I'd hate to get burned." She nodded at the cup. James reached out and took from her.

He said. "I didn't scare you, did I?"

"I'm just a little jumpy." She smiled wishing he would stop glancing at her legs. At the same time, she felt a blush blooming on her cheeks. Suddenly feeling uneasy, she said. "I think I'll rinse this out and take a quick shower."

"Okay." James also smiled, then stretched and sat upright on the couch.

Martha turned and left. She thought she felt his eyes watching her leave, but dismissed it as silliness. Using James to fill up the hole inside, it was just plain wrong. He was a good friend and had answered desperate woman's cry for help. She didn't want to ruin that bond. My God, she thought, was I flirting with him back there? I hope he didn't see it as that. I should have worn my robe.

She entered the shower and turned on the water. Carefully, she pulled the tee shirt off, not wanting the coffee mark to touch her. It would be cold now, but she hated the feeling of wetness slide up her body. Next she removed her bra and pulled down her panties.

The shower door had no lock. Part of her wished for James to push the door open and another part wished him to remain on the couch.

She wondered why these thoughts were popping into her head. The thought of James as her lover had crossed her mind before ... when ... she couldn't finish the thought. James was a friend and that was all. There could never be anything more. She wouldn't let there be anything more. Twenty minutes later she was dressed and heading back to the living room, pushing such thoughts away. Martha would start the day fresh, as if the earlier incident had never happened. James had made them a breakfast of scrambled eggs, toast and coffee. They sat in silence at the kitchen table, unsure what to say, like strangers at a coffee shop forced to share a table.

James spoke first, "Sorry about falling asleep on the couch."

Martha didn't hear him. The sun was beaming through the open window. It shone brightly against her face. She was lost in thought. She was breaking her ritual. It was Sunday and she should be at church now, praying and adding an extra prayer for her family. She moved her head and the sun caught her in the eye, making her squint and she realized James was speaking. She was looking directly at him and not a single word had registered.

"... It might be a good idea. What do you think?"

Snapping away from her thoughts and unable to guess the subject James had spoken about, Martha took a long drink of her coffee and said. "James, I'm sorry, but I was a million miles away."

"Oh," he was prepared to repeat himself. "I had a dream last night. Well, it was more of a nightmare. It was very vivid and seemed very real. I know it was only a dream but I pinched myself and this morning," he rolled up his shirtsleeve to reveal a purple bruise.

Martha nodded, but she had a feeling he'd lied or omitted something, because his voice changed tone slightly, almost strained.

But she ignored it. It was his dream and the last thing she needed to hear at the moment was more horror stories. He looked confused, so Martha asked. "And?"

His expression showed he wanted to ask something but he wasn't sure about how to do it or if he should even ask. Martha knew he was concerned about her and she held the same worries for him. She wondered how he was dealing with the attack. What was going on inside him? All outward impressions showed a person who went with the flow, took things as they came in life and wasn't very worried about what life or fate threw at him. But she knew better. She had known James for three years. He never came across as a carefree type of person. Everything was planned. When they had first met, when Carl introduced him, James gave a detailed explanation of his long-term dream although he called it a goal. He had it all worked out and his plan sounded as if it couldn't fail, but so far it had yet to show signs of taking root.

He was so full of energy and hype back then and she had watched it slowly dwindle, seeping away like mist. And now this. His facial scars were clearly visible, but his neck looked worst and she noticed he had taken to wearing long sleeved business shirts with the top button done up. She was very worried about his mental health. How much anger and regret could a person bottle inside before they exploded in fury and any small incident? How long could James hold it in? Would he hurt her if she were around when it happened? It seemed unlikely. It was not good to dwell on hypothetical questions like the last one. She decided to put all the questions away and take things as they came. God had a plan and she would not question it.

"Anyway, the dream kind of shocked me, so I thought I might give Dr. Stephens a call." James finished, watching her reaction closely.

"Dr. Stephens? That name rings a bell," she said suddenly feeling a little nervous. The hypothetical questions wouldn't go away easily. She forced a smile, showing straight white teeth. "Oh, I remember!" She almost shouted. James stopped eating his toast and stared at her. The sudden outburst embarrassed her she thought she must have sounded like an eight-year-old opening a birthday present.

"What?" James asked, his voice betraying his amusement.

"I remember where I know that name." Her smile was real this time and she relaxed, the thoughts gone for the time being,

"Detective Kerrs gave me a card when you were in your caravan collecting your belongings. He said I might want to give this lady a call. I have never believed in head doctors, but I took the card. It was nice of him to offer."

James looked relieved, "Can I borrow it? I haven't got a clue where mine is. Are you sure it is the same name?"

"Maybe," she replied starting to feel doubtful, "I'll check."

Martha got up and went to her bedroom where her purse lay under the bedside table and removed a small white card. She read it, smiled and was about to return to James when she realized that he probably didn't have any money. Especially having just left the hospital after the banks had closed for the weekend. Opening her purse, she frowned at her own lack of funds, but she had no plans of spending any money today and the fridge was full. She pulled out ten dollars, hoping it would be enough for a taxi to and from the doctor's practice.

A smile was on her lips as she headed back to the kitchen. She stopped in the living room and watched James for a moment. The sun coming through the window, his scruffy hair and business shirt gave him a look of complete innocence. She suddenly felt a strong attraction to him but pushed it back as quickly as it had come. She couldn't believe she was feeling or acting this way, her husband wasn't even buried yet. She thought she knew why these feelings were popping up. She was desperate for something to latch on to, something to take her back to a life she once knew and understood. As long as she controlled these fake feelings, they would in time pass, as she grew stronger in her new life.

"Here it is," she said, breaking her thoughts.

James had a piece of toast on his plate. Martha watched him stare at the 500g tub of margarine next to her plate. She wondered what he was doing. He looked tense. For a moment she thought he was lost in his own little world. He obviously had not heard her and she was surprised to find James like this. He was the one person she thought that had a good long attention span. The one person she thought who didn't have his or her own little world to run off into. If he were an actor or writer then she would expect this or perhaps worry if she never saw it. She had met writers with a small attention span regarding reality, preferring to sit at their computers exploring their story's reality. Diving deep into their imagination.

But not James, he was a photographer he shot reality. She didn't know if he doctored photos or what he did to enhance them, but reality was always there. She knew he needed a break, a chance, but could he have created a little hideaway due to his recent events? Martha didn't know she was not a psychiatrist and had never experienced what she was feeling or what he was going through. Anything was possible.

And Carl had trusted him a great deal, even though James was not a churchgoer and Carl was not the type of person who gave his trust away easily. People they knew for years still hadn't gained his trust before his passing and yet here was James whom he had given it freely and openly. Her husband was no fool, there had to have been something that drew Carl to him.

Still, Martha told herself, it isn't strange for someone to pop out of reality every now and then. Even she was accused of doing that. She even admitted it. She was about to go and sit in front of him and bring him back from that far off land when she noticed sweat shining on James' forehead and something drew her eyes to the tub. What she saw scared her. What was happening was not real, could not be real. How was this happening? Was James controlling it, making it happen? He was a photographer, not a magician and yet he was staring at the tub of margarine and it was shaking and slowly sliding across the breakfast table.

Martha couldn't believe her eyes. This was ungodly. Fear entered her as she slowly approached the table. She stood in front of James and dropped the card next to his plate. She could see he was overjoyed and bubbling with excitement.

"Martha, did you see that?"

"Yes," she replied her voice empty.

A worried expression crossed James' face. He said, "I wouldn't think too much of this. When I was nine I used to-"

"I need a rest," she said coldly, cutting off his explanation. She placed the ten-dollar bill next to the card. "Here's some money if you need it for a taxi or something."

"Thank you."

Martha headed out of the room. Over her shoulder, she said, "Call that doctor today." She felt it was very important to call that doctor. What James had just done, she shouldn't be happy about. It was not natural. It was not right.

"I will" James said, watching her leave.

* * *

The file was interesting.

As Carol Stephens read she tried to remember the patient more fully. She only recalled brief sights. Picturing him sitting there in the easy chair was easy all her patients sat in it. Recalling his quick temper, especially with moral issues, was also easy to picture.

But there seemed to be a cloud of fog covering her memories of his fears and needs. There was one other thing missing from her file, although she couldn't be sure of it.

Carol remembered his time here, she had been very busy back then, as she was now, and he was always the last patient of the day and always in the evening. Had she been too busy or tired to fill out his profile fully? Was she that lazy back then? Hers was not the easiest job on the market and it sure as hell wasn't nine to five, either. In fact it was damn hard and drained her emotions as well as taking a major toll on her physically. She thought it would be an easy job, listening to others people's problems and then giving advice based on what Freud, Crowley or countless others had said, and bring her own interpretation into it.

Not now. That belief vanished early. All the students in these classes were told it wasn't as easy as they thought but she didn't believe the professor and neither did most of her classmates. She also had the problem of attaching herself to her patients, sometimes going against professional conduct to help them, and although in some case she had referred them to other doctors, she did not really want to do that. She knew of only a few doctors who would treat them fairly without their sight set on writing another paper in the hope of attaining a few more letters behind their name. She thought being referred to, as 'Doctor' was great in itself.

God, she wished she hadn't slept so long. What was the time? How long had she slept? How long did she have left? What is the real reason I haven't called the cops? Had she really found him? Was it Allen Sheriff? What would he do? What was his plan? What if ... What if ... What if... Fuck, Carol wanted to call the cops. Terror and paranoia had taken over her bodily controls and she doubted she could even reach the phone let alone call the police.

For the first time in her life, she was running on her gut instinct and it terrified her.

The file was open on the floor before her. Carol sat cross-legged beside the stereo with a cup of cooling coffee to one side, an unopened packet of cigarettes and a clean ashtray at the other side. The smokes were her distraction they should help her concentrate.

She was a non-smoker, mainly because she knew what it did to your body inside, apart from making them black and gooey, smoke also shrunk the lungs, which caused the short breath many of her smoking patients suffered. She understood why so many people still smoked in these uneconomical times. It had been drummed into them since childhood that it helped with stress and nerves and, of course, it was cool to smoke.

Addiction did not exist, there was no such thing, but if someone believed it then for them it was real. Addiction was a habit, and habits took years to break. If a person wanted to break a habit due to peer pressure, then there was a ninety-percent chance they would fail. To break a habit, you really had to want to break the habit, and it was this, which hampered hypnosis.

So, Carol knew exactly what addictions were. At least she thought she did. The subconscious mind was a tricky devil, it lied to the conscious usually in dreams but sometimes when a subject was awake and she was positive that had happened to Allen Sheriff and if he had created a separate persona, it would be his way of dealing with the lies. And it had been her job to separate the truth from the lies - she had failed with Allen when he stopped coming.

Now she had a choice, the smokes or the file. If she chose the smokes she wouldn't light one, she would sit and wait for Allen, if it was him. He was going to kill her, so why fight it?

Because she was a fighter, that was the long and short of it.

Carol picked up the file, placed on her lap, lying open. The tape, which came with it, slid off the smooth surface and fell between her legs. She retrieved it and searched the file for the sheet of notes of his action during the recording. She peeled the top of the sheets back. It was the last page in the file.

She put the tape into the stereo and was about to push play button when there was a knock at the door.

Carol froze. She noticed her hands were shaking. Was her time up, already? Couldn't be, I haven't started yet. It couldn't be him, she thought, why would he knock? To scare the shit out of me, she answered. The she remembered he liked games and this could be one of them.

For some reason this thought pleased her, happiness glowed inside. Fuck him, she thought as she went to the door and opened it with a smile.

James stood on the doorstep. Her smile died.

The afternoon sun beamed high above him and the sky was a clear blue. Birds sung in the trees and insects went about their business. The world went on even though she was unable to enjoy it. She had blocked out the outside world and seeing him standing here brought everything back. Emotions conflicted within her. She still felt an attraction to him but she also felt hate towards him. Her kitten had died because of him, and she was next on the list. Was it all really because of him? He looked small and lost standing here, a business shirt hiding the results of his attack.

Startled, she said. "Hi, James. What can I do for you?" It sounded cold, she hadn't meant it to but that is how it sounded to her. Had he noticed it? His expression did not change so she thought it had slipped by.

"Hi, doc. I was kinda hoping that is if you had the time, perhaps we could talk or make an appointment. I'm sorry I didn't call but I thought that if you had the time, then maybe, perhaps..."

He was talking so fast. His sentences almost ran onto one another. Carol saw this as a sign of nervousness. The sun was at his back and she had to squint while her eyes adjusted. His face was a dark blur, his features just recognizable. She felt something for him but didn't want him around at the moment.

She would have to pass him on to another doctor - had to. The hate was quickly fading the longer he stood here and she was prepared to break every rule just to find out if he felt the same way about her. Deep inside, she thought he didn't, but she had to find out. She was going to turn him away and she was going to do it now.

"Could I come in?" James asked, his voice small. He looked at his feet when he asked the question.

"I have somebody with me at the moment." She lied.

Damn, she wanted him inside. Wanted to talk to him over coffee, get to know him on a personal basis. She had to fight the urge and found it difficult. It was stupid of her to blame him for another's actions. Yet that is what she had done, and she was a fool for doing it, for letting her emotions judge, control her actions and cloud her thoughts and reasoning. But she still had to turn him away perhaps another day would be better timing - if there was another day for her.

"How about ten thirty on Tuesday?" Carol said not sure if she had a patient already booked, she just needed him out of here. Tingles of fear run up her spine. If Allen was watching them, her time was over and she needed to learn as much as she could about him before he arrived. If she succeeded, she might just have a chance.

"Okay, I understand." James replied.

His voice was full of disappointment and Carol understood why.

His emotions were a mess, like hers at the moment and although it hurt her to do this, she had to follow through. Disappointment faded easily.

She faked a smile. "See you then." She started to close the door.

"Yes," James said, "ten thirty on Tuesday. Look forward to it."

Carol closed the door and leaned back against it. She listened as his footsteps hit the gravel driveway, and the crunch of his steps fading as he walked down her driveway. She closed her eyes and took a few deep breaths.

Damn it, she thought.

* * *

After he killed Nick yesterday, an instinctive emotion boiled up inside him and he ran. At first he thought it was adrenaline, which made his heart pound, and his veins throb vigorously, but he now realized he had felt fear. Slightly flowing through him like the tremble of a rail track as a train neared. It was not a fear of being caught, more; it was the fear of being second best again. And it was that which made him run with all his might, right into the deep regions of the forest. He was headed to Opera Sands beach but it seemed the wrong direction so he veered into the forest and felt peace there.

After an hour or so of being with Mother Nature he had returned to the caravan park only to find two squad cars and a bunch of police officers looking about and collecting something. What they were looking for he knew, but was confident he had left no trace.

A beautiful woman stood in front of a detective, constantly wiping her eyes with the back of her hand not using the tissue she held. She was speaking erratically and it looked as if the detective was having difficulty following her story. A strong cold breeze rushed through the area, blowing her ash blond hair behind. The large coat she wore and her solid legs showing below her denim shorts told him she was a strong lady physically, a gym regular no doubt.

Her features resembled the man that he had the pleasure to slay earlier. A relative, he wondered, most likely a younger sister - but what was she doing here? And how did he know someone was coming to the Caravan Park? Perhaps he meant to run here, God had driven him to the park. He couldn't understand why and maybe he wasn't meant to understand completely - yet.

He suddenly remembered the Caravan Park was almost deserted. Everyone had left, even bloody Dennett, so it seemed highly likely that the woman was meant to pick up the final remaining occupant. The man had not packed his things when he went into the caravan to fetch the knife, so she must have arrived very early, either that or Nick was too lazy to pack and was planing to take the caravan with him.

What was he doing back here? What if he was spotted? Allen couldn't understand his reason for returning and being so close. Was he testing fate? That's when he heard it...

"Detective Kerrs, I think we've found something."

The detective turned away from the woman and went to where the young officer stood. Allen couldn't see what they were looking at, even when the detective picked it up with something and gently placed it in a plastic bag. He wondered what it was. Had he left something behind, after all?

It was time to leave. He didn't care what they had found. The Lord had bestowed a gift to him, and he had yet to thank the master he loved and feared. His Lord whose power is, was, and will always be almighty.

With that thought in mind he went back into the forest. His eyes felt better here in the tree-shaded area. The day would be drawing to an end soon. It did not bother him. In the blackness of night he could see clearly. He was the night shadow.

He reached a lake, which ran through the forest. It had been handy many years ago when a fire broke and raged out of control. The lake proved to be a perfect firebreak and helicopters scooped buckets of its seemingly endless supply of water and dumped it on the flames leaping tree to tree.

He stepped into the lake. It was ice cold but he barely felt it against his young skin as he knelt on the murky bottom at the shallow end. His knees sunk a few inches through the soft mud. He tilted his head back and gave thanks to the Lord. Cupping his hands he filled them with water and splashed it on his face. He mumbled and swayed to the rhythm of his words. He ducked his head under the water, kept it below the surface for a full minute, then snapped his head back and inhaled deeply.

Water flew from his hair. His entire being was cold, he felt it eating through him and tried to block it out but his head hurt from the cold. Throwing his arms wide, he said, "Hail the mighty

Lord Jesus Christ and His father, for he has baptized me in the cold clear water of innocence. All sinners must be paid their due. The meek shall not inherit the Earth, for the meek are the sinners."

Make it so, a voice inside his head said. A voice, which had remained as silent as the dead for the past year. A voice that came only in his dreams had joined him now in reality. He felt a joining of sorts like a feeling of wholeness.

PART THREE

Tortured soul,
criminal sign,
Insanity face to
control my mind.
Eyes of blue, I explode
my voice,
In screams of ultimate
delight.
Oh, but what a sight,
Don't be caught out
tonight.
Evil is upon me.

CHAPTER SIXTEEN

Dr Carol Stephens, as tired as she was, went back to the living room. She wanted to call James back but knew better of it. If she ran, she could probably catch him at the roadside. Instead, she sat on the floor, crossed her legs and pushed the 'play' button on her stereo. Life had a way of ruining plans. She picked up the cold coffee and drank it all in four large swallows. Even cold it tasted great. The cigarettes on the other hand did not look the least bit inviting.

Suddenly her voice boomed through the speakers and she reached over and turned the volume down. Her voice came out metallic sounding. She cleared all thoughts about James and what might be waiting for her around the corner. Concentrating was the main thing, now.

The tape spun in the deck:

Carol: All right Mr. Sheriff, the tape is recording.

Sheriff: Okay, so what do I do now?

Carol: I'm going to show you some cards and I want you to tell me what you see. Make up a story, if you like.

Sheriff: You want me to lie?

Carol: No, not exactly. Just say what you think.

Sheriff: This is bullshit, doc.

Carol: Would you like to try something different?

(Pause)

Sheriff: Yeah.

Carol: Okay. Tell me, what is your favorite animal?

Sheriff: Wolf.

Carol: Good. Three words why.

Sheriff: Strong, Leadership, faithful to the end.

Carol: Favorite color, again three reasons.

Sheriff: Blue. Strong. Powerful. Cold.

Carol: Water. Three words.

Sheriff: Um, the ocean. Long. Deep. Lasting.

Carol: Very good, Mr. Sheriff. Now, imagine that you're in a room. No windows or doors. No way in or out. How you feel?

Sheriff: Trapped, but at peace and with the Lord.

(Silence. Two, five, ten seconds)

Sheriff: So how did I do? Did I pass?

Carol: There is no pass or failure in these questions.

Sheriff: Can you understand what all that crap means?

Carol: Please sit down, Mr. Sheriff. You're entitled to see your file, but I have yet to write the date so far.

Sheriff: Hey, I can fucking read. What's with all my answers you got on that pad?

Carol: The animal represents how you see yourself.

Sheriff: Faithful. A leader. Strong. I like that.

Carol: The color shows how you think others see you.

Sheriff: Oh.

Carol: Water represents your sex life.

Sheriff: (Laughter) Long, deep and lasting, huh?

Carol: The last was your perception of death.

Sheriff: Oh, at one with God. I like this test doc. So what does that tell you about me?

Carol: Not much, yet.

Sheriff: Sorry to disappoint.

(Shuffling sounds)

Sheriff: Nice picture doc. Want me to tell you what it is?

Carol: If you would like to.

Sheriff: (Soft voice) Why don't you look at the pictures and tell me what *you* fucking see.

(It wasn't a question)

Carol: (Calm. Relaxed.) It helps me to help you. It's a good way to get to the root of your visits. You came to me remember.

(No reply. Silence)

Carol: Do you like my office?

(Silence)

Carol: It was a real problem. Took me weeks to get it just right.

(Silence)

Carol: This is your thirteenth week here, Allen. You always hint at something. I would like it if you told me what was on your mind. Tell me about the voice again. Do you still hear it? What does it tell you?

Sheriff: This room was a problem to decorate, aye?

Carol: Yes.

Sheriff: You don't even understand what a real problem is.

Carol: Help me understand it.

Sheriff: It's beyond you.

Carol: Try me.

Sheriff: I told you about my father. I told you about his problem.

Carol: Is your father part of the problem?

Sheriff: I love my father.

(Silence)

Sheriff: Life is full of surprises, isn't it doc?

Carol: (Paper being moved. A cough.) You mentioned a while ago about a man named Dennett. Where are you going? What do you see out the window, Allen?

Sheriff: A motherfucker.

Carol: Excuse me?

Sheriff: I told you before dad always said he was better.

Carol: Who is he? A relative?

Sheriff: How do you get rid of a problem?

Carol: You solve it.

Sheriff: How?

Carol: One way is by talking about it.

Sheriff: That doesn't get rid of it. It may make you feel better for ten minutes, but that's all, right?

Carol: You can always write it down and work through it systematically.

Sheriff: A physical problem?

Carol: Most problems.

Sheriff: A person?

Carol: Are we talking about James Dennett here?

Sheriff: I've watched him. I know a lot about him and his life. He's a loser and hangs out with dead beats. He has a friend whose kids are sleeping together.

Carol: How does that make you feel?

Sheriff: Immoral is what it is. There must be a law against it. I know God has a law about that kind of disgusting sickness. (A slightly louder voice) God chose me to be his servant. (Silence) No, not a servant, for I have always been that, but maybe an enforcer of His law. (A thump against the wall. His fist) It would be my pleasure to enforce His law on those heretics.

Carol: Mr. Sheriff. Allen, please take your seat. Thank you.

Sheriff: Ugh, sometimes I just feel like tearing their skin from their bones. (Suddenly calm) He hasn't asked me yet and I must be ready when he does.

Carol: When who asks you? God?

* * *

Carol remembered her first thoughts about their thirteenth meeting. Allen Sheriff had created a fantasy word. He occasionally spoke of a voice, but never elaborated. She was never fully convinced that there was a voice. She often wondered why he came to these sessions. More than not he often seemed more wound up when he left. She had considered at the time to pass him on to someone better suited to help him. Criminal fantasies were out of her league. Sometimes Allen got so worked up she thought her control over the session was about to change. And that would be disastrous. It worried her deeply. Allen had violent tendencies, they were bottled up but she noticed his rises to anger were getting more frequent. She thought he had a double persona, but she also thought he had it under control. Now, she was even more convinced the two personas had blended.

* * *

James headed home. He wrote down the appointment date with Dr. Stephens on a loose piece of paper and shoved it in his back pocket. He was feeling a bit hungry strolling home. He wasn't in a hurry, he had all day and no real plans, in fact he was unsure about his future and he was on edge. He wondered if he would be attacked again and when that would happen. He had no fear during the daylight hours it was the night he worried about. Darkness seemed to last longer than light. He knew that was only perception but he wished for everlasting daylight.

He removed the piece of paper to check the time again and to be sure it was still there. Lately he seemed to lose things. A ten-dollar note and three two-dollar coins came with it. Surprised to find the money, he smiled. He knew where the note came from but the coins were a mystery. At least he wasn't completely broke, his unemployment benefit sat in the bank, but he would have to wait until Monday morning before he could collect it. He hated ATM's so had never applied for a bankcard. No telephone card, no bankcard, he was going to have to change his ways. They were important items these days. He had learnt that the hard way in the last two weeks.

A new cafe was advertising an opening week special by way of a large sign above the window. James had not noticed the place before. He couldn't recall seeing a building in this spot and there wasn't a memory of its construction. His stomach churned, creating a bubbling sound, "Okay, okay." He said to his stomach. "Let's check it out."

Once inside, he realized it was a hamburger and bar rolled into one, not a cafe at all. The place wasn't very full, about a dozen people. Some couples holding hands, a few business type people, who seemed to work seven days a week and always wear a suit, were having a cocktail with their lunch and there were a few average Joe's having a hamburger.

Heading to the counter, he noticed a handsome looking man trying to pick up a young lady. They both had coffees, although he hadn't touched his and hers was almost finished. He watched them from the corner of his eye. James enjoyed watching people's body language. The young man was leaning close to her. Her legs crossed in his direction and she leaned slightly his way, smiling and enjoying his words. The lady gave the impression she liked what he said and was interested. James changed his opinion, he decided the man was maybe a work colleague He was a little too friendly for a first meeting.

James wished he had the ability to talk to people like that.

When he met Zoe, at the law firm, a lifetime ago it now seemed. He saw her the first time in court. She was defending a young man accused of stabbing with intent to cause injury. He watched her closely. The way she used her body to manipulate the men and women on the jury was amazing. Her words were smooth and her body language was the right amount of ... something. He wasn't sure what that something was but he had to know. In the bravest act he'd ever committed, he approached her after the trial and asked her out. She might have refused him if he hadn't told her why he was asking for a dinner date.

At dinner she answered most of his questions and found he was having a wonderful time and learning something as well. What he most liked about her on that first date was her interest in his photography. After dinner they returned to his place to look at some of his photos. His favorites were mounted on card and hung on the hall.

They sat together on the sofa and chatted about everything and nothing, when James noticed her body language, he had learned only a few of the basics over dinner but had decided to explore this subject more deeply at a later date. He saw her legs crossed, toes pointed in his direction, the closeness of her body. He was sitting on her left side. Her right hand held the coffee cup and her left hand rested on her lap. If he remembered correctly that was an open invitation. He wanted it to be so, but was afraid to try. He was never lucky in this department, and Zoe hadn't said anything to make him think of biting the bullet, going full stream ahead. But he really wanted her, wanted to take her on the sofa, hike up dress, roll down her stockings. He wanted to lick, kiss and touch every inch of her body. He had never felt this way before for any woman. His hands were sweating and his heart pounded against his chest, he had to do something, it was getting late, already 11:30pm, but his body refused to act on his wishes.

Zoe put the cup on the table, turned to him and said.

"James." A big innocent smile spread across her face, then she jumped at him. That night they made love on the sofa. In his mind they didn't just fuck, they made love - twice. James couldn't get enough of her, but he was careful not to appear that way. Zoe was an independent woman from a rich family, so he figured she knew many men who'd wanted her for the money and connections only. James was confident she knew he was the opposite. He was almost happy with life. If only he had the courage to take a chance and follow his dream.

The next morning they made love on the kitchen table, knocking the morning toast to the floor. She had wrapped her legs around his waist, and for the first time in both their lives, they were late for work. Everyone was amazed he had scored the ice maiden, as she was known.

Later that day, he learned she also worked in the same building, but on a different floor. Their chemistry never faded or died and the only disagreement had come at the end of their relationship when he had finally found the courage to follow his dream. It was ironic in a way for it was Zoe who had unknowingly helped him make the decision. If they had never met perhaps he'd still be at the law firm today, working as a clerk.

He never blamed her for leaving, how could he? She was everything to him. They lived together, worked together, did everything together. It was a Hollywood movie romance, and he had fucked it up. Although Zoe was modern minded in most aspects of life, the one thing that did bother her was a workingwoman with an unemployed man. At first James assumed she lacked confidence in his ability but it wasn't that at all. It was her belief that if you worked hard, studied, you would sooner or later hit the big time.

She was an analytical person and couldn't bring herself to believe in James's dreams of grandeur. And within two months, she had left.

James had met a couple of women since Zoe, but it was never the same. He picked them up at bars or cafes, wherever he saw someone he thought attractive. He used the body language skills he had learnt, but he never made love. Only fucked. It took a while but he realized he was trying to replace Zoe he was on rebound mode. Instantly he put a stop to it. He could never feel the same way towards any woman the way he felt for Zoe she was a one off.

He would never find a person like her again. If only he had another chance.

All opportunities were now gone, he could never swallow his pride and return to the law firm in the hope of starting afresh with Zoe and he was sure she would have found someone to replace him. She would have found someone easily. It was best to put his thoughts and wants in the back of his mind, on a wish list as it were.

The way he looked and the things he had seen lately, he doubted he could cope mentally with the demands of seeing Zoe again and the heavy workload of a law clerk. In fact he wondered if he could cope with any type of work again.

"Hey, buddy, what can I get you?"

The counter assistant broke through his thoughts. James looked at the menu on the wall behind the man. The prices were very good.

If the food were as good as the prices, he would be here often.

"Just a burger and fries," he said, then spotted a sign claiming 'BEER -- $2 TODAY ONLY'. James liked the sound of that it had been a long time since his last beer and at this price he could afford a couple. He had to be careful as he was still on medication from the hospital. Beer was the best analgesic for bad memories. He quickly added, "And a glass of beer, please."

The man behind the counter asked, "Twelve ounce or eighteen?"

"Twelve."

"Okay." He stared at James. He seemed to be waiting for something.

"What?" James asked. He had feared this, the open staring from strangers. Had better get used to it, he thought.

The counter assistant pointed at the beer taps. "What'll it be?"

"Oh, sorry. Um," he read the handles, "Our beer," he said. It sounded homey.

"Advertising." The man laughed, "Double Brown coming up. Regular, Natural or bitter?"

"DB Natural thanks." James wondered if they sold 'Flame' beer, which was his all time favorite. He wouldn't bother asking today. It's Sunday. Can't sell beer on Sundays, can you? When the man returned with the twelve-ounce beer, James asked that very question.

"It's perfectly legal as long as we serve food." He smiled. "Take a seat and I'll bring over your food order."

James watched the young couple as he waited for his food. He sipped the beer. He was a slow drinker. He could never get into the habit of having a beer after work. He had never been much of a drinker when he thought about it. He was more of a coffee and Pepsi man. The counter assistant brought his order to the table. It looked very good. The proof was in the taste. He picked up the burger and took a big bite. It was juicy. He absent-mindedly wiped the juice off his chin with his shirtsleeve.

He would have to tell Martha about this place. He asked a woman sitting at the next table what this place was called and she said. "Two Angel Faces."

"Really? Thanks."

"Strange name don't you think?"

James shrugged, "Everything has two faces. But this a damn nice food." He looked down at his plate and kept his eyes there as he continued eating. The lady looked like she wanted to say more, she had three empty glasses at the table and was nursing a fourth.

He didn't want to talk to her.

"You're right." She said, "We all have our angels in disguise."

James thought about that for a while then threw the idea away, he wanted to enjoy the beer, burger and fries.

Earlier that day when the young man returned home, he went straight to the shower and turned on the hot water only. His legs, chest, feet, shoulders, arms and insides felt stiff, numbed from the cold river. It had been a hard trek home, dripping wet, he was thankful to the Lord for providing a good Samaritan who didn't ask questions and offered him a ride to his door step. His clothes were as wet and stiff as he was and he had to peel them off.

The shower stung. The water wasn't yet hot enough to burn but it felt like burning water against his ice-cold body. He fumbled with the cold tap and added it to the water flow. He thought about his plans remembered Carl's death. That had been too easy. It was a shame to kill such a good, God-fearing person. It had to be done though.

He wished James were as religious as Carl was, then he could use the same ploy, but he wanted to hurt James also. His bladed glove was the best weapon. He would continue to use that.

Martha Rothsins came to mind. He truly felt sorry for her and consoled himself with the thought that it was Martha's fault; she did raise the two children. Martha wasn't a part of his plan it was best to forget about her.

The hot water felt exhilarating against his face. In a way it felt the same as when he had disposed of Carl. He had followed Carl to work, then James's caravan. He looked happy when he left, as if on a mission, with his trusty old bible in his large hand. The man was heading to church. Where else would he go? Allen knew what Carl had discovered about his children. The man would have been very confused. The church was the logical place for him.

The large concrete church wasn't far from Opera Sands. It boasted the tallest church tower in New Zealand, looking as if it reached the heavens above. Carl headed to the large Oak doors.

This church was one of the few, which still kept its doors unlocked during the night. And it had never been vandalized.

Before Carl had reached those doors, Allen ran up from behind and shoved a hypodermic needle into the back of his next. Shocked Carl remained still as the liquid flowed through his veins. It was taking affect quickly.

"Who are you? What did you do to me?" Carl asked.

"Only a little acid mixed with coke. You're about to take the ride of your life." He left then, running down the path. Carl's pupils had a strange look when he left and Allen wondered if Carl even knew he was there.

Standing in the shower he wondered what the hell Carl was tripping out on. What did he see, hear, feel? He had returned to the church a few minutes later and saw Carl running out, waving his arms in the air, yelling about demons and devils and that God had fallen. He stopped dead in his tracks when he saw Allen and calmed down.

Carl said. "You're in my way."

"Sorry." Allen replied and stepped to the left. Carl's eyes were bloodshot. He watched the large man calmly walk away.

That had been interesting, Allen had thought at the time.

He turned off the shower feeling fresh and warm and relaxed. Fresh clothes were in his room and he changed quickly into black jeans, black tee shirt and black denim jacket. Occasionally he felt like wearing different colored clothes, but those times were rare and he reminded himself that when his plan was finished, then he could change.

He glanced in the mirror on his way to the garage to get his bladed glove. The time had come. No more games, and no more fucking about. If the good doctor had worked it out or not, it no longer mattered. In the garage he turned off the police radio. He had not used it like he planned. It didn't matter. He would take his chances.

God was with him.

CHAPTER SEVENTEEN

Carol listened intently to the tape. Allen Sheriff was telling of what he had learned about his father rummaging through a box in the attic. He told of his father's first marriage to Jenny Dennett, told of the divorce, and his feelings of no longer being an only child. The day his life changed:

Carol: If Dennett is your half brother, why don't you visit him? You might discover how well the two of you interact together.

Sheriff: He won't remember my father. He was only three when he left. James won't believe me. Besides...

Carol: Besides what?

Sheriff: He's a loser.

Carol: Why do you say that? You've told me this twice.

Sheriff: Because he is, that's why. Did you know he believes in myths, demons and the like?

Carol: Really?

Sheriff: Yep and he is terrified of mean looking dogs.

Carol: How do you know that?

Sheriff: I've watched him, I should know. A dog killed the man he called 'Dad'. I read that in an article from the local paper. That is why he is scared of them.

Carol: I hear a lot of hatred in your voice. Why do you feel you must hate him?

Sheriff: I've told you doc.

Carol: Tell me again.

Sheriff: Because in my father's eyes I was always second best to that piece of shit. Dad said James did everything better than me. If I got a grade B, James would have a grade B+. It never ended. I tried my best, but I always came second. Is that how a father should act?

Carol: It wasn't right for him to do that. You're just as good as the next person, if not better. Why blame James for your father's-

Sheriff: (Angry. Sounds of footsteps) You don't get it do you doc?

Carol: Get what?

Sheriff: My father is James' father. Different mother, that's all. Dad kept an eye on James. Found out his grades at school. Compared me to that loser. He is a major sinner. Burnt a bible after his father's death.

Carol: How do you know that?

Sheriff: He is a sinner who licks the sweat from Satan's armpit. He must pay.

Carol: But you said he has religious friends.

Sheriff: So?

Carol: So, religious people don't interact with that type of person.

Sheriff: Carl Rothsins didn't know. (Voice tone changes. Relaxed again. Anger gone) Look at the time doc, my hour's up. See you.

Carol pushed the stop button on the stereo. That had been his last visit. Flicking through the pages of the file, she came across a letter sent by Allen a few days later. It read:

Sorry but I am not returning. All your talk is giving me a headache, not helping. In fact I don't need your help anymore. I'll get past this. In fact all my problems will be solved. In time God will tell me when to take action. Thanks for trying.

Allen Sheriff

Jesus, Carol thought, it has to be Allen. I'm 100 percent sure about it.

All the pieces of the jigsaw puzzle fell together. Fitting nicely into place. She had to make a decision and she had to do it quickly. Her time, she was sure, had expired. Fear danced up her spine.

* * *

The knifed glove.

Blades razor sharp.

A perfect fit.

He smiled at the reflection in the stainless steel. That bitch of a doctor should know by now, no one needs forty-eight hours when they have all the information at hand. She better not have taken the chance and called the cops. If she had, her death would come slowly, painfully.

Swinging open the side door of the garage, his eyes did not need to adjust to the shadows of the setting sun. The air was cool.

Allen whispered, "Out of the darkness I will come in search of sinners blood. God's wrath shall be felt. In the dead of night, I will come, ripping and tearing flesh."

Allen's smile was fixed on his face. It was his favorite poem he had written after his father's death.

The sky was darkening.

Darkening as if in his wake.

It was indeed a good time to do the Lord's work.

He was filled with joy.

God was at his side.

* * *

It didn't take James long to realize his money had run out. Four jugs, a hamburger, french-fries and good conversation had followed. He had spoken to nearly everyone there. The couple he had watched earlier, following their body language, which he'd been reading, had left together. No one at this place seemed to notice his scars or they were too kind to say anything. Perhaps all his worries about being stared at or being teased were only in his head. Worries that amounted to nothing except stress and that were one thing he didn't need or want anymore of.

The light was fading into dusk and the cafe's fluorescent lights ripped apart the darkness forcing it outside.

James had just finished telling anyone who would listen about Zoe and how he was to blame, when the bartender/owner/counter assistant called for all to finish their drinks and please leave, but come back soon with their friends. James looked at his watch it was 8:15pm. He hadn't realized how fast time passed. He quickly finished his beer. Said his good-byes to people he doubted he would ever meet again and headed out the door.

The cool night air pinched at his skin and he shivered, crossing the road. He thought about his appointment with Dr. Carol Stephens and wondered what he was supposed to do in her office. How could she help with words and thoughts as her only weapons? Would she be able to help? He had never been to a shrink before, although he most likely needed one now. The prospect of "Talks" scared him. Could he tell her about his ability to move objects with the power of his mind? Would he tell her? Would she believe him or just smile and nod her head, saying, "I see." and, "I understand."

He was having second thoughts now. The morning's dream seemed miles away. Its affect on him had left. James was sure the beer helped that. Perhaps, if he stayed drunk the rest of his life, the problems would be gone forever.

A car drove by and tooted. The window was down and he saw the couple that had listened intently as he told his story about Zoe.

The car pulled to a stopped on a small mound of gravel at the side of the road. Tara got out the passenger side and ran across the road. Her blond hair bouncing on he shoulders.

"Hi." She said, standing at his side.

"Hi." He replied feebly.

Tara smiled and swept hair from her face and said. "Ted wants to know if you'd like a lift. He hasn't had that many, so he is okay to drive."

James noticed her eyes were desperately trying to avoid his attacker's marks. It didn't bother him as much as he thought it would.

"No thanks. I think I'll walk. I only live ten minutes away at Orewa."

"You sure, we don't mind a detour."

"Yeah, I'm fine, thanks." James smiled in return to hers and added quickly. "Besides it's a lovely night for a walk."

"Well, if you're sure?"

"Yeah," he lied. He wanted the lift badly, but couldn't bring himself to accept. The darkness was thick around him. He realized that anything could be lurking there. Waiting for its chance.

"Okay. Then we'll see you next Saturday, for a few drinks?" James nodded. "Great! Hey, why don't you bring some of your photos? Ted's friend Sandra owns a photography magazine. We'll bring her along, if you don't mind." Tara winked. "She's single too you know." A slyness crept into her voice. "Who knows what the winds of change will bring, aye?"

"Not a problem."

James couldn't believe what he had just heard, and shook his head in amazement, his smile remaining. Tara was his junior by at least five years and she was trying to set him up. He wasn't interested in a relationship at the moment. The time just wasn't right. He waved as the car sped off into the night.

A new opportunity arose, and he decided not to give photography the flick yet. During his first drink he had considered calling the law firm for his old job, or any job for that matter but he doubted they would offer him one, they had a policy not to re-hire employees who had quit. But if he begged...Who knows? Life had a funny way of working itself out, although it sometimes came late.

He was almost at Orewa, heading down the long hill that led to the "Welcome to Orewa" sign. Something was moving towards him but he was lost in thought and didn't notice it at first, but as it came closer he saw the paws, fangs, red eyes. Black fur moving slowly, steadily toward him.

James froze. The time had come. He would never realize his dream. Never meet whomever it was Tara had planned on bringing to meet him. Such a short life.

He stared in the eyes of the beast. It was taking its time. James thought, surely it would charge at him once it had caught his smell. It didn't. Instead its head was dipped to the ground, searching for something but not him. It was his chance to hide and pray for the best. He quickly moved off the road, ran over mounds of gravel and ducked behind a tree. A cow lowed at his intrusion and snorted in the cool, but growing chilly air. It moved up to James and nudged his shoulder. When he didn't move the cow followed his gaze.

A lifetime seemed to pass before it rounded the bend and was in sight. It stood on two legs. It was a man dressed in black. The cow lowed again, turned and ran as quickly as it could. The young man looked in James direction. For a second their eyes locked. Then the man moved on. He had a jacket draped over his right hand. James swore he saw fire rage behind the pupils.

He watched the man walk to the next bend and disappear from sight. Am I going crazy? He thought. Seeing werewolves would certainly fit into that category. He remained hidden for another ten minutes, just in case he wasn't crazy.

Heading back to the road, his mind wandered back to Dr. Carol Stephens. He found her very attractive and she reminded him of Zoe. Smooth legs, rounded figure, a little bit of meat in all the right places not a stick person that was the latest fad. Like Zoe, Carol was short and came across very intellectual and strong willed. It was the first time he had thought of Dr. Stephens in this light. And found he wasn't sexually attracted to her. She was beautiful and her eyes shone kindness or understanding, but that certain something was missing.

Anyway, there was a problem he had to overcome if he was going to try living a normal life once again. He had to know if he was heading for a breakdown. He didn't want to continue living with crazy thoughts. A lot had happened recently and he felt the pressure pushing on his back, trying to force him to his knees - trying to make him quit. He would not give in to this pressure without a fight.

And he knew he needed Dr. Stephens in his battle.

Suddenly, James couldn't remember the time of the appointment. Was it 10:30 or 11:30? He thought 10:30 but needed to check. He rummaged through his pants pockets and came up empty handed.

Where had he put it?

Behind him he could see the corner of the cafe/bar. No lights shone in through the thin curtained windows. He wondered if he should go back. He needed the slip of paper with the appointment time on it. He was sure everybody would have left by now. He still needed to check the place out. Perhaps a cleaner was there, who could help him look, if they let him in that was.

He quick paced back. His first thought was correct. The place was locked up tight and as quiet as a graveyard at midnight and as dark as a bottomless well, saving the neon sign flashing in the front window facing the road.

James knocked on the front door above the closed sign.

Cupping his hands, he peered in. The counter and a few chairs and tables were in view. Not a living soul, only the ghost image of his-self reflected off the glass.

Damn it!

That option gone James checked his watch. It was 9:10pm. A lot of time had passed since he had left.

Looking in the direction of Dr. Stephens's place. Stars sparkled in the black sky and from the West, clouds were moving in. He hoped she wasn't one of those people who went to bed early. He was unsure whether to go or not. He could always phone in the morning. No he couldn't. The worry would keep him awake.

He nodded his head in decision. He would go. If she slept, or if the house looked empty, he would just have to grin and bear it. Take the chance. He started the long walk up the hill. His eyes scanned the darkness and his ears listened for any sound different to what he normally heard at night.

James had already glimpsed the wolf tonight, even though it was only his imagination, he would be careful. He didn't want to meet the real thing.

* * *

Dr Stephens placed the Allen Sheriff file on top of the metal file cabinet. She stared at the phone. It seemed to be calling to her, urging her to pick up the receiver. She took a few tentative steps towards it and froze. Her heart pounded in her chest, ever aware that someone could be watching her right now.

What would happen if she picked up the phone and dialed Detective Kerrs number, which was committed to memory? Would Allen came charging in and cut her? Could she take the chance?

All the curtains were drawn. There wasn't any possible way to see inside, and yet she felt eyes on her, crawling all over her back and dancing on her spine. And making me paranoid, she thought as she picked up the receiver.

Dr Stephens knew she had to take a chance. She knew she was dead if she did, and most likely dead if she didn't. She was facing a catch 22 situation, no escaping it this time. The familiar tone of an open line greeted her and she punched in Detective Kerrs phone number.

Kerrs answered the phone on the third ring.

"Who is it?" He barked down the line.

Carol fixed her eyes on the drawn curtains. She had an irresistible urge to open them. As Kerrs repeated himself, Carol pushed the speaker button and headed to the curtains. She grabbed the two joined edges and threw the curtains apart with as much force as she could muster. They were heavy and black connected by large silver rings on a pole, which clinked together as both sides bunched at the ends.

She stared outside, searching for any sign of movement. She needed to see, to prepare herself for him, to be ready. As ready as anyone could be prepared for a maniac. Maniac. That was a word she hated to use, but it seemed to fit Allen very well.

Outside, the grounds were black and dead. The silence seemed different somehow, a dense deep silence, more foreboding, scarier than a haunted house she had been dared to enter as a ten year old.

A silence, which radiated substance and then something moved - quickly, and Carol swore hard eyes in the blackness watched her.

Kerrs barked into the receiver again, breaking Carol's concentration on the outside world. Keeping her eyes fixed on the window and scanning the outside regions, she finally spoke her voice nervous and on the verge of cracking and her eyes darted from side to side.

"Detective Kerrs?"

"Yes." His voice was dull and sounded tired.

Carol guessed he was coming off a long shift when she called.

Her pulse started racing. She noticed her hands shaking slightly like a smoker trying to quit cold turkey.

"Detective Kerrs. It's Carol Stephens here. Please you have to listen to what I am about to tell you and don't interrupt until I'm finished." Her voice had gathered speed. She was desperate to get it all out in the open before she heard her door crash inwards and come face to face with the horror of what would follow.

"Carol, calm down." Kerrs said.

She kept talking, her words joining. She realized she was babbling.

Louder, Kerrs said, "Carol, for the love of Christ, will you calm down. I can't make out a single word you said."

Carol silenced herself; she had gone overboard and for a person in her line of business that was unforgivable. She had heard that it has happened to the best of them, but unfortunately only the best of them even made a return to the profession. It was like a hit man thinking about the consequences of his actions.

She had to get her emotions under control, physically calm herself. She had a patient once who sliced her wrists in front of Carol. Blood gushed everywhere. She had not lost her cool then, but this was a totally different situation. It was her wrists that were sliced.

Taking a few deep breaths, trying to bottle up the loose emotions and some of her fear at the same time, Carol said. "I believe I know who killed the kids at the beach, detective. And I think I have proof, to back up my claim."

"No shit, aye." He sounded happy and alive again. "James came through, did he?"

"No. I found him going through my old files."

The line was silent for a bit, then. "Your old files."

Carol didn't answer and it wasn't a question.

"Who?" Kerrs asked.

"Allen Sheriff."

CHAPTER EIGHTEEN

The gravel crunched under his feet, the sound echoing in the night bouncing off the trees. James was tired as he headed up Dr. Stephens's long driveway. He had drunk too much beer and it had reacted against his medication, making him feel dopey and overly exhausted.

He inhaled deeply the cold night air in an attempt to clear his head.

The night was unusually bright and it made the journey up her drive all that much easier. He rounded a curve and saw the house up ahead. It was still a distance off.

Light lit up the ground ahead. He saw the open curtained window and Dr. Stephens on a phone, her back to him. She turned as a dark figure ran towards the house, the figure jumped and he heard breaking glass, followed by an intense scream. A sound he knew well. A sound he had voiced not so long ago.

He stopped and stared at the broken window. His energy returned and nerves twitched. He couldn't just stand here. Action had to be taken and he felt himself drawn forward but not by his need to help but by a thought. A thought that his entire life, a turning point, had lead to this moment in time. Cautiously he moved closer to the window. And as he got closer, the image of the beast took shape.

* * *

Carol pinned herself against the wall. She felt faint, but the blackness would not come. She had been so very close moments ago and his words had brought her back. Surely detective Kerrs would be on his way. He must have heard her scream. If she could fend him off until help arrived then maybe, just maybe... This had to be a dream, a nightmare. It wasn't real couldn't be.

She had been working extremely hard the past two days. She had suffered the emotional loss of her kitten. It was that thought which reminded her off the message on the fridge: No dream doc, no dream. It popped into her head like a light bulb exploding.

Allen looked happy. His eerie smile was disgusting. Seconds ago he was angry, now he seemed so full of himself, so god dammed proud and so at ease with his glove. The way he twisted it downwards, light reflecting off the blades, sparkles jumping from one the next, calmed her. It had an almost hypnotizing effect.

He was talking but she was only half listening, trying to find a way to stall for time. She was lacking in that precious commodity, and had to think of a way to expand it, gain a little more.

"I defeated the Hell hound." Allen said, "It lead me onto a road. Then jumped. But God took me away from the Devil's claws and put me in a safe area. The beast was killed, of course."

Carol nodded, she could not think of anything else to do.

"You don't understand. But how could you? I could smell Satan's breath."

Carol's throat was tight, but she found a way to speak. Trying to keep calm and speak clearly without showing how scared she truly was. She said, "What are you," she stammered, "do doing here." She failed.

"Doc, in the good old days, witches were burnt at the stake and the human remains of a werewolf were also thrown into the blazing fire. This was done out of pity, so their poor souls could enter the gates of Heaven." Allen moved closer to her. "Besides," he added, "I don't have any matches. Have you?"

Carol was confused. What was he talking about? Witches. Werewolves. Fire. He had smelled Satan's breath. She looked at the clawed glove, saw a longing in his eyes and asked. "Are you a werewolf?"

"I am God's chosen one."

"Has God made you a werewolf?"

He looked at her long and hard.

Carol thought she had found a way to gain some time. If she could ask the right questions and get him talking then she had a chance. A puzzled expression entered his eyes, like he was asking silent questions to another person and wasn't getting the answers he liked.

"Think of me as a Human-Beast." Allen said.

"What is a Human-Beast?" Carol asked. She felt her time had just run out.

"God's creature!" Allen screamed, raising the glove high.

* * *

James reached the broken window. He saw the beast standing on two legs, but the vision was blurred by a second of a young man dressed in black. He shook his head and squeezed his eyes shut. What was he seeing? It was not alcohol induced. The two images were one, but which one? He opened his eyes and saw the clawed glove.

His attack at Opera Sands flashed before him:

The claws of the beast sweeping through the air-something shining in the moonlight-

The fur-

The howl-

The pain-

Something attached to leather-

Glowing eyes-

A face, young and smiling.

Suddenly he saw clearly. He saw the image of the beast. It was a wolf. The hairy body blurred and changed into that of a smiling face. The face of a young man. A man he had seen before. A person he knew. An intense anger, born of fear, raged inside him. Erupted.

Photos fell from the wall. The pins, nails and tacks, which held them, flew at the man with the glove raised. Newspapers and books followed. The television screen flashed into life, the volume high. A second later the tube exploded, spraying glass in a widening arch.

Allen about to strike spun around in shock and saw James climbing through the window. Fuck me, he thought, and said. "Two birds with one claw."

James didn't respond. He stood, staring at the easy chair. It wobbled but would do more. He feared he wasn't strong enough mentally to hoist such a large object. He could feel the strain on his brain like a pair of hands pushing a block of wood against a sponge and a wall.

Allen strode towards him. "What's the matter, still seeing werewolves?"

He swung the claw at James, who ducked barely in time and came up with a clenched fist and drove it in an upward direction, into Allen's ribs. He screamed out. In pain he dropped to the floor on one knee clutching his side.

James watched him for a couple of seconds. There was no movement. One punch was that all there was to it? No. He knew that, the attacker was not a weak person of body or mind. Quickly, he slid past and made his way to Carol. Helping her up, he asked, "Are you all right?"

She nodded.

"Good. Get somewhere and call the police."

A strange look came over Carol. Her eyes widened, mouth dropped open then snapped shut. It looked like she was trying to say something but no words came out.

James stared into her frightened eyes and saw Allen reflected back at him. He spun around as the glove jabbed at him. He moved to the side as the bladed glove slid into the side of his shirt and exited leaving four not so very deep cuts bleeding in its wake.

Allen gave a cry of frustration as he stumbled past James and landed against Carol who had remained motionless against the wall in shock. She gasped. He pulled away from her, his blooded blades sliding easily out of her stomach. He looked at her, smiled as she slowly slid down the wall leaving a red smudge behind. His gloved hand fell to his side and he swung it up, ripping through her tee shirt, smashing through her jaw, tearing her clear smooth face leaving four thin cuts running up her face.

Charging him, James struck Allen on the side with his shoulder forcing the gloved hand above his head, locking the elbow using his neck and the side of his head as a vice making it impossible to move his arm.

One arm punches flew as the two struck the wall. Allen's nose bled from two well-placed strikes.

Pinning him to the wall, James brought up several knee strikes to Allen's tight stomach area. Squirming against the attack, Allen found an opening and delivered a knee to the groin. James doubled over and dropped to his knees. Allen grabbed him by the hair and forced James's head back until their eyes met.

"Time to meet your maker." Allen hissed, blood dripping from his cut lip. Light danced off the blades as they hovered half a foot from the exposed neck. He smiled.

"Do it!" James screamed, having passed the point of no return, no longer caring if he lived or died. He had fought his battle and he had tried his best. "Fucking do it you malignant cunt!"

Crying sirens screamed in the night as police cruisers tore up the driveway. The blue and red flashing lights bounced off the trees and faded into the night sky. Headlights beamed through the darkness, shining into the living room. Covering Allen's frame.

"Do it for Christ sake!" James cried.

The smile faded from Allen, he had to made a decision and quickly before the cop cars stopped and the cops reacted. He had to act now.

He said, "You and I will meet again. During midnight."

With that he ran into the hallway and disappeared around the corner. James heard a window smash. He hobbled to the hallway, across it to the bedroom. He saw a dark figure vanish into the darkness.

He returned to the crumpled body of Dr. Carol Stephens. He knelt beside her and lifted her head onto his lap. She was covered in blood. The slashes from her face and neck were visible through the oozing red muck. He whispered her name.

Her eye fluttered and flicked open; the other was a sliced mess.

She looked at James, but he doubted if she saw him clearly if at all. She coughed, upper body jerking in reaction to the wet vibrating sound. She coughed up some blood and whispered, "He ... is ... your ... half ... brother." She shuddered against him and lay still, her eye staring at him.

Two officers appeared at the window, one at each side, arms stretched out in front holding pistols. At the same moment two more entered the living room. They shouted at James but he refused to move. The two officers pulled him away from the dead woman and pushed his face into the carpet.

"Don't move, pal." One said while he removed handcuffs from the back of his belt, then snapped them against James's wrists.

"Who we got here?" the other said pulling out a wallet from the back pocket.

Detective Kerrs entered, saw James and ordered the two officers to remove the cuffs. He stood over Carol's body. He had once fancied her and had put up with her reluctance to help in an investigation, but looking down on her now he felt sickened. He reminded himself to remain professional.

Unhooking the large walkie-talkie clipped to his belt, he pressed the red button on the side and mumbled into it.

James came up beside him. Her death had brought pure rage, a force James had never felt before. It had made him act in a way that he only dreamt about, thoughts, which made him the hero or anti-hero in countless dramas of his imagination. Strangely, he felt little or nothing as he looked at the lifeless corpse of his doctor.

Detective Kerrs said, "We'll need to get a description."

James didn't reply.

"As soon as possible. Perhaps now while he is still fresh in your mind."

Silence, but James did look at him. A tired look of a man pushed to the limit.

"Or perhaps after you relax a bit."

James smiled. "Relax?"

"Calm down. That's what I meant."

James inhaled deeply, "I'm as calm as I'll ever be."

Detective Kerrs smiled inwardly. He removed a small note pad and a pencil, and then had a second thought. "Perhaps you would like to come down to the station. I can get an artist to meet us there, how does that sound?"

"Like a waste of fucking time."

He's your half brother.

Carol's words echoed and thumped in his head. Surely he would have been told about a brother. Why would that have been kept a secret from him? And why would someone carrying the same blood want him dead? It didn't make sense, but not much had made sense lately. The whole world had tipped itself over and lay on its side. It seemed unreal. Years of wanting a brother, some one to play with, grow up with. He had wished for it to happen when he was younger, cried for one when he was lonely and emptiness ate at him.

Now suddenly, he had a brother, a half brother who wanted him dead. Who had attacked him, scarred him, and left him for dead. The one thing he desperately needed all those years ago had suddenly become a reality. A reality and a nightmare all rolled into one.

"Well?" Detective Kerrs asked.

It was hard to remember. He hadn't concentrated on the face. He had snapped, having given his self-control over to rage. And he had been busy trying not to get killed.

He did remember a slight resemblance to himself, so he said, "Dark hair, shoulder length, I think." He struggled hard to recall anything he could, but replaying most of what he could remember, he couldn't mention any specific details. In the end he decided to describe a twenty-year-old James Dennett dressed in black.

Detective Kerrs wrote fast. When James finished, he looked up from the small note pad and said. "That it? No marks or visible tattoos?"

"You can't miss him." James added. "He's got four blades stuck on his right hand."

Kerrs spoke into his walkie-talkie. He saw James headed toward the couch and knew he was about to sit down. "I wouldn't if I was you," he said, "why don't you follow me out to my car, we can rest in there."

James nodded.

"I'm going to call a police artist now to get a more detailed description."

James sighed. "I just gave you one."

Detective Kerrs smiled, "We cops like pictures." His joke came out deadpan.

James stared openly at him. "What?"

"It was a joke." He replied. "Just humor me, please."

"Fine."

James headed out the front door into the cool night. It was getting late and he shivered, not due to the cold. Allen's last words came back to him. He decided not to tell the detective, and he had no idea as to why he wanted it to remain a secret. He did not believe Allen would return so soon, and if he did maybe he could talk to his brother. It was a long shot, but he had so many questions that needed asking.

Deep down he knew he wasn't going to have the chance to ask them. Their next meeting would be their final. James wondered if he would survive.

CHAPTER NINETEEN

Allen ran through the bush, tree branches pounded against his head some weaker ones snapping. Twice he was felled by protruding roots, both times he realized how close to the upturned blades he had landed, his head centimeters from the sharp steel. He removed the glove and folded the blades inward to the leather straps. It was a lot easier to remove than it was to attach. His black shirt was torn in several places and in the moonlight he could see his scratched body, most had come from the trees and his fall.

His ribs hurt making deep breathing troublesome. James had scored a lucky punch that time. There would be no more. He was surprised at the ferocity of his half brother's attack. Many times Allen had witnessed James back down and give-up when confronted. Perhaps age gave him confidence in his actions, or he had passed a certain point within himself. If the latter were true, then it was because of him and Allen felt a hint of pride. He had helped his brother break free from fear. He smiled in the moonlight, then another thought came to him: James had stumbled onto a scene he could not control. He hadn't thought about anything except perhaps trying to help the doctor. He had run on instinct.

A deep breath shook Allen's body with pain and he doubled over, dropping the glove and clutched his right side. Sonofabitch.

James always caused problems. He prayed to God that this pain wouldn't interfere with his plans for later tonight. He was going to have to tape his side up, which would restrict his movements, his flexibility greatly reduced. But James was a pussy at heart. It wouldn't require a great deal of trouble to take him out.

James had surprised him tonight, although he had been sort of happy to see him there. The sureness of his brother had also surprised him, but he was ready for their next meeting. He would change his tactic again. Since he killed Carl Rothsins, his plans had continuously changed. And the worst part of it was he couldn't place the mistakes. He had spent two years devising the end of James, had thought of every possibility. Even included him turning up at some strange places and he had been right to include him as he did indeed turn up. First at the beach but that had not turned out badly, as his work was finished. Now he was at the doctor's house. Why did he have to turn up tonight? Why couldn't he stay at Martha's place where I knew where to find him? And how the hell did he make those books fly and TV explode? Was the Devil working through his half brother to stop him, like he had put that dog in my path?

"It won't work, you crafty old son of a bitch." Allen hissed, his anger again rising.

He doubled back, careful moves, eyes watchful. He had to get back into town, tape his side and prepare for Dennett. He had spoken too soon and promised a final midnight meeting. He thought seriously about taking the dirt road back, but it would take too much time and he needed as much of it as he could get.

He saw flashing blue and red lights in the distance and moved in a wide arch around them. Time was against him and he had to take the chance that God would hide him away from the police in shadows and hopefully they would be busy and inattentive to his actions.

"Dennett," he whispered, clutching his claw glove tightly, "you're history. I'll be waiting for you, if you can work this out. You know my plans, you've always known deep down. I will wait for you."

* * *

James wasn't sure how long it took for the police artist to arrive, some moments of time dragged on forever, while others flew past. One moment he was talking to Detective Kerrs, the next he was looking at the forest, which bordered the property. Police activity dragged on at times and shot by at others.

When the police artist finally showed up, he looked haggard and as if it was past his bedtime. Bags drooped under his eyes shadowed by thick black rings. Overworked, underpaid and in a rut. He approached James without hesitation, knowing exactly who he was. He carried a small soft computer case.

"I'm officer Ruby. Andrew Ruby."

James shook his hand. "How did you know to come straight to me?"

"Look at how you're dressed, and besides, you look like you have been in a war." He smiled as he placed the case on the car's hood. He opened it and removed a small computer and switched it on. There weren't so many keys and the screen was very sharp. "I had this specially made, cost a fortune but it helps my work."

"I thought you used a pencil and paper." James replied wondering what operating system was used. It wasn't Windows CE or Lynx or any other that he knew.

Officer Ruby pulled out a blank sheet of A4 paper and feed it into a pair of plastic claws at the back of the machine. He smiled up at James, "Who said paper was old fashioned?" The computer had a small ball and he used it to scroll and click, "We're in business."

James liked this guy. He was friendly and a people person. If he had his camera he might ask to take a few snaps. Still thinking about photography, that shocked him. It was in his blood after all these years and he guessed it would be a part of his life, till the day he died. And that could be before tomorrow, he reminded himself. He had already decided to give the office the exact same description as he had given detective Kerrs.

"Right." Officer Ruby said. "How well do you remember the offender?"

"Well, I'd remember him if I ever saw him again."

"Good enough. It's a start." He punched some keys and clicked the ball. A number of faceless heads appeared on screen, "Did he have a square face or an oval one?"

"Oval."

"Fair enough."

What the hell did that mean? Fair enough? What was fair about all this? James suddenly felt tired. Exhausted. Not physically, but mentally. Had he been in shock and this is what it felt like coming out of it? Or was the opposite true? His eyes felt like they were heavy, hanging from his sockets.

"What's the time?" he asked.

Officer Ruby checked his watch. "Almost ten."

"Almost equals what?"

"Do you have to be somewhere?" James had his full attention.

"Yeah."

Officer Ruby frowned. "Three minutes to."

James leaned heavily against the car. His mental tiredness was becoming physical. From the house he saw two paramedics wheel a gurney out of the house. A plastic bag lay on top. They started along the gravel driveway but ended up carrying it. That's because of me, James thought, it's my fault she's dead. What a way to die.

Detective Kerrs said they believe the attacker was a former patient, one Allen Sheriff. James had never heard of former patients killing their doctors, so if Allen was the man at the beach, what the hell did Carol have to do with this? Would this Allen character commit murder because she was helping him? Was it as simple as that?

Officer Ruby asked many questions and he answered them smoothly. As the picture developed, James saw similarities between that picture and him. Far too many to be just a coincidence. Although he gave a description of a younger him, when he saw the end picture, he pointed and said, "That's the son of a bitch." The picture looked like a photograph, very lifelike.

James accepted Carol's death was because of him. He could not think of any other reason for her to die. It wasn't a trap to lure James there. He had stumbled upon the attack. He thought about Carl's death, had that been orchestrated? The kids murders, also? It seemed that everyone he cared about had died recently. Well, almost everybody. Martha was still alive. He was thankful for that. She was the last person he truly cared about. The last person left, that was.

Then the thought struck him like a thunderbolt smashing into the earth.

* * *

Every Sunday night, Martha would curl up in bed with the bible reading the pages that were already committed to memory, with the bedside lamp providing the only light. But recently, she had forsaken the bible for fictional novels. The bible no longer held any real meaning for her. It had taken a week to break the habit, a twenty plus year habit. She still loved God, even though he had taken her family, she just didn't trust Him anymore. The old expression, "He works in mysterious ways." didn't work for her now. Until recently that answer had sufficed. It was what people like her always said when they couldn't understand why such and such happened. That answer wasn't sufficient any longer. She wanted solid answers, but she would have to wait until it was her time to go before she received them. She was willing to wait. What else could she do?

Two weeks ago she had entered the local bookshop. Martha loved to read at night and for twenty plus years the bible was all she had needed. It took three hours to find something. She had also asked a couple of ladies who looked about her age what they thought was good. One suggested romance novels and she skim read a few pages of some, but found them too rude for her taste.

Another suggested horrors but that was totally out of the question, she would never sleep at night. International espionage was too real or too flamboyant, 007 type books did not appeal. She remembered as a child that she had read a couple of murder mysteries, so she headed to the 'Who-done-it' section. There were so many titles and different types from when she was younger that she felt a headache coming on. She grabbed the first one off the shelf with a woman's name and bought it.

Martha was almost finished. The book was different to what she remembered murder mysteries were. The killer was identified early on and the book seemed focussed on the relationships between the characters and how they discovered the killer. She saw no point in continuing on, but she was determined to change habits, even if it was only switching one book for another.

She closed the paperback and placed it beside the lamp.

Suddenly feeling thirsty she struggled out of her warm bed and headed to the kitchen for a drink. She had left the lights on for James. She didn't want to be awakened by him crashing into something He was clumsy at times, especially when he tried to be quiet. She looked up at the wall clock. Fifteen past ten. Where was he? She hoped nothing had happened to him. The poor man had had enough trouble for one lifetime.

Martha found a coke in the fridge. James must have bought it. She didn't care for soda but decided to have a glass anyway. A friend of hers always drank a glass of it first thing in the morning, claiming it wet her throat and made her morning cigarette not taste dry. She carried the bottle to the sink and poured half a glass. It was a gustatory sensation on the way down but she remained thirsty and she remembered why she had stopped drinking it many years ago. It never quenched her thirst. She replaced the bottle and saw a quart of orange juice at the back. James must have bought this also. Martha preferred to buy sports drinks, they were so much better than cordial. The carton was open and Martha drank a mouthful from it. It tasted good.

She closed the fridge and headed back to her room. On the way she decided to turn off the lights and if James did crash into something and wake her up, then so be it. At least she would know he was safe at home. Secretly, she hoped he would stay for a long time, the company was pleasant. The loneliness had been heavy before James agreed to stay for a while.

Reaching her bedroom door, she glanced back at the dark hallway and living room. For some strange reason the darkness frightened her. She thought she heard the sound of clattering garbage cans outside, followed by breaking glass and other wee sounds. A shoe scuffing the pavement. The gate squeaking open, banging shut.

Martha pushed her bedroom door open slowly afraid that some deformed creature from Hell was waiting to pounce and have its way with her. Perhaps it was the same demon that took her family.

Stop it, she scolded herself, you're a grown woman act like one. She pushed the wood wide open and had a good look. Empty. Just like it should be. She glanced back at the darkness enclosing the hallway and living room before entering her bedroom and closing the door behind her.

She sat on the bed and brought the paperback to her lap. The cover was gruesome it showed a knife slashing through the word murder in a downward angle heading towards a blue eye surrounded by blond hair. If she had looked at the cover before buying the book, she would never have forked over the money. The cover was more macabre than the story itself. And she blamed the book cover for her anxiety. She sighed and tossed the book back, it hit the side of the cabinet connected to the headboard and fell to the floor. She had never been a good... Clatter.

Clatter. Clatter. Scrape. Clatter.

There it was again. The sound she had heard earlier, only this time it sounded closer. Could she really be imagining it? It was doubtful. A book cover never brought sounds. The house took on an unusually silent emptiness. Martha suddenly felt very alone and exposed; she had taken to wearing one of Carl's old shirts as a nightdress.

Something at the door.

Clatter. Clatter. Scrape. Bang.

Creaking hinges ... the soft thud of a door closing.

That's my door. Fear rose up inside like a tidal wave, washing through her entire body. Tingling sensations suddenly down the lower part of her body. The need to run to the bathroom was strong.

"James?" She whispered, her voice cracking as she stared at her bedroom door.

On tiptoe she crept to the door and put her ear against it. She waited a few minutes but heard nothing else. Slowly she opened the door. A heavy metal drummer high on acid pounded away in her chest. She scanned the hallway and the part of the living room she could see. Nothing. No one. A faint light from the street outside pushed its way into the living room through gaps in the curtains. The hallway dimly lit from her bedroom lamp.

"James?" She repeated a little louder. "Is that you?"

No reply.

Again. "James, is that you?"

Still no reply.

"Please answer me."

Nothing.

"Is anybody there?"

Silence, like a heavy blanket.

Did she really expect an answer?

A sudden noise outside made her jump and Martha spun around and quickly went to James' room, too scared to look behind her into the darkness. Visions of blood and terror flashed before her.

Visions she had pictured reading a few of her sons favorite authors: Dean R Koontz, David Martin, and Stephen King, Christopher Pike.

She had only read the first few chapters of these books and that was all the evidence she needed to never touch these writers again. Martha did not fancy being frightened by ghosts and ghouls and undead things, why did thousands of readers like these types of books if all they did was put fear into you. There was enough real horror in the world as it was. Why add fake horror?

She didn't want to be frightened by things, which weren't real, but it was these images of ghosts and ghouls that flashed to mind as she quick stepped to James's room. He wouldn't mind finding her there, especially if she explained why.

She wasn't sure if there was someone in the house. After all, the sound had originated outside. She could have imagined the sound of the door closing.

She pushed through the ghosts and ghouls and James's bedroom door. It was empty but his curtain was open. She'd never noticed she could see the neighbor's house and driveway all the way to the street before. She looked for a place to sit. It seemed inappropriate behavior for a woman of her age to be waiting for a man while sitting on his bed. She remembered there had been a stool in this room at one time long ago and she had put it in the back of the closet in case her son needed it for any reason. She hoped James had not removed it or placed it out of her reach on the top shelf.

Martha crept to the closet. She stopped short. She had the strangest feeling that if she opened the door an ax-wielding killer would greet her. The thought made her shiver but she opened the door regardless. Behind his suitcase, she found a little stool, smaller than she remembered.

She pulled it out, closed the door and sat with her back against the closet, staring out the window facing her. She saw her neighbors return home from an evening walk, arm in arm, they were a young couple new to the area. She had never met them and doubted she ever would, people just never introduced themselves to their neighbors like they used to. She watched them enter their house, when she spotted a darkly dressed young man stop at their gate and look directly at her. He stared for a minute before continuing on his way, kicking a soda can as he went.

Tightness closed around her chest and the heavy metal drummer returned. There was something wrong about the man. The light thrown by the street lamp had lit up only part of his face. His eyes were clearly visible. In them she saw hatred. A pure undiluted hatred.

"Hurry up, James." She whispered.

She had never felt this scared before, but then she'd always had Carl to protect her, but now he was dead and gone. A warm wetness spread around her groin and she saw the liquid run over the edge of the stool, felt it dribble onto her ankles. The warmness of her urine quickly cooled. She hugged herself, letting tears of fear run freely down her cheeks.

* * *

Detective Kerrs mulled around near the upturned coffee table where the phone Carol had called him on, lay cracked on the carpet surrounded by a sparkling array of shattered television tube glass. The beep was just audible over the ruckus inside. A vanilla colored folder lay open next to it. The pages were scattered. Putting on a pair of white latex gloves he picked it up after asking if it had been photographed. When a "Yes" came, he showed it to James, "Allen Sheriff, a former patient of hers. Carol told me this on the phone." His voice came out slightly strained as if he was unloading a bundle of feelings about a woman he knew well, but was trying to hide it with details and James was the only person he could do it to. He offered the file to him.

James took it but did not look inside.

"You're mentioned quite a bit in here," Kerrs added. He opened it in James's hand, easing the covers apart. "This," he said selecting a sheet from the uneven bundle, "this tells us why he came after her. A former patient that feels more bad has been done than good."

"But it doesn't make sense."

"Why he killed her?" Kerrs asked quietly.

James didn't reply, as he had not intended to voice any questions. He needed to get home quickly. The feeling that Martha was in great danger also, nagged at him, trying to force his body into action. He had to find a way to convince the detective here to listen to his intuition, but how could he do that without sounding crazy or like he was trying to cause panic. The police had their hands full here. Something was missing or had been overlooked. He didn't know what it was but it felt like he was staring right at it. Think, he cursed himself, think dammit.

Kerrs broke into his thoughts.

"He killed Doctor Stephens, 'cause she hadn't helped him. According to her notes he was obsessed with God, a religious zealot, one might say. And, he tried to kill you because you're a witness to his frenzy."

That didn't sound correct to James, there was more to it. Allen attacked James before he came after Carol.

He asked. "Then who killed Carl Rothsins?" He pushed the file back at Detective Kerrs, holding it inches from his face. An idea struck him, like a thunderbolt between the eyes vibrating behind them. He flicked through the file; skim reading the pages instead of just glancing at them like last time.

"Carl committed suicide, plain and simple."

James wasn't listening, he had not told the police about Carl's 'felones de se', had no intention of doing so anytime in the near future. He read through page after page, growing angrier, his face showing the advancing tempestuousness with each sheet he finished.

He pushed past the detective and put the file on the car bonnet. His hands held the sheets against the cover bracing against the curling breeze, which was growing stronger. Scanning a page reading: Recent conclusions, James found what he thought he was looking for. At the bottom of the page, Carol had written: 'I have come to these conclusions based on the events of this tape recording, numbered six.'

Looking at detective Kerrs, James said. "Where's tape six?"

Kerrs looked surprised. "What tapes?"

"The tape mentioned here." He handed the file page to Kerrs who read it slowly.

"I haven't seen any tape." He headed inside. A lot of the officers had left on other duties, but the lab technicians were still at work. To them he asked. "Any of you boys see a tape?"

"Yeah, over there in the cabinet." He nodded in the direction.

Both James and Detective Kerrs went to it and started searching for the tape numbered six. They found one through five and seven through fifteen. No number six.

Kerrs said, "Maybe he took it."

"Doubtful." James replied, "He would not have had time. I saw him jump through the window, then saw the attack. I got involved in the fight. I tried to save her, and thought I had." He shook his head. "Allen had no time to get it."

"So where is it?"

A female technician who didn't mind being called 'One of the boys' heard their conversation and said, "Have you checked the stereo?"

James thought, No way, it couldn't be so easy to find.

Yet, there it was, staring at both of them through the small see-through plastic compartment marked: Deck A. Kerrs made it there before James and pressed the play button. There was a long moment of silence before:

Carol: A perfect example of misused trust and self-loathing. Combined, this has led to a projected hatred of James Dennett. Perhaps what Allen's father had planned all along.

Kerrs and James both looked at each other, they both had the same idea in mind. James pushed the stop and then the rewind buttons before Detective Kerrs had a chance to stop him from spreading his prints over evidence. The tape spun back a bit and Kerrs held a hand up to James in warning and pressed the play button himself.

Carol: Are we talking about James Dennett here?

Sheriff: I've watched him. I know a lot about him and his life. He's a loser and hangs out with dead beats. He has a friend whose kids are sleeping together.

Carol: How does that make you feel?

Sheriff: Immoral is what it is. There must be a law against it. I know God has a law about that kind of disgusting sickness. (A slightly louder voice) God chose me to be his servant. (Silence) No, not a servant, for I have always been that. But maybe an enforcer of His law. (A thump against the wall. His fist) It would be my pleasure to enforce His law on those heretics.

Carol: Mr. Sheriff. Allen, please take your seat. Thank you.

Sheriff: Ugh, sometimes I just feel like tearing their skin from their bones. (Suddenly calm) He hasn't asked me yet and I must be ready when he does.

Carol: When who asks you? God?

James pressed stop and fast-forwarded a little:

Sheriff: Do I have to spell it out for you?

Carol: No, but I do feel it would be better for you to hear it in your own words and your own voice.

Sheriff: (Sighs loudly) Fine. James's father is my father. We just have a different mother that's all. Do you feel better now?

Carol: The question is do you feel better?

Sheriff: I don't feel anything.

James stopped the tape. "Jesus, he wants to kill everyone including me, whom he feels has fucked with his life."

Kerrs had trouble believing it. It wasn't logical and it didn't make sense. There had to be a better reason for Allen to do what he was doing. Some kind of hard evidence, some kind of proof, he needed proof that he could hold in his hand, show a judge. James's idea was largely based on assumption and he could not go to court with that. But he did have an eyewitness to Carol's murder and that was enough to get the guy behind bars, then they could look at the other findings and make sure he never sees freedom's sunlight again.

Making a quick summary, James said, counting off his fingers. "First, he killed Carl Rothsins."

"He committed suicide."

"You want hard evidence? Well, so do I. I bet the autopsy show trace elements of some kind of drug. Right? I thought so. Carl hated drugs, never took anything stronger than aspirin."

Kerrs ejected the tape. "Cathy," he said, "bag this for me, will you?"

"No problem." She said with a smile.

"Second, Carl's children."

"You're a witness, he wants you dead. Can't you see that?"

"Third, a message left with the dead puppy."

"Pranksters."

"Fourth, Mrs. Clemm."

"Dog attack. Michael Fratscure, almost got it."

"Whose dog?" James asked, "How do we know it wasn't Allen's"

Kerrs shook his head. "I doubt Allen would train a dog to attack only one person. Remember there were a lot of wild dogs lately until Michael got most of them."

"Are they still around?"

"One or two. But look, what makes you think Allen had anything to do with Mrs. Clemm? You're a more likely suspect, if you weren't in hospital."

"And finally," James plowed on, "Dr. Stephens, ripped apart with the same weapon used to attack me and probably the same exact weapon used on Carl's children."

Detective Kerrs sighed deeply. "You're right, there are a few instances where Allen could be connected. But that's all. Key words here are: could and be."

"He wants to kill everyone associated with me."

"Highly unlikely."

"Fuck you!"

James made to leave but Kerrs grabbed his arm and spun him around. Their face inches apart, Kerrs said. "Look at it from my perspective for a minute. So far you've said everything from what you believe to be happening. I've countered everything you said. And when we catch Allen, we'll get his perspective. Then, " he held up a finger, "and only then will we be able to put this whole mess together. Don't jump the gun and don't get yourself killed."

James shook off Kerrs hand and moved past him and the car headed down the drive. The cool air swished at his hair and he brushed it back absentmindedly. In the house was an abyss he did not wish to enter or look into again in case it did in fact look back.

But that sight, oh God, that fucking sight. Blood smeared on the wall, carpet blotted by the liquid of life. It didn't seem real, like a horror movie Nick would watch.

He cursed himself for storming off like that but Kerrs had infuriated him. James realized he hadn't thought things through as well as he usually did. He had made many mistakes tonight and had cursed himself more than usual. If had hadn't paused when he saw Allen jump through Carol's window, things might be different. She might be alive now answering all his questions about Allen. Most importantly, time was running out and Martha's house was miles away, at least an hour's walk and his energy was lacking. He must get Martha out of the house and someplace safe before he faced his half brother. It was at times like this he wished he had not sold his car. It was a necessity of life. Walking everywhere sucked and took too long.

"Hey, Mister Dennett."

James turned to his left and saw a young officer leaning against his car door. He had been lost in thought he hadn't noticed it. The officer smoked a cigarette in such a styled way. He thought he must have practiced for years.

Smiling, James nodded a hello and went back to the problem about Martha. He could feel his hair turning gray at the stress and adventure. Yes, he thought of it as an adventure although he knew he shouldn't, but he was acting in ways he only daydreamed about. He had always wanted to be the hero or the underdog finally winning but reality was very different, his adventure was out of control and had turned into a nightmare.

"Would you like a smoke?" The officer asked.

James stopped next to him. "No thanks."

It suddenly hit him.

He surveyed the area. They were almost at the end of the drive with no other cars or people in sight and the bend in the driveway hid them.

"Where's your partner?" James asked.

"Inside. He doesn't like smoke and I drove down here." The officer smiled, "Sometimes I have to be sneaky about it, one here, one there. This no smoking policy is discrimination against us smokers, but we can't act on it. Well, not really."

The moon sent cold beams of light flushing against the scenery.

James dragged his hands through his hair. An idea blossomed fully. Unable to believe what he was about to do, mainly because it was against his character, he acted fast trying to keep his voice smooth and calm and the adrenaline that pulsed through his heart in control.

After a few short deep breaths, James said. "Actually, I wouldn't mind a cigarette now, if you don't mind."

"Always willing to help out a fellow smoker."

He kept control hoping the officer didn't notice the shake in his voice. If he had noticed it, he must've brushed it off and he dug a cigarette from the packet and handed it to him. Putting it between his lips, James said, "Thanks. Have you got a lighter?"

"Sure, no worries."

They were the last words he spoke for a while. James clenched his fist as tight as possible and swung as hard and as fast as his strength would allow. He connected with the officer's cheek with the sound of two planks being struck together. The officer looked stunned. The butt of his cigarette dropped from his parted lips and for a second James thought he would have to hit him again, but the cop's eyes rolled back and he collapsed to the ground. James caught him before he hit and gently laid him down.

He quickly looked around. No one had seen him.

He jumped into the cruiser, happy to see that it was automatic. He hadn't driven in years and wondered if he still could. Turning the key, it fired up, the motor quietly vibrating, eight pistons shooting up and down. He eased the vehicle down the driveway watching the officer in case he should come to quickly. He knew he had only a few minutes before the officer was discovered and increased his speed. The act of driving came back to him easily as if he had been behind the wheel all his life.

CHAPTER TWENTY

Allen stood on the porch at Martha's little yellow house. He was inhaling deeply and rapidly, trying to calm himself. James had to be here by now, he thought. He had returned home, wrapped a bandage tight around his waist after taking a very quick cold shower to sooth the aches and pain. James had dealt him a few solid blows.

He had decided that Martha should also be punished, for she too, as a friend loved James and her punishment would come from his glove, as all punishment should.

It was a close call at the doctor's house. He hadn't planned on James turning up and he thought the police would take longer to arrive. He surmised that a police cruiser must have been close. Dennett had turned into a life long problem and today was the day he would end the problem.

He tried the doorknob. It was locked.

Too much of his life had been wasted. It was time to take back his life, no more fucking about. Dennett was never going to catch him unprepared ever again. James would never see the sun rise. Carol's house had been the last time he would ever let James get the better of him.

Allen took half a step away from the door, took a deep breath and kicked. The sound seemed incredibly loud in the quiet hours of night. The door remained intact. Frustrated, he repeatedly kicked with all his might. The third kick split the wood around the doorknob, the fourth cracked it and the fifth tore it away from the knob, which hung momentarily in the jamb before falling to the floor.

He smiled as he entered Martha's house and adjusted the glove so that it sat more comfortably and more secure. He had made the glove in such a way that it resembled a dog's claw; after all, that was James's weakness - dogs. But somehow, that night on the beach, which seemed a lifetime ago, his half brother saw a wolf, a werewolf of all things. So be it. The illusion had protected him. Now it would kill him.

* * *

Martha's heart skipped a beat at each kick against the door, and when she heard it give way, she thought her heart would never start again. She left the stool and tried to hide in a dark corner, doing her best to remain quiet. Her heart thumped loud and hard against her chest. Squatting down, the smell of her urine was strong and she feared it would give her away.

The sound of objects falling and doors being pushed open penetrated her eardrums above the sound of her heart.

She could hear him getting closer, and with each step he took, she found it harder to breathe. Fear was crippling her lungs. She had to leave and get out of the house before he found her and did whatever he wished. Knowing she would be powerless to stop him.

A feeling of impending dread had hung above her since this morning when James had performed his magic trick but she had shrugged it off. He had scared her this morning, and she blamed that for the cause of the feeling. She now knew better.

Martha found the ability to move. Her legs were like rubber but she was able to stand and edged her way to the window with her back against the wall for support.

"Martha, where are you?" The voice was just above a whisper as it floated under the crack of the door and into the room. Light also shone through the gap. He must have turned on the lights as he went.

A scream erupted from Martha almost drowning out the sound of screeching car tires outside.

The bedroom door flew open.

"Nice scream. You must've awakened half of Orewa." Allen said advancing on her, "What were you trying to do? Escape through the window?" He laughed while he watched the fear shake her like a rag roll.

Martha tried to speak. If she pleaded with him, maybe he would find some kindness in his heart. Maybe he would leave if she spoke kind words to him? She realized she didn't want to die, even if that would lead her to Carl and her children, lead her to eternal happiness. She didn't want that yet. She wanted life. But as she tried to speak, forming the words in her mind, she found her vocal cords would betray her. Her fear gripped them in a vice so tight they weren't able to vibrate the sounds into understandable words.

"You can't escape the wrath of God, whore of Babylon."

"Neither can you, Allen."

He hadn't bothered turning on the bedroom light but he had turned on the hallway and other room lights. He spun around and saw a dark figure surrounded by bright white light. No features distinguishable. Allen knew who this was.

"My Lord." he whispered, "Have you come to bare witness?"

* * *

James floored the cruiser. He sped along the empty roads. The car handled the corners very well, the tires gripping the road like spit on sand. They screamed in protest as he took tight corners only slightly relaxing his foot on the accelerator. He knew he should slow it down. No point in getting himself killed, yet he couldn't. His nerves were tight and his hand gripped the wheel tightly enough that the whites of his knuckles showed beneath his tanned hands.

He entered the Orewa city limits and forced himself to slow down. A few cars were still on the streets most of them filled with teenagers. James ignored the shouted insults and the raised middle fingers aimed at the car as he flew past the kids. The dashboard clock showed: 11:17 as he turned onto the street leading to Martha's house.

He used the hand and pedal brake to stop. The car slid to a halt blocking the neighbor's driveway. He jumped out and ran to the door. He stopped at the gate. The front door was open and he saw the doorknob lying on the porch connected to a piece of door.

Anger raged inside. The bastard was here. He kicked the gate open and froze. He was unarmed. The gate swung back, bouncing off its hinges and returned slamming against his leg. James barely noticed. He stepped back, looking at the police cruiser. A million police dramas flashed through his mind. Hoping it was true he ran back to the car and popped the boot. Protected by a padlocked crossbar was a vision of beauty. A chance. He took the keys from the ignition and tried three before he found the one he was looking for. He entered the house with more confidence and the feeling he had a chance.

The living room was dark but the hallway was soaked in light. He hurried. He heard laughter coming from his room. He ran to it, stopping outside the door as he heard Allen speak.

"You can't escape the wrath of God, whore of Babylon."

"Neither can you, Allen."

Allen spun around and looked at him. James saw a man pushed beyond his limits, pushed over the edge of sanity. He felt pity for his half brother. A person he never knew existed until tonight. The pity quickly departed when he saw the bladed glove.

"My Lord." Allen whispered. "Have you come to bare witness?"

"No I haven't." James said stepping into the room. He knew his face couldn't be seen before from the light but in the room, he was clearly visible.

Allen's features changed from wonder to rage.

"You mother fucker!" He screamed. "How dare you!"

James didn't answer.

Allen looked down at what James was holding with both hands. It was rounded at one end and shaped like a triangle at the other. It looked like a short boat oar. He smiled. "Always the hero. You are quick these days."

"Not quick enough I see." James was surprised, he felt remarkably calm. He could feel his anger bubbling inside. Facing his brother, his anger had subsided a lot but it was reaching boiling point quickly. He came to realize he hated his brother.

"No. Nowhere quick enough." Allen raised the glove. In one nice, even, smooth action, he spun around and brought the razor sharp blades slashing downwards cutting the air where Martha was.

She had moved when his back was turned and was now near the bed.

Allen's claw glove ripped down the wall leaving gouges in its wake.

James took advantage of the distraction and charged Sheriff from behind. He dropped what Allen thought was an oar. The shotgun landed with a heavy thud. He pinned him against the wall and shouted at Martha to get the fuck out of here. She didn't move until he screamed a second time. He was having trouble holding his brother in place. It was like pinning a wild boar to the ground as you struggled to get your hunting knife out.

Allen swung his arm around. His elbow made contact with James' cheek. One of the scars split open, warm blood dribbled down his neck. Intense pain ripped through his body. His hold on Allen faltered as his hand went automatically to his face. Sheriff elbowed him in the ribs and brought the glove upwards. It barely missed its target.

James felt the air change, as it swept past. He replied with an uppercut punch. It connected but not with enough force. He followed it with a left fist to the stomach. It felt padded. He backed away.

Allen almost ran at James swinging the glove from side to side. It swept through the air as if it had a life of its own, brought into this word for one purpose only - to kill.

James ducked each passing sweep. Allen was aiming for the head only. He moved backwards as quickly as he could. He saw no trace of sanity in his brother's eyes. They burned brightly with madness.

Allen started yelling, not words, just primal screams of anger and pent up frustration finally loosed. He changed the course of the glove. Instead of side to side it now swung at an angle towards the legs.

He spotted the change just in time and side stepped. His left foot clipped the edge of the bed and he hit the floor. The shotgun was no more than two feet from him.

"Yes!" Allen screamed, bringing the blades down. "You're no longer the best!"

James rolled out of the way towards the weapon. The blades dug into the carpet. Allen quickly pulled then out and raised the glove high.

He felt the cold steel and it felt like heaven. James pulled it to him, flipped onto his back and fired blindly. The spray of pellets struck Allen below the neck. His left hand grabbed at the wound.

He looked like he was trying to pull off a jumper. He started choking and stumbled towards James who quickly rolled out of the way.

A new look entered Allen's eyes. What was it? Disbelief? Amazement? Wonder?

The sound of sirens and screaming tires came from outside. James pumped the shotgun and fired a second time. The final shot with his eyes wide open and his aim perfect.

The force of the shot spun Allen around, his back facing James again. He stumbled along the bed to the far wall and fell against the shelf. He gripped the boards with his one free hand, trying to hold himself up. His closing eyes focussed on a green bottle marked: Exonpet 2000. "Fuck it," he mumbled and collapsed bringing the shelf down with him.

The bottle of Exonpet 2000 cracked when it hit Allen's forehead. The clear liquid spilled onto his face. The acid started eating away at the flesh around his nose. More liquid ran into his eyes. Allen didn't scream out or shake in pain. He was unresponsive. Body unmoving.

James knew he had killed the man. His brother no less and thought something was wrong with him because he felt no remorse, no pity, no shame and no anger. He felt nothing, except empty.

Spent.

Two police officers burst into the room their guns drawn and aimed at James's head. "Drop the shotgun, asshole! Do it! Now!"

Stunned, James muttered, "What the fuck?"

"Drop the fucking gun, asshole!"

James obeyed as Detective Kerrs entered. He glanced at the dead body of Allen Sheriff. The blood covered neck and shirt, partly melted face and empty eye sockets. He felt sick, "What the hell happened?" He wasn't looking for an answer to the question yet, "Arrest the wanker."

James stared open mouthed at Kerrs, an expression of puzzlement on his face.

"You should have let us deal with it." Kerrs answered the unvoiced question.

"You were busy."

"Get him out of here," Kerrs said flatly.

EPILOGUE

For a week headlines flashed in the newspapers across the country.

One headline read: *Killer's brought down with acid.*

James appeared in court four months later. His trial lasted two days. It was a jury trial and the twelve citizens who judged his actions and listened to the facts and reports took four hours to return with a "Not guilty" reply to the manslaughter charge, but the judge did impose a twenty-four month probation ruling for auto theft. He also recommended James to seek professional help to deal with his ordeal.

He left the court through the front doors and was surprised not to see a hoard of reporters clamoring for answers, comments.

It was disappointing. At the bottom of the steps he saw Tara and Ted leaning against their car. During the past four months they had been incredibly helpful and given their time and advice freely. He believed he had found two great friends and was glad he had entered the cafe/bar that fateful night. It was hard to believe it was all over.

Standing beside them was an attractive lady in her thirties. The way her hair was styled and the manner of her dress reminded him of Zoe.

Tara came up to him. "So, how are we today?"

He smiled. "We are fine."

"I've always wanted to meet a famous person."

"Well then, I hope that one day your dream will come true," James replied with a smile. He knew she meant him. Since the newspaper articles about his life before the attack, he had received many offers for his photos. Collectors were offering top dollar for his lost photos of the night at Opera Sands beach. His bank account was growing healthy once again.

Tara walked him to the car.

Ted shook his hand. "What'd they give you?"

"Twenty four months for nicking a cop car." He couldn't take his eyes off this new person standing next to Ted and looking a bit nervous. "Who's this?" he asked.

"James," Ted said. "I'd like to introduce you to Miss Sandra Clarke. Sandra, this is James."

"I would never have guessed," she replied, her voice soft and smooth.

"Hi," James said extending his hand.

"Hi there." They shook.

"Excuse me, Mr. Dennett?"

James turned and saw a middle aged man with a camera pressed against his eye. "Yes?"

"New Zealand press, mind if I get a shot?" He didn't wait for an answer and clicked five times. "Thank you. Take care, Mr. Dennett."

* * *

One year later, with Sandra's help, James held his first exhibition with remarkable success. The place was small but filled. Many people were buyers, some others were just curious. He couldn't believe how fast some of his more expensive photos were selling. Of every photo he took, there was no copy. Only originals were sold. He destroyed the negatives.

James sipped on a glass of champagne he held in his left hand while nervously playing with a piece of smooth green glass fashioned into a pendant on a silver chain, hanging around his neck.

Sandra leaned to him and whispered, "Stop playing with that thing. Everything is going well." She placed her hand on his shoulder and light glistened off her engagement ring.

James replied with a soft kiss. "Let's get out of here."

"You want to leave?"

"Well, I'm not doing anything, my agent's taking care of matters pertaining to my money. Let's leave it in her hands, besides, I feel like some fresh air." James started off knowing

Sandra would follow.

She did.

Outside Spring was in the air, just. It was still cool outside but not bitterly and the coolness was refreshing. She caught up with James when he stopped to light a cigarette. Sandra joined him and said, "Aren't you worried about your health?"

"No."

"Okay," she answered. Then: "Where are we going?"

James stared out into the night. "Two Angel Faces," he said walking past his new car. "It's a nice night for a walk, don't you think?"

She wrapped her arm in his. "I agree one hundred percent."

They headed up the hill, a fifteen-minute walk ahead of them.

They walked in silence. James was as happy as he had been for years ago. Life was good once again and he felt like the king of the world, especially with Sandra on his arm.

The lights of 'Two Angel Faces' glowed in the distance. They were regulars there and had become friendly with the owner, which wasn't difficult. Patty had a friendly disposition and he was the most likeable person James knew. A couple of his photographs graced the walls from time to time. They always sold, but James never asked for any money from Patty.

Sandra stopped cold, forcing James to halt also.

"What is it?" he asked.

Then he heard the sound. A soft rumbling growl coming from the bushes across the road. He stared in the direction and saw two yellow eyes watching him. "Keep walking," he said, "Try not to look at it."

"James," she whimpered, pointing ahead of them at a large black deformed dog standing in the road.

The animal from the bushes walked out slowly, cutting off any retreat. At the same time they both howled.

Sandra pushed herself up hard against James. He could feel her shaking, her hot short breaths hitting the side of his neck.

"James, what are we going to do?"

"I don't know," he whispered as both dogs closed in, low

growls rumbling from their throats. He looked ahead and behind. There seemed to be no help from anywhere. No car lights in the distance headed this way. He couldn't count on help coming. He had to think fast, the animals were getting closer and gaining confidence. Nothing came to mind, so he screamed and ran at the dog in front.

It turned and ran back a few yards, stopped and turned to face him. James heard Sandra scream and turned his back on the dog.

She was struggling and doing her best to fight off the dog that was behind them. For a second, James thought they had been set up by two very smart animals.

Then it came, a feeling he had ignored for almost a year. His eyes narrowed and lips pressed tight together. In his mind, he whispered: *Push.*

The beast on Sandra was flung high into the air.

The other one rushed forward.

James heard it...in his mind. The rapid breathing, pounding paws on the tar-sealed road. The rush of wind as it jumped at him. The click of the jaw opening. Saliva flying from it's mouth, lashing the night air.

He spun, swinging his arm in a downward motion. The animal folded in two as if sliced with a sword and dropped like a dead weight to the road. The body twitched. Sharp cracks of broken bones reforming filled the night.

In his mind, he saw the other animal, rise to its feet. There was time. He rushed to Sandra's side. Blood coated her shoulder. "Can you stand?"

She nodded, then froze. The two animals were standing side by side. Fuck they were quick. Their snarl rattled the air; yellow eyes harsh in the night. As one, they rushed forward.

"Stop!"

The voice commanded authority and the man spoke with a faint accent. Scottish. The animals skidded to a halt.

"Who are you?" James asked, holding Sandra close.

"I am your blood." The man motioned the animals at his side. "We are the same. We watched over you."

"Let's go," he said to Sandra.

"Come here," the man ordered.

Something pushed in his mind. A desire washed through him, a desire to do as the man commanded. James complied. His legs felt like rubber but he managed. He heard a scuffing sound behind him and turned. Sandra moved with him, her hands at her side. Tears welled in her eyes but did not fall.

"We are of the same blood, James." The man's voice sounded almost hypnotic.

Sandra stopped and looked at the man.

"Who the fuck…" James hissed. He was fighting the desire, pushing it back. He kept his face slack, hiding his inner fight.

"I'm a very distant relative. You may call me, Duncan. Duncan McDennett."

The two dogs morphed quickly into human form. A man stood on his left and one woman on the right. They were naked but not ashamed; they seemed unconcerned about events around them. They looked at James and Sandra with disinterested eyes. They stood slack, not erect and proud like Duncan.

"Werewolves," Sandra muttered.

"A commoner's term, which I hate to hear. James has always been one of the blood. You my dear are nothing."

A little more, just a little bit more. James struggled with the desire emotion. It could feel it ebbing from his veins and muscles. His strength was returning in a rush of ice filled shivers.

Calling Sandra a 'nothing' enraged, James to the point of making, what he feared could very well be an error. But he couldn't control himself and drove an uppercut to the man facing him. It was deflected easily, like shooing a fly. He tried to 'push' Duncan with his mind, but that also failed. He realized he was facing a most powerful man. A relative.

The man smiled at him.

He shook his head. "My life is complete at the moment. I don't want this."

Duncan looked at the woman's shoulder. His lip curled up.

"I'm afraid you have little choice in the matter."

The naked man and woman squatted into a sitting position and morphed back into lycanthropes. Duncan McDennett knelt beside them and locked his arms around their thick bulky necks.

James backed away, keeping his eyes locked on Duncan and the Lycanthropes. His hand held Sandra's upper arm and he pulled her with him.

The werewolves rose.

"No, my children," he said. "Let them go. The bloodline will survive. Pure."

Duncan McDennett led them back into the edge of the woods. Dennett's woman would change with the next harvest moon. It would be interesting watching James's reaction.

He looked back and saw that James had stopped backing away. He was moving forward. Duncan stared hard at him and saw the facial expressions were different. Pulsing under the skin, he saw the image of a pure wolf. But he hadn't been bitten.

James stopped under a streetlight and the blood covering his mouth and chin was plainly evident. He had cleansed the woman by drinking the infected blood.

A new light burned in his eyes.

Hatred. Pure and simple.

The Lycanthropes at Duncan's side whimpered. His attention went to them. Their thick black coats were smoking; white streams rose into the darkness.

The whimpers turned into cries of pain.

Duncan stumbled away from his two only companions. Suddenly their coats burst into flame. The animals howled, rubbed themselves against nearby trees, trying to douse the killer fire.

They failed.

Their master looked on, helpless.

He turned to James and rushed forward. Raged pumped though his veins. He knew James felt the same rage, but for a different reason.

They both charged one another. Both jumped in the air at the same instant. Both morphed in flight...both fought savagely.

Sandra watched as the two animals tore at each other. Her body was weak. James had taken a lot of the injured blood. Roars of anger and pain filled the empty street.

Shouts ahead grabbed her attention. She looked up toward the café /bar and saw Patty and several others approaching In Patty's hand was a shotgun. Others also carried weapons.

Shots were fired. The werewolves continued fighting. She had no idea which one was James. They looked the same. She had to do something quickly, before James got hurt.

The men stopped.

"What in the name of god..." Patty cocked both barrels. Leveled the shotgun and tried to get a line on one.

Sandra jumped in front of him. "No!" she shouted.

The shotgun exploded, sending the woman stumbling back. Pellets from both barrels opened her chest and face. She fell backward onto the warring animals.

The rest fired blindly at the two beasts.

One reared up at the men. Several blasts ripped its chest wide open. The other ran into the woods. No one followed.

The wounded animal morphed into human form. His chest was torn apart. He tried to speak but blood rolled over his lips, chin, silencing any words.

One of the men stepped forward, placed the barrel of a handgun against the center of the forehead and fired.

From the safety of the trees...James watched. Watched and cried. Once again he had nothing. He raised his head to the star studded night and screamed.

END

About the Author

Lee Pletzers is a writer who is very active in the genre world, online and off. Over 40 short stories have found publication in anthologies and magazines, zines and online.

In September 2009 his first novel was released by BBS books. Lee is an avid reader and writes reviews for HarperCollins and Hachette via SFFANZ (Science Fiction and Fantasy Association of New Zealand). He is also a member of AHWA (Australian Horror Writers Association) and a founding member of SpecFicNZ.

He has edited 4 anthologies, worked as editor and reviewer for Sinisteria horror magazine, has translated one novel from Japanese to English and edited several novels for small press authors.

In 2003 he created the popular social site for horror writers at:
http://moh.spruz.com/ Feel free to join in. Masters of Horror is not just for horror writers, but a home for everyone who loves/likes a little bit of darkness in their lives, be it through books, s/stories, movies, artwork, for just a general fan. This site was created for you guys.

You can find him online at: http://terror.co.nz
Lurking on twitter: http://twitter.com/Lee_Pletzers
His Facebook fan page is located at: http://is.gd/4vGOJ

www.ingramcontent.com/pod-product-compliance
Lightning Source LLC
Chambersburg PA
CBHW070104260626
47160CB00004B/1311